Dear Doctor,

Once you have secured
the secret nested
in the girl R. T., her
continued survival
is no longer required.
It is, in fact,
no longer preferred.

DO AS YOU MUST.

KENT DAVIS

A RIDDLE IN RUBY

THE CHANGER'S KEY

BOOK TWO

GREENWILLOW BOOKS

An Imprint of HarperCollinsPublishers

A Riddle in Ruby: The Changer's Key
Copyright © 2016 by Kent Davis

The text of this book is set in 11.5-point Sabon MT.
Book design by Sylvie Le Floc'h
Library of Congress Control Number: 2016950344
ISBN 978-0-06-236838-6 (paperback)
17 18 19 20 21 OPM/BVG 10 9 8 7 6 5 4 3 2 1
First paperback edition, 2017

 Greenwillow Books

To Dianne,
who taught me what was right

CHAPTER I

Nothing is more wonderful than the art of being free,
but nothing is harder to learn how to use than freedom.
—Elizabeth de Toqueville, *Travels in the Colonies*

If they put a bag over your head, they mean business.

"Sorry about this, miss, but our route must remain secret." The bald man pulled the fabric down over Ruby's eyes, and it erased his smile, along with everything else. The burlap stank of mice and scratched against her cheek. The fine leather of the seat squeaked under her bum, and the shackles chafed at her wrists. The cuffs hung heavy, crafted from friar's iron, the toughest steel in the colonies. These reeves—elite warriors and spies, the lawful arm of the crown—had spared no expense to protect themselves from a thirteen-year-old girl.

"Best not to squirm, you." That was the younger reeve. In Ruby's mind's eye she scratched at the pink pockmarks on her flour-pale cheeks. Her voice carried the slightest trace of a lisp. Ruby ground her teeth. Two reeves and manacled hands in a barred black carriage headed straight into the heart of hell. If only Gwath could see her now.

Before today her former mentor would have seen nothing special. Seven days and nights bored out of her skull in a well-appointed stateroom in the upper reaches of the great Tinker man-of-war ship *Grail*. Not fifty steps away was the balcony she'd almost thrown herself from. It had been a desperate gamble, her opponent none other than the combined forces of the crown and the Tinkers, whose arcane science had transformed and dominated the colonies. She had bet her life to bargain for the release of her father and friends. A moment of madness—she still wondered if she truly would have jumped from that balcony to her death—but she had won.

However, what exactly had Ruby Teach won? Her father only had time to whisper, "We will come for you," before they tore him away and hustled him and her companions out of her life.

One of the reeves—the big woman from the groan of the carriage seat—shifted forward and fiddled with what sounded like a latch. The creak of hinges and a rush of brisk winter air announced the opening of a hatch in the ceiling. "Stuffy in here," she lisped. "What we waiting for, Cole?"

"You know," Cole replied.

The first reeve blew out her breath.

The two watchful guards had never left Ruby's side, sleeping in shifts in an adjoining stateroom. One friendly, one menacing, they had been her only companions, save occasional visits from their terrifying lord captain, Wisdom Rool. Rool had captured her father. He had pursued her for days like some terrible hunting cat through the narrowest alleys and across the steepest rooftops of Philadelphi. He had killed Gwath. Possibly.

And what was this all about? She had sworn her service to Rool in exchange for her father's freedom, and then nothing. Seven days of stillness. Of solitude. She had spent her life surrounded by family, a big, boisterous crowd of thieves and pirates, all joking and bustling and teasing and working on her father's ship. And then all of a sudden she'd been encircled by an empty, echoing nothing. The reeves almost never spoke. Sometimes Ruby hated the silence, and sometimes she feared it. Mostly she struggled with a boredom so profound she felt she might stab her eyes out with one of the delicate teaspoons.

Instead, she had stolen one. It took four days until the big reeve had sneezed, squeezing her eyes shut for just an instant. An instant was all Ruby needed. Before the reeve opened her eyes, Ruby had palmed the little spoon. She had filed its handle down on the iron bedframe at night, and the sliver of metal now rested snug in the fold of her cheek like an unspoken prayer.

She had held on to it, hope dwindling, until this morning. A few hours before dawn they had woken her and led her down the stern steps, across a makeshift gangplank, and into a deserted corner of the Benzene Yards docks. They quietly hustled her over to a horseless tinker's carriage, hidden at the beginning of a high maze of crates and barrels, and it was into the coach and on with the bag.

They were taking her somewhere in secret, that much was clear, and Ruby wagered her salt for scurvy she didn't want to find out where.

She doubled over, coughing, and reached up under the bag to pass the spoon sliver out of her mouth and into the palm of her hand.

"You all right, Teach?" That was Cole, the smiling one. He had generous eyes, but they were always moving.

She crouched away from his voice, managed a shiver. "I fear I may be coming down with something."

"Dove," he said, "close the trap. We don't want her catching a chill."

The other reeve muttered to herself, and the seat creaked again as she stood up.

Quick now.

Ruby twisted the spoon in the lock, and the shackle

sprang open. She tore the bag from her head and flung it into Dove's pimpled face. With her free hand Ruby swung the chain to the right as hard as she could. Cole caught it easily, but the distraction gave Ruby the instant she needed to pick the other lock. He yanked on the chain, but it flew free from her wrist.

Ruby planted one foot on the windowsill, one foot on Dove's shoulder, and she was through the trap onto the carriage roof. Cries came from below, and the carriage door crashed open.

Ruby vaulted down the other side into the alley of boxes and sprinted with all she had. She didn't care where or how; she just had to keep moving. Seven days was enough, was it not? Seven days was plenty for her father and friends to have made it clear and into hiding. The tangle of crates and chests would soon release her into the dark streets of UnderTown, and this time she would disappear without a trace.

But she had given her word she would not run.

She skidded to a stop, sucking wind, next to a crate as tall as she, labeled ACID OF SUGAR.

She had given her word to save her friends, her family.

So why was she running?

The cries and calls came closer, and Ruby bit her lip. She was free. She could escape. Find her family again and then sail with them over the edge of the world and into the mist. But Rool was relentless. If she ran, he would never stop trying to find her, and wouldn't that put her family in even more danger?

At the same time, the Reeve and their Tinker allies were the only ones who could discover the secret in her blood, the only ones who could unlock the truth about her. Freedom or knowledge? For a moment the strain of those two ropes threatened to pull her in two.

She turned back the way she had come. She had to know. She had to know the truth of herself, no matter the risk, no matter the cost. She took a step back toward the carriage.

Someone chuckled.

Ruby whirled, and around the corner strolled Wisdom Rool, empty eyes dancing. He leaned against the crate and smiled, folding one thick arm over the other.

"Decided to keep your word?"

Her feet itched. Even if she ran, he could catch her. He was stronger, faster, more relentless than anyone she had ever known. She never could have escaped. This had been his plan from the beginning. He had wanted to see if she would scarper off. "Yes," she said, and the fear closed over her.

Rool nodded, a smile interrupting the horrific scars that crisscrossed his face. "Well then. I'm glad we got that out of your system. Up for a wee excursion, Ruby Teach? There are some people I'd like you to meet." Rool took another burlap sack out of his belt, just like the first. He tossed it to her.

She caught it and pulled it on, and for a moment she was grateful. It kept him from seeing the fear. "Does this sack look fetching?" she said. "I hear burlap is all the rage in Paris."

Ruby Maxim One: "Show Wisdom No Weakness."

—

CHAPTER 2

Keep your friends close. Keep your enemies tied up in the hold.
Or dead. Or both.

—Precious Nel, scourge of the Seven Seas

Henry Collins ran his acid-stained fingers back and forth along the edge of the journal page, locked in desperate battle with its maddening cipher. It was as impenetrable as the first moment he'd seen it. Wayland Teach had given it to him with a dark look and a warning: "Our only hope to find Ruby lies in this."

Henry leaned back in the rickety chair and rubbed the grit from his eyes. The deserted little balcony on the rear of the King's Bum tavern looked out east over the swamp and the madcap collection of shacks, houses, taverns, and towers that made up the pirate haven of StiltTown. When a strong wind blew, the buildings swayed and swung, lashed together as they were with rope, seaweed, and prayer. They dotted the water, indistinct shadows against the night, connected by a sorry patchwork of walkways, all the way out to the sturdy docks where the ships of thieves and murderers lined up as orderly as you please.

He sighed and rolled his shoulders. The journal lay open on the makeshift table, laughing at him. Seven days of constant study, deep into the night, and deeper into the morning, and he still had no idea what the ciphers hid. Shame heated his cheeks. The captain had entrusted the journal to him because Henry was the only member of the crew who had even the remotest chance of solving its chemystral riddle, but he had not even cracked the first line. Ruby's mother had crafted a perfect puzzle, and if Henry could not solve it, their chances of saving Ruby from the Reeve were apparently next to nothing.

He took a sip of tea out of the battered tankard,

straightened up to his full height, and shook himself awake. No use moaning. All he could do was try again.

Henry went back to the equation about two-thirds of the way down the page. His grease pencil danced across the scrap parchment next to the journal, trying to pin it down. Wait. A candle lit in his head. Did he have it? Suddenly his vision blurred, and no, the coded algorithms and chemystral equations on the page pulsed and rearranged themselves, dancing away. All in a waterfall it came to him.

The ink itself was charged with chemystry.

Henry laughed. Of course. He reached for his Source, the inner strength that fueled all chemysts, and trickled out a bit into the journal. The equations stilled. He copied a few lines to his parchment, the numbers and sigils straining against his control. Then his vision blurred once more, and it felt as if a mule had kicked him in the belly. Gasping, he opened his eyes. The journal had changed yet again. But everything he had copied lay still on his scrap parchment.

He dived in. Some time passed. It might have been minutes or hours. Finally, in a burst of inspiration, he discovered the key to the section, and the symbols unlocked. Pink kissed the sky. Hours indeed. Two lines had taken him most of the night, but he had done it.

A wave of weariness washed over him. He finished the bitter tea with a grin and stowed the journal in an inner pocket of his tattered wool coat. There would be no more work tonight. He would barely be able to get back to his room. He levered himself up on the crutches the *Thrift*'s carpenters had made for him and gingerly maneuvered his broken leg away from the table and chair. The sunrise had gone red in the distance, and it lit up the mast and rigging of the *Thrift*, the ship of jovial smugglers that had carried him to this place.

The sunset flickered. It flashed orange. Cries and clamor came up from the shore over the wind. The chem pot on his table still burned, and the sky above him was still black as pitch. It wasn't dawn. The *Thrift* was burning.

Henry whirled, heading for the door.

And stopped short.

Two women stood between him and it. One was the new serving girl from downstairs, the friendly one who quoted Shakespeare and Calderón. Her clocklock pistol was leveled at his heart. The other he had never seen before, but she was tall, almost as tall as Henry, and in close breeches and a sleeveless vest. She carried no weapon and was soaking wet, a trail of water leading to the edge of the platform.

Bells rang in the streets below. Calls and yells rang out, and the village sprang to life, banding together to fight the seaman's worst enemy: fire.

He took a breath, but the serving girl—Jenny—cocked her clocklock and shook her head.

The soaking wet girl said, "Now, Mister Collins, we cannot have you calling for help." Her English was careful, and her accent was Catalan, from the east of what used to be Spain. "Otherwise, what use would it have been for me to set fire to that lovely ship of yours?"

Henry faced the two women and scratched his ear. "Who are you?" he asked. He barely heard his words over the pounding of his heart.

Jenny motioned at his coat with her gun. "We need that journal, alchemyst."

"I'm not certain I know the journal of which you speak," Henry lied. He was a terrible liar.

The tall one chuckled. "You are playing for time. Perhaps one of your new friends will burst in from below to save you. The captain with all his rage, or the buffoon, or the lithe one with the sword. Athen, yes? However, I set a *crashing* good fire, Henry Collins, and every one of your companions will be busy putting it out far into the night. By the time they find your body, it will be cold and clammy. Perhaps the seagulls will have had a go at your pretty eyes." She smiled. "That is, if you resist. If you give us the journal and leave with us, no harm will come to you."

Henry scratched his ear again.

This time he was able to grasp the tiny vial Cram had helped him sew into the collar of his new coat. The little clay container rested just between his thumb and forefinger.

"Very well," Henry said. "It's right here in my coat—"

"Vera, look out!" Jenny cried.

Henry hurled the vial at the ground between them as he threw himself out of the way. The pistol fired, and the ball grazed his shoulder. A razor of pain almost scattered his focus. The vial of carbon fluid smashed, and Henry gave it a push with his Source, activating it. Jenny threw herself to the deck, and sticky gray threads sailed above her head and smacked into planks of the wall. The tall one, Vera, was not so lucky. The thick strands shot around her and affixed themselves to the wall. They contracted, and within a moment she was stuck fast next to the door: an immovable statue.

Henry clawed across the floor, but a wild beast in the form of a serving girl pounced on him, punching and biting, smelling of stale ale and, strangely, marigolds. They rolled back and forth across the balcony, neither able to gain the upper hand despite her small frame and his injury. He rolled over, one leg hanging over the edge of the deck, trying to get at his crutch, but it was just out of reach. Jenny rolled with him onto her back, and her legs snapped around his throat.

"Wrong target, simpleton," she gritted through her teeth. "She's the one who wanted to spare you."

Sparks shot off in Henry's head, and red crept in at

the edges of his vision. His fingertips brushed the crutch, but it slipped away. He flailed his arms about as the world grew darker and darker. It was just Providence that he struck the back of his hand on one of the chairs. His fingers closed about the chair leg, and he heaved it over his head in desperation. It struck something.

The vise was gone.

Air poured into his throat, and he scrambled onto his knees, ready for the next attack.

It didn't come. The chair was gone, as was the girl. He crawled to the edge and looked over. Ripples in the water.

The tall girl shouted as he stumbled through the door. She was yelling in Catalan at the top of her lungs, but the carbon over her mouth muffled most of the sound. "*Lo siento*," said Henry. He tumbled down the stairs.

He labored through the deserted common room, cursing the crutches and his injured leg in equal measure. The chilly night reeked of smoke, and he picked his way with rushed care from the Bum's platform over the slimy planks of the empty bridges.

Henry still had no idea how to navigate the chaotic

maze of switchbacks and cul-de-sacs. Was the sound of the fire . . . that way? He rushed around a corner and barely ducked under a low-hanging sign. How had he come to this? Three weeks ago he had been apprentice to one of the most powerful chemysts alive. The road ahead had been lined with purpose. If he had died, at least it would have been a noble death. But now? He shook his head and burned those thoughts away.

Turn after turn he forced himself through the heaviest clouds of smoke, until he careened around a corner at the top of the stairs that led down to the docks.

Below, a beast of fire gorged itself on the *Thrift*.

Her mainmast glittered like a candelabrum. Part of the main deck had burned away, and some of the forecastle as well. Teams of townsfolk tended to the small fires that had started on the surrounding ships, but the *Thrift*'s crew was on its own.

They were losing.

Big Shem and Little Shem led a bucket brigade from below. Up on the forecastle Cram, Athena, and the captain beat at the raging fire with blankets, coats, whatever was at hand. Frog Jerky and Pol the Gizzard yelled at the bystanders, pleading for help.

Henry tottered down the stairs and through the crowd on the wharf. A giant hand of heat pushed at him. As he reached the gangway, someone grabbed him from behind and whirled him about. Skillet held his arm, soot-black face tracked with tears. "She's lost!" he yelled. "Get back!" Henry could barely hear him over the fire. He struggled, but the old steward's grip was stone.

"I must get closer!" Henry pointed up at Fat Maggie, the figurehead, just in time to see the captain, Athena, and Cram jump over the edge into the water below.

Skillet shook his head and dragged Henry back the way he came.

Then the mast cracked. It was a pistol shot, if the pistol was the size of the wharf.

Slowly, ever so slowly, the mainmast leaned. It was falling. Time slowed, and every eye on the wharf, even Skillet's, tracked it. That was probably why he didn't see Henry's crutch fly up to strike him square between his legs.

"Sorry!" There was nothing else to say. At the edge of

the gangplank, the heat of the fire stopped him. He had little time.

Henry wrapped his sleeve around his hand and drew a sealed pewter pot out of his coat, then popped off the little wax lid. Balderston's Vapors was a complex equation, and he was drained already; but he had to risk it. He cleared his mind and triggered his Source, the force of it bringing him to his knees. A rushing sound surrounded him, and a whirling rope of fire—*all* of it—spiraled from the *Thrift* toward Henry and into the impossibly little jar. It was too much fire. Without a heat sink it would scorch him to cinders. He stepped off the dock. The water closed over him, the heat of the fire spreading from the little flask into the surrounding cool. The serpent of fire, however, still spiraled down into the jar, whirling through a cone of vapor moving so quickly it held the water at bay. Faster and faster he guided the fire and the air that fed it into the jar, now glowing an eye-searing crimson.

The tail of the fire hurtled over the brim.

The jar cracked and went dark.

Henry couldn't breathe.

He sank into the sea.

CHAPTER 3

No trace of the package can be found throughout the colonies, despite the best efforts of numerous agents. We have exhausted our capacity for inquiry. I am sorry to report that the package has disappeared.

—Chemystral missive from M. Hearth, Bluestockings,
to Lord Godfrey Boyle, Sc.D., Worshipful Order of Grocers

"Apple, Ruby Teach?" Rool's voice pulled her out of her doze into blackness. Rough fabric scraped the tip of her nose.

"Thank you, but something seems to be blocking my mouth."

Rool chuckled. "Pride perhaps? Or a touch of anger?"

She made a face at the burlap. "A cursed sack, if I'm not mistaken."

"Here." There was a snick, and something moved

toward her. Light crept in under her chin, and scarred fingers appeared, holding a slice of apple. She fought hard to not flinch. It smelled delicious, even over the soapy scent of Rool's fingers. She considered biting them but didn't. She had to cooperate.

The apple slice was sweet and crisp on her teeth, and then it was gone.

The carriage rattled and bounced. The hours ground past. The flip of cards sounded on the leather seat, punctuated occasionally by the two other reeves arguing over the stupid rules.

Finally the carriage slowed, and then it crept up a steep incline.

Horses whickered, and calls echoed outside. The carriage stopped.

Powerful machinery clashed and ground somewhere up ahead, and then the coach moved forward again but only for a few moments.

The door opened, and a chill wind rushed in, along with the bustle and noise of busy people about their business.

"Come, Ruby Teach. I have a surprise for you," Wisdom Rool said, and held both of her hands in one of his. He guided her down the steps of the carriage onto flat, hard earth. "Look to your eyes," he said, and whisked the bag from her head. She squinted as the sun shot in.

Through the blur she caught a glimpse of high gray walls and cold blue sky.

"Welcome home," said Wisdom Rool.

The dirt yard was crowded with boys and girls standing in ranks, all in gray. They held a single pose with varying degrees of success: crouched on one foot, knee bent to chest, with the other leg stuck out long, heel hovering. Hands clasped behind their necks. Besides a chestnut-haired girl in the front who had the knack of the thing, the rest were wobbling and flopping like fish on a deck. One boy, about Ruby's age, panted in and out through his clamped teeth, clenched hands wound up in his white hair. He fell over onto the ground but scrambled right back into position, grunting under his breath. All of them stared straight ahead, eyes on a woman with a blaze of red hair at the front. She held the same position, still as carven stone.

Beyond the crowd, two reeves were sparring, spinning and kicking with hummingbird grace. A mountain of a man rushed a slight, pale woman with short black hair. She was cornered, and Ruby was sure the man had her until she leaped up sideways and planted her feet on the side of the wall. Where she *stood*, parallel with the ground. It was an impossible thing, and no one in the yard gave it a second glance. As the man rushed past her, she planted her hand on his shoulder and spun over him in a cartwheel. Flushed with triumph, she looked up across the yard, and her eyes met Ruby's. She nodded as if Ruby were an old friend. Then she turned away to help her partner up.

Ruby blinked. "All this for me? Kind of you. Do they do parties as well?"

Rool chuckled. "Not exactly." He turned to the bald reeve from the carriage. "Cole?"

"Yes, Lord Captain?"

"Please take over for Ward Corson."

"My pleasure, sir." He gave Ruby a grin, ran up next

to the woman, and folded into a motionless replica of her pose, save for the cool, clear smile on his face. The woman unwound herself and trotted over to bow to the lord commander.

"Edwina Corson, Ruby Teach," said Rool.

Green eyes flicked over her, leaving Ruby feeling plucked, weighed, and shelved.

"You will be instructing Ruby Teach as a new Reeve cadet in all manners."

"Sir—"

"She is our prisoner, yes, but I have spent time with this girl; she may be an asset to us."

"Doctor Swedenborg—"

"Leave him to me," said Rool.

"Yes, sir," Corson said. "Trained in all manners." Her eyes snapped back to Ruby's, then to Rool's. "Would you like us to begin now?"

Rool chuckled. "Tomorrow, I think. Are the quarters I requested ready?"

"The cell, sir?"

"Yes."

"Absolutely, though I still believe bunking with the other cadets would—"

"This is how it shall be."

"Yes, sir." Edwina Corson bowed and made her way back to her charges, who were now performing some kind of hopping dance, aping the grinning Cole.

"I am so excited to learn from her. Soon I will be a whooooole new girl," Ruby piped in her best urchin's voice. Rool smiled and began to walk. She kept up.

"Who was that?" Bald-faced curiosity first. Who knew what stray information it could drum up?

"She is Ward Corson, one of your teachers."

"Ward?"

"Call them all ward. And you are a cadet."

Fair enough. "What is this place?"

The big man did not answer as he stalked across the courtyard. Ruby took it in, searching for weaknesses. The palisade walls were gray wood of some kind, patrolled by men and women in Reeve blacks. Next to the stable loomed a big three-story log building. There were no guards on the front door; that seemed good, until

Ruby passed a few people in the hallway and realized something: besides the gray-clad girls and boys Rool had called cadets, everyone else was in black.

This was a fortress of reeves.

Her mouth went dry as they passed two more reeves, who bowed to their lord captain. There were no official jailers here, no hardhearted overseers. What need was there for turnkeys when the entire place was a prison? Ruby chewed on that as Rool led her down a long hallway to a door.

"This is where you will sleep," said Wisdom Rool, and he stood there, waiting.

He wanted her to ask him. Very well, she would. "What's this about?" She could not bring herself to call him Lord Captain, and she wouldn't be caught dead calling him Wisdom. "Where are my irons? My cage? Am I not an enemy of the crown?"

Rool matched her theatricality, glancing up and down the corridor, an overcareful conspirator. "You trusted me, Ruby Teach. Back on the *Grail* when you almost threw yourself to your death for your friends. I gave you my word that I would release your people. I took you under my care, and I want to train you. I am loath to waste an opportunity."

"Opportunity?" He looked at her, waiting. "You said a war. You said you wanted me so you could win a war."

He leaned back against the wall of the hallway. "All in good time." His empty eyes ranged up and down the hall. "Think it through, Ruby. Freedom of movement. Your own cell instead of a crowded dormitory. The tutelage of the Reeve. If there is one thing I have learned since I met you, it is that you have the makings of a consummate spy. I have positioned you so that you may infiltrate the laboratory of Doctor Swedenborg, who will be leading the effort to extract the secret you carry. I want you to steal that secret for yourself. And for me, of course."

"You want me to steal it for myself?" He nodded. "And then give it to you."

"Yes."

"And what will you do with it?"

He smiled. It stilled her breath. "I need a catalyst, Ruby Teach. Someone like me. Someone who starts fires.

And since I need you"—he snapped his scarred fingers—
"I must have you trained." The way he was looking at
her, like a prize pig at a fair: she did not like it.

He nodded, as if hearing her unspoken questions.
"If you refuse, or worse, if you fail, well then, you will
sacrifice your one protector in a den of wolves. There is
more than one person in Fort Scoria who will be delighted
if you fall short of the mark." He crouched to chuck her
under her chin like a grandfather.

She whipped her head back, avoiding his touch.

She swallowed her rage. Best to play his game for
now. "No. No. I will do what you say."

He showed her his teeth. "Excellent! I see great things
in your future, Ruby Teach!" He walked down the hall,
whistling a jig. "Great things!"

Ruby opened the door behind her.

The room was close, well made, and exceedingly
secure. It reminded her somewhat of her hidey-hole on
the *Thrift*, but it was no refuge. The gray wood walls
had not been constructed to keep people out. They were
there to keep her in. A single barred window hung above

the straw pallet, which lay upon a flagstone floor. The view from the window was beautiful: a sheer vertical drop down to a river valley hundreds of feet below. Her hidey-hole had been a refuge, a calm, quiet secret in the heart of the *Thrift*, but its silence had lain surrounded by the steady beat of the waves, the creak of footsteps on the deck above, the scattered laughter of her father and the crew. Here there was no family. Her heart rang in the silence.

She pulled her feet up under her knees. The cold of the stone floor crept in. The empty walls stared back. What had she done?

CHAPTER 4

Place yourself at the disposal of Doctor Swedenborg, and assist him in his all of his endeavors. Despite his quirks, he is a Treasured Asset to the Crown. Please consider this an Order.
—Enciphered Letter, James Stanhope, Lord High Intelligencer, to Wisdom **Rool**, 1718

There was no introduction. No orientation.

Someone pounded on her door. "Teach! Break your fast and hit the yard!" That was all.

Ruby struggled out of bed. She had slept poorly under the scratchy wool blanket, and she hopped from foot to foot on the cold stone floor. A gray getup had been left outside the door, and she pulled it on. It was simple: breeches and a homespun shirt. She got turned around in the twisting passages and lost precious minutes. By the time she found the dining hall a line of cadets was filing out the other door, already having broken their fasts. She cast a longing look at a half-eaten apple, rushed to the end of the line and then out into the yard.

No one spoke to her.

Ward Cole, head freshly shaved, waved Ruby over to the back corner of a formation of cadets. What followed was hours of grueling physical effort. Jumping back and forth on top of poles that had been sunk into one corner of the courtyard. Cadets in pairs, one carrying the other on their shoulders across the yard, then switching for the carry back. Ruby paired up with a wiry girl whose white hair matched that of the boy she had seen yesterday. They didn't speak the whole time. Well, there wasn't much time for breathing, let alone speaking. Perhaps if she just keeled over? She thanked Providence for Gwath and his training.

At least Gwath's relentless instruction had made her body strong and her balance true enough to be able to survive the grueling pace. It still hurt to think about her former master sharping and thieving. He had been dear to her, an ally and a friend, and his loss was still an open wound. Worse, he seemed to have been the only one who could have explained a strange discovery: she had recently, completely unintentionally transformed into a barrel. Ridiculous and impossible, but it was true. Ruby was convinced that the changing was part of the secret everyone was so keen to get at.

All morning her mind kept returning to Gwath. Her teacher had fallen to Wisdom Rool defending her escape from the *Thrift* months ago. Was he alive, imprisoned somewhere like her? Was he lying at the bottom of the ocean, food for fishes? Rool had hinted that he knew more about Gwath but had said nothing since Ruby had turned herself over to him. She used the anger to push herself harder, to help her run faster.

The unsettling part? Even with her training and her anger, she could barely keep up.

A few boys and girls shone, lifting more and running faster than all the rest. The girl with chestnut hair was one of them, long limbs flashing, curls pulled tight on the back of her head. The rest of the cadets formed a kind of pack, jockeying for position behind the leaders. All morning long Ruby fought with all her will and all her fire to stay out of the rear.

What was this madness? Some sick joke? Bring children to a far-off mountain just to turn them into piles of quivering paste? And where was Rool? She snuck looks at the walkways atop the palisades, but no sign of him. Was he watching from some secret platform? Weighing her worth? Testing her mettle? Ruby had no idea, but whatever this test was, it would not find her wanting.

Someone else looked on from a walkway, however.

Thin. All in white. The turned-up collar of his long coat and his broad-brimmed hat screened his face, but he was watching her. She could feel it. After more than an hour he disappeared into the main building.

With the sun high in the sky, Ward Cole called them all over to a corner between the main hall and the thick gray wood palisade. The cadets moved like a school of fish or a herd of deer, shifting as one. Covered in sweat, legs shaking, Ruby followed at the back of the crowd. She found a perch on some boxes so she could see.

Two ropes snaked down the side of the building. Ward Corson and Ward Cole stood at the bottom facing the cadets. They were of a height, but the muscled red-haired woman was half again as wide as the skinny bald man.

Ward Corson stood with one hand on the rope. "Are you tired?"

Nods traveled the group. Several cadets were bent over, hands on their knees. Two had been sick while jogging over. No one paid it any mind.

"Tired is good. Focus on that. Let everything else drop away. Let the work burn away your need for water, your yearning for your beds. Your anger at the wards." Breathless laughter rippled through the herd. "It is the Void for which you search. It is the emptiness that fuels us. The Tinkers have what they call the Source, their name for the life energy that catalyzes their amazing works of science. But they use it like a tool, like a hammer or a saw. A reeve does not manipulate." She twisted her hands like kneading dough. "A reeve channels. A reeve is a *vessel*."

She clapped her hand to her chest. "This. Is waiting to be filled. If you are not empty, the great deeds will not find you."

For a pitch, it was pretty good. But the carnival barkers in New Roanoke were better.

Cole grabbed the other rope.

"Two goals. Firstly, climb to the top as quickly as you can. More important, you must reach the top together. Use the wall, your hands, your feet, anything and everything. Questions?"

An older boy, sturdy and muscled, raised his hand.

"Stump," said Edwina Corson.

He looked scared. "Ward Corson, er—what if we fall?"

Corson turned. "Ward Cole? What if Stump falls?"

The younger man nodded, as if this were a very interesting question. "You should probably land on your feet."

Ruby laughed. No one else did. The yard glared at her. She forced herself to stare back.

"Yes, well," Cole said. The two wards turned to the

wall. They scurried up the ropes like spiders and then over the top. Somebody whistled, a low, respectful sound.

The chestnut-haired girl clapped her hands. "You heard them," she said, and she grabbed one of the ropes. The big cadet, Stump, went to grab the other, but the fierce little white-haired boy beat him to it.

Ward Cole leaned over the edge of the roof, high above. "Go!" he yelled.

The two cadets scrambled upward, the girl using her feet on the wall, the boy with his legs wrapped around the rope. Quick as two sailors before a storm.

Two by two the cadets raced up, until Ruby and the white-haired girl were the only ones left.

Ruby stuck out her hand. "Teach."

The girl looked her up and down. "Keep up, Teach."

"Go!" came the call from above.

Well, if that was how she wanted it. Ropes were Ruby's friends. She had grown up on a ship after all. Three stories was a climb, but she had topped higher masts. She tore upward.

The girl fell behind. She was trying, but maybe her

arms were not strong enough, or she did not understand the technique. Ruby was just an arm's length from the roof before she realized: they both had to get over the top. She cast a glance below her. The girl had stopped about five feet below, feet against the wall, arms wrapped in the rope.

"Come on!" Ruby said.

"I am!"

But she wasn't. The girl's arms were shaking like a sail in a storm. It would not be long before she fell.

Ruby cast her eyes up. Ward Cole peered over the edge, as did Ward Corson and the rest of the cadets. Why should she play their stupid game? It was an easy thing to climb to the top, leap over the edge, and spit in their eye.

A cry sounded from below.

The girl was yelling at her arms. Not words, just howls, her mouth inches from her forearms, as if trying to scare them back into motion. They did not seem interested in listening. It was a ridiculous sight, but fierce. Brave even.

Before Ruby could think about it, she climbed back down, just a little bit below the girl. She steadied herself in the rope, a trick Gwath had taught her, wrapping it around her bum and her shoulders. Then she grabbed the other rope and hauled her body over, until her shoulder was right under the girl's foot. "Here," she gasped. "Put your foot here."

Fear gleamed in the white-haired girl's eyes. She did it, though. She found purchase on Ruby's shoulder, levering herself up. Ruby gritted her teeth, she stared at the wall, and she did not fall.

That was how they climbed. Foot by foot, inch by inch, the two of them huffing and grunting like two beached sea lions.

The girl climbed over the edge, and Ruby groaned in relief. Only then did she look up. Ward Cole's hand was seamed and weathered, tough mahogany against the rough yellow twist of the rope. He hauled her up.

The roof was empty, save for an open trapdoor and the girl with white hair. She gave Ruby a nod and disappeared down the trap.

"Saved your skin. You're right. Don't make too much of a fuss," Ruby panted.

Ward Cole laughed. It was open laughter, though, no malice in it. "We train your body, Teach, but we train the mind, too. A reeve's weapon is not only strength but guile." He motioned over his shoulder to the empty trap. "The cadets do not know what to make of you, and until they do, they will keep their distance."

"What to make of *me*?" Was he serious? She waved her arm behind her. From their vantage on the roof, past the walls in every direction the trees and forest lay far below, uninterrupted by barns, houses, or the smallest sign of habitation. "What should I make of this *place*? Is it a prison? A school? A fortress?" Before he could answer, she pressed on. "And please do not tell me, sir, 'It is what you make of it, my pupil.' I have read my share of books, and that claptrap will not fly."

Ward Cole's smile disappeared, a candle snuffed out. "I will not tell you that, Ruby Teach. I wager this place can be all of those things to you, but my money is on laboratory."

"Laboratory."

"Yes. You are a specimen. A fly under a magnifying

lens. You will be examined until they have accomplished whatever purpose they wish."

"And then what?"

His smile eased back into place. "I suppose that depends on *your* purpose here, does it not? What is it you wish to accomplish?"

"You mean, there's more to it than hopping about like a one-legged chicken?"

He laughed.

But he was right. It was a laboratory. Everyone was observing her. And who was that man on the walkway? Was that the doctor? What did Rool call him, Swedenborg? More important, what *did* she want out of this place? She had to decide, and quickly.

CHAPTER 5

A Tinker cannot afford fellow feeling.
It clouds the eye and dulls the mind.

—Foreman Ambrosius Jecked, MCS, GmSS,
Boston Chapterhouse

"Henry." Something feathery brushed his face. "Henry."

Henry's mind stuttered. What was it? Classify. Feathers. Owl? *Strigiformes*. Crow? *Corvus*. Feather duster? What was the Latin word for *feather duster*? He took a deep breath, setting off a chain reaction of coughs and then memories. Smoke, fire, the *Thrift*. "I'm alive."

A strong gloved hand covered his mouth, and the

familiar, if not entirely welcome, voice of Athena Boyle whispered in his ear, "Quiet. You are in the King's Bum, in a room upstairs, and the captain is downstairs, bargaining with the chief pirate or mayor or what-have-you of Stilt Town, as well as the entirety of the populace. We are eavesdropping."

Henry opened his eyes a slit and immediately regretted it. Pain lanced into his head. Guttering chem pot light cast strange shadows on the pockmarked plaster wall and bisected the strong chin of Athena Boyle. Athena had somehow acquired a fur-lined tricorne hat, and her jeweled waistcoat glittered in the gloom. She placed her other index finger to her lips and pulled her hand from his mouth.

Henry rolled onto his elbow. His stomach grumbled, and pain blossomed at his temples. Someone steadied him from behind. A scent of cheese lay on the air. He whispered, "Thank you, Cram."

"Professor," came the whisper, and a cup snuck into Henry's hands. He gulped half of it down before he realized it was the hard cider they called applejack.

Luckily his coughing fit was masked by the sound of

an argument filtering through the cracked door.

An angry voice cried out, "Enough of this dillydally! Say your piece, Teach. Why should we let you stay?"

A crowd called, "Mercy!" Others responded with "Out with him!"

"Can you stand?" Athena asked.

"I think so." It turned out he could stand, barely. He refrained from reminding her that a push from her had broken his leg for him in the first place. Athena and Cram helped him over to the door, and all three peered through the gap.

Henry had never seen the common room of the King's Bum so full. The two-story hall was packed with pirates, filling the tables, standing against the walls, lined up along the balcony. A few even perched in the rafters. A tiny woman stood on the bar, legs wide and fists on her hips. She wore salt-crusted leathers, sported an empty rapier scabbard at her hip, and had her silver-streaked golden hair tucked into a little pink bonnet. She raised her hand, and the room fell quiet. "You know the question before us." Her high-pitched scalpel of a voice cut to every corner of the room. "The fire was set by outsiders. Captain Teach and the *Thrift* are hunted, and we meet to decide if we should still offer them the protection of StiltTown or if the danger to us all is too great."

"That's Precious Nel," Cram whispered in Henry's ear. "They say she's killed more seafolk than the Royal Navy and the Reeve combined."

Wayland Teach also stood on the bar. In the almost a fortnight since they had escaped the *Grail* he had lost weight. There was a hollow, hungry look to the man. He had shaved away most of his beard, leaving only his bushy mustaches.

"Wayland, speak your piece." Precious Nel gave him a nod and then dropped to the floor.

Where Nel's voice was a scalpel, Teach's was honey. "Mates. Captains. Chieftains of the Sanguine Seas. You know me, and you know my folk." Jeers at that. Henry picked out Skillet and Frog Jerky in the corner. Skillet was frowning, and his sharpened frypan was nowhere to be seen. None of the *Thrift*'s crew had weapons.

"You ain't even a pirate anymore, Teach! You're a *taximan*," called a big fellow with a mouthful of tarnished tin teeth, glowering next to the door. Laughter and catcalls erupted.

Teach nodded, genial. "That may be true, Dogsilver Sam, that may be true. You should give us a hulloo for a taxi ride the next time you run your ship aground. I reckon that happens about once every moon." More laughter and pounding on the tables.

Teach rode the wave. "Lads and lasses, my crew has fallen on hard times, and we have no other place to run." He looked up to the rafters, then down at the floor. "Many of you know my girl, Ruby. She has been taken by the crown into the shadows." Murmurs and whispers crossed the room. "We need a burrow to lie low and plan our next move. I had thought StiltTown a likely place, but we have brought danger down upon you. I beg you for a little more time, special since the *Thrift*, she is sorely wounded. We are at your mercy. I'll leave it at that."

He hopped off the bar like a man half his size and strode, flanked by Skillet and Jerky, straight toward the door. Dogsilver Sam snarled and stepped aside.

Memories of the two women on the balcony flooded

back into Henry's mind. "Come on," he said.

Athena whispered, "Wait. We can observe and report back."

The journal's familiar weight comforted him as he pulled on his coat. "I have to get to the captain." He hopped over to his crutches, stowed in the corner behind the door. The room spun for a moment, but he had to keep moving.

"But we will miss the verdict!"

"It does not matter." He pushed through the door into a small crowd of Ottomans, their rich scarves tinkling with interwoven tiles. Athena and Cram trailed him as he clunked down the steps and out into the night. The cold mist chased away what little warmth he had gained from the room; but he had business to attend to, and that business would not wait. They found the captain with Skillet and Frog Jerky under the tavern sign, a painting of a monarch with his elegant robe up over his shoulders and his kingly breeches around his knees. King's Bum indeed. The three smugglers were smoking pipes and looking gloomy.

"Henry." The captain gave him a huge bear hug,

very different from the distant "Mister Collins" he had employed in the past. He was a big man, yet he still had to look up at Henry, as a brick wall might to a willow. "Good to see you fit and moving. We were worried for you."

The captain's friendliness had caught Henry off guard. "I am well."

Captain Teach said, "You are more than well, lad. You saved our home, and I owe you a debt."

A pistol shot rang out from inside the Bum.

Henry jumped. Guns put him on edge. Athena's hand snapped to her hilt. Skillet tapped his pipe on the sole of his boot. "Calm yourselves, urchins. That's the sound of pirate democracy in there, nothing more." And indeed, the sound of a pitched battle rang out from inside the tavern: fists and grunts, kicks and clashes. Once a woman came sailing through the window to land on her back at their feet. She dusted herself off, spat out a tooth, and ran straight back in, yelling at the top of her lungs, "You mistake my premise!"

Henry cleared his throat. "So, they fight over whether we stay or go?"

Skillet quirked his mouth, squinting. He was always squinting. "That's right," he said. "How dear a body cares for a thing is how hard they'll fight for it."

Frog Jerky nodded. "Thy vote be thy life."

He uncapped a leather bottle and handed it over to Henry. Whatever was inside tasted like sugared liquid tar.

Henry kept it down, barely, and passed it on. "What is that?"

"Lemonade." Skillet made a face. "I know it. I ain't no Gwath."

"Who?"

"Long story."

The captain cocked his head at Skillet. "I hope that particular story hasn't ended."

Cram coughed most of his "lemonade" into the air beside him and then delicately replaced the cap before passing the bottle along to Athena, who returned it to Skillet untouched.

"Captain?" Henry asked.

"Yes, Henry?"

"Last night—"

"Two nights ago." Teach corrected him.

"Oh," Henry said. He had been unconscious for two days? "Two nights ago then"—he began again—"before I came to the *Thrift*—"

Frog Jerky snorted. "Before you called down a sou-wester outa the sky and saved Fat Maggie?"

"Yes, well." The praise caught him flat-footed. He didn't know what to do with it. "The fire was set as a distraction."

"What?" Athena said.

Henry took a breath. "I was on the back balcony, studying Ruby's journal, and I was attacked by two women."

Frog Jerky nodded. "You do cut a fine figure, sir."

"Listen to me, please." Frog Jerky quieted. "Captain, one had already been in disguise here: the clever one who served in the bar."

"Jenny?"

"Yes. The other one climbed up the side of the tavern to the balcony from the water, I think. She said she set the fire to draw you all out."

"They were coming for you?"

"No, not me. For this." Henry pulled the journal out of the pocket of his coat.

Teach reached out a hand involuntarily. "What happened?"

Henry told them about the ambush and his escape.

"Where are they now?" Skillet scanned the darkness around them. He had drawn a smaller version of the sharpened cast-iron pan he usually wielded, summoned from some secret pocket. He flipped it absently by the handle.

Cram pulled his eyes away from the shadows. "The potboy was saying the next morning they had a spider colony up on that balcony. A huge web the like he'd never seen before."

"But no woman?"

"No, just all the strands hanging there," Cram said. "No spiders, neither."

"So she escaped," Henry said.

"We need to move, Captain." Athena's eyes lit up. The girl fed on danger the way Cram fed on griddle cakes. "Someone is obviously hunting us, and we have been found."

"Who?" Henry asked.

"Does it matter?" said Athena.

"Well, I think it might," said Henry.

They all looked to Wayland Teach. "Patience, Lord Athen." It had shocked Henry to see how easily the entire crew remembered to use her public face. Liars cottoned to lies, he supposed. The captain hooked his thumbs in his wide leather belt. "Let us concern ourselves with these hunters after we see what the rest of the night brings. Meanwhile, we keep a weather eye out for trouble and keep close with one another. Frog Jerky, spread the word among the crew."

"Aye, Cap'n." He disappeared into the night.

They clustered a bit closer under the chem pot after that, jumping at shadows.

Just after moonrise the door creaked open, and the woman called Precious Nel stumbled out to the steps. Her bonnet hung stained and torn, and she held a haunch of raw meat over her left eye. She plunked down on the steps and looked them all over for a moment. "Sorry, Wayland," she said. "I did my best, but the tide of discourse just wasn't with ye. With the French and the British circling each other like mad killer whales out in the drink, the town won't accept one more risk. They want ye out, by midnight tomorrow, and you're not to come back."

"Banished." Skillet spat.

"Wait." Nel smiled. "Not all. Only the captain there. The rest of you lunkheads have leave to sign on with another crew or scrap the *Thrift* or, Providence help you, try to salvage her." She pulled herself up to standing by the railing. "Where will ye head?"

Teach stroked his mustache. "The Wild, I reckon."

Nel spit. "Careful out there. It's madness on dry land." She held up her left hand, and the pinkie finger was gone.

"I will take that under advisement."

"I always liked you, Captain Teach."

"And I always found you precious, Captain Nel." He doffed his hat and bowed to his boots.

She laughed and staggered back into the lit-up room. The door closed.

A frog glorped somewhere.

Wayland Teach scratched at his mustaches. "Well, *Captain* Skillet, I trust you will begin repairs immediately on her jolly majesty the *Thrift*?"

Skillet eyed Wayland Teach. "It is only for a man such as you, sir, that I would ever lower myself to join the slugs and ne'er-do-wells that do style theyselves Captain."

Teach laughed. It was the strangest thing. The man had just lost his ship and the rest of his family, and he laughed as though it were his birthday. He took in Henry, Athena, and Cram. "My friends, I have no ship to offer, but will you journey on with with me to search for one Ruby Teach, apprentice thief and daughter to scoundrels?"

They exchanged glances. It was never really in doubt.

"Yes, sir," Henry said, "but you might be following me."

Teach blew out his mustaches. "Is that right?" Henry nodded. "And why is that, Henry Collins?"

"Because I have solved the first two lines of the journal."

"Have you now?"

"Yes. It is a set of directions."

CHAPTER 6

The words we Say we cannot Unsay.
The acts we Do we cannot Undo.
—William Keith, governor, Pennswood Colony

The girl with the chestnut hair sat down across from Ruby with a bold look. Skillet might have said she made the bench her own. And she had plenty of room. Ruby had come down the stairs to the dining hall to find the tables packed with cadets, save one, which was completely empty. She took the hint. The porridge tasted just like Gwath's—if Gwath had thrown a pot of porridge into a pit filled with rabid weasels, ashes, and a snail.

Ruby stared back and used all her will and cunning to down another spoonful of the stuff.

"Avid Wake." The girl said her name like a challenge, loud so the whole room could hear.

Ruby pitched her voice to carry just a wee bit farther. "Ruby Teach."

Quiet fell so completely, Ruby could hear herself chewing. Eyes on her from all corners. No reeves or wards about at all. This was an interview. Well, Ruby had been sharping for folk since she was old enough to walk. Whatever this band of feral urchins was on the lookout for, she would give it to them. She let the world fall away and focused on her mark with the chestnut hair.

"How is your breakfast, milady?" Avid asked.

"Somewhere between the refuse pit and sweaty rat cakes." That got a chuckle from the room. Ruby Maxim Two: "Always Mock the Vittles."

Wake smiled as well, nodding at the white-haired girl, Ruby's climbing partner. "Keep a watch out for Never. She has brains to burn and will never show you her full hand."

Ruby tipped an invisible cap to the girl, who stared

back, expressionless. And creepy. "I'll remember."

Never jumped up on her bench. "See that you do!" The cadets about her stomped their feet in appreciation, none more energetic than the white-haired boy sitting next to her, the one who had raced Avid on the ropes. Her brother?

Avid looked her over. "So where did you come from? They haven't told us anything about you, but that was some entrance yesterday. Tinker's carriage with the lord captain?"

"That's not how everyone arrives?" That got another laugh from the hall, but not from Avid.

"Hardly."

Too much bravado. This was the queen, and she wouldn't be upstaged in her own castle. Ruby toned it down. Humble. That's what this girl wants, for me to scrape and for her to be the one who shines. Ruby dropped her eyes to the table, then brought them up, stark. "What's past is past. They brought me here to train. That's all I want to do." She couldn't exactly say, "I want to discover the secret forged into my blood by my grandmaster alchemyst mother, who then abandoned me, and oh, by the way, stumble on how to activate some kind of hidden ability to change my very shape," now could she?

Avid nodded. "I saw you out there today."

"And?"

Avid smiled. "I've seen worse days."

Ruby ventured a small smile back.

"What happened to your parents?"

Was this about her father? Her stomach tightened.

Or her mother? Marise Fermat had left Ruby far behind when she was a baby, but not before branding her with *something* that so many people wanted: Wisdom Rool, the Tinkers, the Royal Navy, and for all she knew the high mandarin of Cathay. Was this girl having at her? Ruby cast a quick eye about the room, and saw nothing but interest. They wanted to know her. She took in their faces: plain lines, hard living. A regular girl, then, that's who she needed to be. "My parents are fine, as far as I know. Father a second mate, mother a milliner." Milliner sounded good. "Said good-bye a few weeks ago. They miss me, I hope. What about you?"

Avid Wake's face closed like a jailhouse door.

She grabbed Ruby by the collar, two cadets swooping in to help her, and before Ruby could even protest, they were back in the yard.

The fist tore into Ruby's cheek. A light flashed somewhere, and she hit the ground. She blinked the cobwebs away, and a circle of plain gray boots came into focus. Just past her nose, red blood spattered the white of the yard. Hers.

Ruby's pulse pounded in her head, and the mix of snow and mud stung her face. What had she said? What had she done? The mud had no answer for her.

"Get up," said Avid. "Get up, girl." She kicked Ruby right in the small of the back. Pain lit her body.

Gwath would forgive her for playing possum. So would her father. Cram would urge her to stay down. Athena might actually jump into the fray, running to her defense.

None of them were here.

Ruby Maxim Three: "They Feed on Weakness." Somehow she made her way to standing. Surrounded by watching cadets, the tall girl was circling her fists.

Ruby spit out more red. "You'll need more than that to lay me out."

Turns out Avid had more.

At some point it stopped.

Unknown hands pulled Avid away, but no one reached out to Ruby. She fought her way to her knees in the chill calf-deep mud of the courtyard. The circle of cadets hung back, as if she were carrying some manner of plague.

Ward Cole half carried her back to her room. A boy about her age sat on her bunk, restless olive eyes skittering about. A clean linen bandage lay unrolled before him.

"Hale here will fix you up," Cole said. He squatted on the balls of his feet, back against the wall. The boy ran a cloth over a cut above her eye.

Ruby stifled a curse.

"I am sorry," the boy said. "It must be cleaned."

"What are you using on that cloth, acid?"

"Don't worry, Teach," said Cole. "Everyone fights when they first get here. It will hash itself out. You fought well today."

"Really?"

"No, not really." He laughed. "But a fight you walk away from is a fight well fought. Or crawl away from. You

KENT DAVIS

didn't quit. That is something."

It hurt her pride to ask, "Why did no one stop it?"
Why did no one pull her off me?

Cole's smile turned rueful. "The wards try to stay
apart from cadet matters. We find it more useful to let
these things work themselves out."

"Is it useful to allow someone to be murdered by a
curly-headed giraffe?"

His face went still. "Are you deceased, Cadet?"

The swiftness of the change caught her flat-footed.
"No. No, Ward."

"Then 'murder' doesn't really fit, now does it?"

"No. But I still don't understand why she came after
me. We were talking about our parents—"

Cole started. "Your parents?"

"Yes. She asked about them, and when I told her who
they were and what they were doing now, she snapped."

Cole let out a breath. "Ruby Teach, we are orphans."

"What, the Reeve?"

"Every last one of us."

They sat in silence as the boy, Hale, rubbed something

cool that smelled like pine on her swollen knuckles. He cleared his throat as he moved to her back. "I need to pull up your shirt, please." He was up close, but his voice stayed far away, as if it were watching everything happening from out in the hall. As he pulled up the shirt about her waist, he gasped. Light fingers probed the place where she had been kicked, and Ruby choked off a moan, twisting. The twist set off a whole cannonade of other pains in her back and legs, until she could do nothing but stay as still as possible.

"Ward." Hale backed into Ruby's view, face concerned.

Ruby did not hear Cole rise, but his hand was suddenly on her shoulder. "Teach, I'm going to help you. It may cause you some pain."

"And that is different from now how?" she gritted through her teeth.

Hale hustled over to the far corner of the cell, as if to avoid a snake. Caution warred with keen interest across his features.

"Hold on, Ruby," Cole said from behind her.

What was he going to do? Whatever it might be, Ruby

gripped the bedframe in her fist for dear life. Just in time.

At first, she thought it was hands on her back. Cole's hands. But no, it was mud. Cool, liquid, gummy mud. On her back. *In* her back. It did hurt, but the hurt came with something else. Ease.

The pain wasn't gone, but it had changed. She was sore, sure, but she could move. She used her newfound flexibility to turn on the bed to face him. He was squatting again, hands held palm up.

Ruby frowned. "What did you do to me?"

Cole was sweating as if he had run from Charles Town. "We call them Works. They are the core of being a reeve."

Before she knew it, her head was on the pillow. She tried to form a question, but her mouth just said, "Wuuuuuu?"

Cole tucked the blanket around her shoulders. "No more questions tonight. The healing is taking your strength, too. You've had quite a day. Tomorrow, be certain that you will discover more, and that more will be asked of you."

She had a smart reply primed, but she was asleep before she could say it.

CHAPTER 7

FARNSWORTH: *I'll be deviled! Without your mask you are the spitting image of Lady Catherine!*

CATHERINE: *I am Catherine, you daft ninny. I have taken a disguise so that I may steal the heart of Gerald Bumblebuffle. Now, boost me up this wall.*

FARNSWORTH: *As you say, my lady. If I may offer my opinion of that young "gentleman"?*

CATHERINE: *You may not.*

FARNSWORTH: *As you say. Boosting.*

—Marion Coatesworth-Hay, *A Game of Vials and Vapors,* Act I, sc. iii

The captain and Henry waited for them at the bottom of the hill. Cram, breath steaming, slogged up the path behind Lady Athena. He rounded a switchback to find her standing in front of a little wooden sign, painted red with writing.

Cram was not much for letters. "What's it say?"

Athena read, "All who cross this line shall beware. You leave your safety behind."

"Ah, well then." Cram turned around and headed back down the trail.

"Cram, stop," Athena said.

"You heard the sign there," Cram said. "Beware the line and we leave our safety. Just 'cause the captain claims this woman as an old mate don't mean nothing up here in the heights. Mam always says, 'If you jump down the chimney, don't be moaning if your nethers get burned.'"

"Fine. Let us stay out of the fire. Let's go back to the inn, shall we, and sit about the hearth telling stories of Ruby Teach and how we wish we had had the courage to walk up a Providence-forsaken path." She turned and trudged on up the trail.

Down below, the captain had wheeled the handcart about so the professor, his busted leg sticking out at an angle, could see. The tall boy stared up the hill at Cram, eyes full of woe. No doubt in Cram's noggin that even on his crutches the professor would never have been able to make it even halfway up. The captain had stayed with him for protection.

The little crossroads outside the town of Harris's Ferry sat empty save those two, no farmers or trappers to be seen. It was a chilly gray morning, and the fallen leaves smelled of rot. The town itself was abandoned, two buildings smoldering in the morning, both with signs in front of them. Lady Athena had read them aloud. BACK TO FRANCE WITH YOU, OR UP IN SMOKE WITH YOU.

"Burning out foreigners," Teach had said. "Bad business." The captain had talked them past a small barricade across the road, and once they had even pulled the professor's handcart into a pond to hide in a stand of cattails as a roaming band of bravos had marched past, muskets and masks and hard looks. The countryside was rising. But why? And for whom? Among them his companions had a passel of sense, and none of them had been able to answer. Cram shook his head. They had other fat to fry.

He sighed and turned himself back around, struggling to catch up with Athena, who was making good time up a devil of a steep trail. The trees loomed in like tight shelves in a larder.

Was the trail yet more steep? "Lady A.?"

She turned, impatient as ever. "Yes, Cram?"

Cram stopped next to her in a little clearing and put

his hands on his knees. "A moment for my bellows, if you might? This trail is tolerable sheer."

Athena Boyle wiped the sweat from her face with a silk handkerchief. Her waistcoat and topcoat were free of the stains and tears that marked the rest of their duds after months on the hunt. Cram was proud of that. It had taken every ounce of ingenuity and gumption he had to make it so. Not to mention professor-level experimentation with cleaning substitutes. Who knew that goat's milk could make leather just that shade of ivory? And it were best not to speak of the various cleansing uses of crushed slug. No matter. Athena looked every inch the wealthy young gentleman, and that was just how Cram preferred it.

"I've caught glimpses of a dwelling farther up the hill, I think. Just a bit farther, and we should be able to get a better look."

"And this woman will guide us to the place in the professor's journal?"

"Supposedly."

Cram sat. And he thought. Something still nagged at

him. "But ain't we going *away* from the Ferret?"

Athena pressed her lips together. "Must I go over this again?"

"Yes, please."

She gave him a Look and ticked off on her fingers. "None of our contacts in Philadelphi can find Ruby. We don't even know if she is in the colonies anymore. Collins's mentor is imprisoned in his own underground tower"—she nodded back down the trail—"and our good captain knows of only one other person who may be able to help us pick up Ruby's trail. His wife."

"His wife who left him and his daughter when Ruby was a baby?"

Athena nodded. "Yes."

"Who is one of the more powerful alchemysts on this continent?"

"Yes."

"Who no one has seen in thirteen years?"

"Yes."

"How we going to find her?"

"The journal and the guide."

"The journal and the guide will take us to her?"

"If Henry Collins can decipher the rest of it, he believes so."

"And then what?"

Lady Athena shook her head, disbelieving. "And then we all pray she is in a mood to help us find Ruby." She cinched her hat back onto her head. "Better now, Cram?"

He smiled. It was nice to be back to the two of them, even if it took scaling a mountain. The lady and the professor still only talked if they had to, and when they did, it was all pins and stickers. And the captain, when he thought no one was watching, had the look of a sinking ship. This whole journey felt to Cram like a rickety old tinker's carriage: holes in the floor, crank wheel smoking, and all four wheels fixing to fall clear off. All he could do was keep tightening, keep cinching, and keep smiling and hope that they got somewhere soon.

He jumped up. "I am indeed better, milady. Right as rain. Let us mosey."

"Well, come on then." Lady Athena started back up the hill, grabbing a tree trunk to pull herself over a shelf of mossy rock.

She swung around the tree, out of sight, and then

there was a strange sound, like something in the brush rushing at her. She yelped, "Cram!"

Cram scrambled over a rock to get a better view.

Athena's hat had come off. She hung upside down in front of him, swinging back and forth by her ankles, rope rising into the trees. Cram split to the side of the path to see if he could help her down.

"Wait, Cram!"

Something struck Cram's feet, yanking them out from under him. Lady A. whirled in front of him and then back and forth like a pendulum. He now was hanging upside down as well, and twirling to boot. Hunting snares, he reckoned.

On the path to a guide's house.

Should have seen that coming.

The ropes disappeared up into the trees. The furious face of Lady Athena rotated into view and then disappeared again. Then reappeared.

Athena cursed. "Do you have a knife?"

She disappeared.

He shook his head, then realized she couldn't see him. "No," he said.

"Why not?"

"The captain needed it for his cheese this morning."

"So you left your knife with him?"

"Well, I didn't surmise I was going to need it."

"What do you mean?"

"Well, with your sword and the professor's flippity-flips at hand, I haven't drawn that thing in anger in a month."

"Well, is it at all possible that it might be useful at this moment?" Athena said.

"It might indeed," Cram admitted. "What about your sword?"

She pointed to where it lay just out of reach, glittering in the wintry sun.

"Hard cheese that it fell out over there. Just inches from your grasp. Worst of luck really."

"Yes." Athena turned back into view, and from the face she was wearing, he was right pleased when she spun back out of sight.

This was not good. "What now? If we keep swinging like this, I might lose my breakfast, and I'm a mite hungry already, so that would make things doubly—"

"Cram . . ."

"Yes, milord." It was important that Cram call her milord, in public, and that was right fine with him, because deciding between *sir* and *lady* had taken up far too much of his very valuable time.

The birds started tweeting, and their swinging slowed until it was more hanging. That's when the little voice snuck into his ear.

"Are you meat?" it asked.

He craned his head about. The little voice, like a piccolo, belonged to a boy, all in buckskin. He wore a beaver head hood, so it looked as if the beaver were chomping his noggin from behind.

"No, young sir, we are certainly not meat," said Cram.

The boy stared for a moment and then turned and ran back up the hill as if he had been shot from a musket.

"Well done," Athena said.

"I had to say something."

" 'Not meat' is most decidedly a solid stance."

"But what if you are meat?" another voice asked.

Cram was pleased that his yelp was not very loud. The

boy was back, and standing next to him, leaning on a spear, was a woman. She was dressed the same as the boy, leather breeches and knee-length hunting shirt, with a wide leather belt around her waist. She had a similar hood to the boy's, but this one was a white wolf's head, and it was propped back over the top of her dun-brown hair. Her skin was that outdoor-seasoned leather that marked her somewhat between five and thirty years older than Cram. The hand on the spear was layered with scars, animal ones, not the kind you get from cooking. She looked positively iron.

"I'm a mite gamey," Cram offered, "and my companion"—he shrugged his shoulder at Athena—"is positively stringy."

The woman barked a laugh. "I like you," she said. "We might eat you last." The little boy licked his lips.

"Madam," Athena began.

"Madam!" The woman hooted. "Madam. Do you see a 'madam' anywhere around here, Cubbins?"

The boy shook his head solemnly and then poked Athena in the shoulder with his stick. She began to sway slightly.

"Very well then," Athena said. "My name is Lord

Athen Boyle. A pleasure to meet you. This is my servant, Cram. We have been sent to secure an audience with you for our captain, Wayland Teach. Would you be so kind as to eat us, or let us down, as you choose, but by all means let us get on with this kerfuffle."

The woman walked over to Athena; the little boy stayed perched on his rock. "Not my fault you came up our hill."

"No, it is not. It is ours." Athena's words came slowly and full of care. "It is our fault, and I would like to apologize for myself and on behalf of my companion for our trespass. It was not . . ." She was searching.

"Neighborly," Cram finished.

"No, it was not neighborly." The woman reversed her spear and stabbed it into the ground. "However, it would neither be neighborly to eat you for breakfast before hearing why you come up all this way. And bring me that Wayland Teach; I have not set my eyes on a good liar in years. By the by, we don't actually eat folk. That's just Cubbins's way of saying hello."

Cubbins threw his arms in the air and blew out his cheeks in frustration.

CHAPTER 8

*A quinsy is a Fever attended with Difficulty of
Swallowing, and often Breathing. For curing, place a
large White-bread Toast, half an Inch thick, dipt in
Brandy, to the crown of the Head till it dries.*
—John Wesley, Primitive Physick

"When a reeve makes a Work, it is an expression of
one's duty. A gift, if you will." Ward Corson tapped
her two jade fingers on the gray wood ledge that ran
around the roof of Fort Scoria's keep. They were actual
jade, rumored to be souvenirs from some dustup with
shamans in the Far East. Ruby sat on the balls of her feet
with the rest of the cadets, crouched around Corson in
a loose semicircle. She had made certain to place herself

as far as possible from Avid. A fierce wind blew up this high, and it stung the cuts on Ruby's face. There were no mirrors here, but from poking and prodding, Ruby was fairly certain she had a blooming black eye. Her back, though, where Cole had done that thing to it, felt only a little sore. Ruby stifled a yawn. The flame-haired ward looked at her. "Teach."

Caution burned away any trace of tiredness. "Yes, Ward?"

"You are new to our company, so you may not understand a Work. Is that correct?"

Should she talk about what happened the night before with Ward Cole? "Well—"

"Very good. A practical demonstration. And a refresher for the entire group. Ward Burk?"

Another ward stood up from her place behind the class. The one sparring the big reeve on Ruby's first day. Her short black hair ruffled in the wind as her eyes searched the rooftop, passing over Ruby's for a moment with a flicker and then coming to rest on the roof in front of her. She held up two fingers. Then she began to breathe out: long, deep breaths. She placed the two fingers, tips first, on the roof.

Then, quietly and slowly, she pressed herself into a handstand! A *finger*stand? It was impossible, but there she was, arm fully extended, feet up in the air, staying upright on only two of her fingers.

Corson's voice wound into Ruby's ears. "A Work of Flesh such as this helps to position yourself or to smite your enemies. A Work of Spirit could heal your wounds or even enable you to walk through walls. They all require you to *give* a piece of yourself, to sacrifice for your cause. But you must first empty yourself of your life before this time and place—"

Ward Burk was still doing a fingerstand in the back of the group, and her face was like glass. Empty, as if she hadn't a care in the world. Like Wisdom Rool's eyes.

Empty yourself? Of what?

Someone knocked on the trapdoor.

Ward Burk flowed back to her feet and opened it.

Mouse brown hair and pale olive eyes stuck up through the trap. It was the boy Hale, who had tended her wounds from the fight with Avid. The rest of him remained hidden, as if he didn't want to expose himself to the sunlight. Cadets giggled.

"Yes, Hale?" Corson said.

His voice was muffled by the wood of the roof. "The doctor has sent me for Ruby Teach." Whispers broke out among the cadets.

The doctor?

Something flitted across Corson's face, but it was too quick for Ruby to nail it down. "Very well," she said. "Teach, you're with Hale."

The smaller boy waited at the bottom of the ladder. He held out his hand, very grave. She shook it. He nodded. "I did not introduce myself last time. I am Evram."

Ruby followed Evram Hale into the depths of Fort Scoria. They soon passed from gray wood corridors down into the rock of the bluff, lit only intermittently by chem pots.

"Where are we going?" Ruby asked.

"The laboratory," said Evram, and he wouldn't say anything more.

Ruby swallowed hard and took extra care to remember their route. Evram led her through a room occupied by a wide stone pool, filled entirely with sand. Double windows with strong storm shutters hung open, and a stout wind was sucked into the chamber. Two reeves—she recognized them from the walls—stood waist deep in the sand, both wearing muslin shifts, scrubbing themselves vigorously. She and Evram circled the sand pool close to the windows, and as they passed, Ruby took in a glimpse of what lay beyond: rock and sky.

Evram unlocked a stout timber door, and after they went through, she helped him fight it closed against the wind. It cleaved into the door frame, and silence fell.

They stood at the top of a little flight of stone stairs, which led down to a long, narrow corridor, two doors on each side. Instead of the restless chem pots that had lit the rest of the fort, tinker's lamps of a style Ruby had not seen before hung at regular intervals, casting a harsh white glare over the hallway.

"Evram—" Ruby said.

"Follow me, please."

She did. The door at the end of the hall opened into a wide, bright room.

The laboratory of Fort Scoria was the most orderly place Ruby had ever seen. It was big and windowless, and there were tinker's lamps here, too, emitting the same bleak whiteness. Alloy and glass tables sparkled grimly, and the shining white walls were so deeply polished that Ruby's blurry reflection stared back at her from several places. There were basins. There were drains in the floor. There were gleaming cages of many sizes, all of which were empty. Rows of spotless prods, pokers, and cutters lay in orderly array, marshaled for action. The air was very still, as though the room were waiting for something.

A man worked at a counter across the room, back to Ruby and Evram. He was of medium height and wore a white frock coat, white breeches, white tights, white shoes with white buckles. He was the one who had been watching her the day of the ropes.

Evram cleared his throat. "Doctor Swedenborg, I have brought Ruby Teach."

The man turned about. He had a handsome, symmetrical face, but most of the skin below the left cheek was gone, pocked and eaten down to the bone. He stared at Ruby. A pink tongue flicked out between his exposed teeth. Much of his neck on that left side was covered in a fine, silvery mesh. It made a tinkling, hissing sound when he breathed. He wore slim white leather gloves and looked her up and down as if she were made of sweetcakes.

"So, Miss Teach. We meet at last." Swedenborg's voice, slightly accented, was an odd mixture of wind and sunshine. It was very pleasant, making things somehow worse.

They sat across from each other at a brushed metal table. Evram set a bowl of watery broth that smelled of leeks in front of the doctor. Swedenborg did not offer her any, but he sipped a spoonful as he looked at her.

"I am Doctor Emmanuel Swedenborg. I am an chemyst. You know what that is?"

The soggy jingle of his breathing unnerved her. She waved her hand at the assembled equipment. "What do you take me for? You're a Tinker."

"Well, yes"—he waved a finger—"but I am not fond of the term. It indicates a low person who sells his art for money."

She could not resist. "So what do you sell yours for?"

It was a solid jab, well aimed, but he barely blinked. His eyes flared wider, and he smiled. "You have spirit. Excellent! I favor test subjects with a certain fire. They last longer."

Her heart leaped into her mouth. Test subject? Last longer? "What will you be doing to me?" She fought to keep the quiver out of her voice.

The spoon rang on the metal table, and Evram was immediately there, whisking away the bowl and delivering an inkwell, a feather pen, and a stack of pristine white parchment.

"What will *we* be doing together, Ruby? That is the question." He dipped the pen in the ink, and it hovered above the parchment.

Did he expect her to just *tell* him the secret? Even if she could, she wouldn't. A spark of defiance cut through the fear at the bottom of her belly. He expected absolute obedience from Evram. He said he liked spirit, but just how much would it take to spoil his soup?

She smoothed her face to seamless innocence. "I

don't know. I thought maybe studying the hunting habits of the common river otter?"

He smiled thinly. "No. I am waiting, pen in hand, for you to tell me all that you know about your passenger."

"Passenger?"

"The famous secret, yes? I have a taste for secrets." His pink tongue quested against the mesh on his jaw. "I have been told by folk at the highest levels of the crown that this chemystral secret can offer the world unparalleled fuel for invention, creation, and destruction." He savored the last word. "And we shall discover it together, you and I. Doesn't that sound delightful?"

There really was only one acceptable response to such a strange and intense request.

"Of course!" Ruby said. She didn't need to force her smile. *The highest level of the crown. Fuel.* Small words. Tiny facts. But she had tricked those words out of him. She could not just sit here and give him secrets. She had to earn them, too.

CHAPTER 9

WANTED:
Mountain Guide of No Small Measure
for travel to Pointes West
Ready Money for True Skill
Inquire at Stores Room, Blistered Heel Inn
Srs. inquiries only

Athena covered her nose. Discreetly.

Muttering under her breath, the beast woman had resplinted Henry Collins's leg and plastered a mat of foul-smelling herbs and fir resin on top of it, then wrapped the whole biscuit in what was unmistakably her (filthy) shirt. The whole of this doctoring, if it could even be called doctoring, was worthy of suspicion. In point of fact the dwelling, if it could be called a dwelling, was equally worthy of suspicion.

It was a cave with a front porch.

The "cabin," as the woodswoman called it, held a series of snug chambers, carpeted with furs and strewn with roughhewn furniture. A smoke hole peeked out of the ceiling of the largest chamber, referred to as the kitchen, and a fire burned hot in an oven made half of scraps of iron, half of a ring of stones. On the walls hung the skins of all manner of creatures, and various implements of forest travel and beast slaying lay strewn about in various states of disrepair.

The woman had handled Henry gently enough, carrying him easily up the hill in her leather-clad arms. She had offered no such aid to the captain, who had followed wheezily and at a snail's pace. The woman and her boy laid Henry on a pile of furs by the fire and then covered him with strangely patterned blankets before tending to his wound.

"Dear lady—" Wayland Teach began from his stool in the corner, but the woman turned a ferocious look on him, and he raised his hands in surrender.

"First, we eat," she said, and Athena fought a brief spike of panic when she thought to herself: Eat whom? "You left me high and dry on a snake-riddled island, Teach, but it will not be said of Winnifred Pleasant Black that she was not hospitable."

"Winnie, we had to go. Three French man-of-wars bearing down on us—"

She threw a pan at him. He ducked. "We eat!"

The beast boy threw a pinecone at the captain. "We eat!"

The woman doled out plates. On each lay a wooden cup. The steaming water inside was accompanied by a floating stick, possibly some weak mockery of tea. Next to it lay a chunk of what seemed to be spiced shoe leather. Well, a Boyle knew how to be a guest. She somehow downed the terrible tea and unchewable meat with gusto and a host of appreciative noises and nods. Cram did the same, but he meant it. Finally Winnifred Black sat in her rocking chair and lit up a corncob pipe. The boy crouched next to her, watching Athena, gnawing on something that had a tail.

She released a gout of smoke from her nostrils. "So. What is your business here?"

"Well, madam—" Teach said.

"Not you, Wayland." She waved the pipe at him. "You sent these babies up my hill to do your dirty work, so I'd soon as hear them say their piece, if you don't mind."

"Fine," said the captain.

"Babies?" Athena said.

The woman slid her eyes over Henry, who was unconscious, and Cram, who was wrestling with Cubbins over the last piece of jerky (and losing), then back to bear on Athena. Now she knew what it was to stare down a mountain lion.

"Babies." She took another long, slow pull from the pipe. "Now, tell me true, young gentleman. What brings you here?"

"We need a guide to travel west."

"You need a guide. I am a guide. Well, me and Cubbins here. We are a team. We can take you into the Endless Mountains, but your captain there is a man who can speak out of both sides of his mouth and many more besides, and I've had my dances with him."

"Now, Winnie—" said Teach.

"Quiet, you." She turned back to Athena. "It just so happens I need work. You may have noticed that my town has been completely rid of humans. I am bereft of a compelling avenue of financial advantage. However, I am also an impatient woman and have no truck with fools, so tell me true just why it is so urgent that you launch yourself and your friends here into the dangerous lands beyond."

Captain Teach waved his hand for Athena to proceed, as if it were the easiest thing in the world. Athena nodded and tried not to think about their other options, which summed up very evenly to zero. Perhaps an appeal to her sympathy? Threats? Status? But these wilderness folk refused to be lorded over. If she tried to command as Lord Athen, this woman would be done with her before she finished her first sentence.

So she tried a stranger tactic. She told the truth.

"A friend is in danger, and we have to go into the mountains because apparently that is our only choice if we wish to save our friend."

"Your friend is in the mountains?" the woodswoman asked.

"No, but information regarding her whereabouts is." Black's gaze bored through Athena. "I need more."

Was this a story that should be told? It was impossible to know who was with them and who was against them. Would the Reeve have just let them go? Athena had abandoned her father's agents, the Bluestockings; would they just *allow* her to dissolve their association? Agents unknown had planned the attack on Henry and the burning of the *Thrift*. It would be the height of stupidity to think that they were not pursued. Leaves fluttered about on the floor. Was this some strange sort of ambush, created just so more information could be got out of them? Athena looked to Captain Teach, who nodded his permission.

So she told the story. How she, Cram, and Ruby had met in a botched carriage robbery in Boston. Meeting again on the *Thrift*. The revelation that Athena was there to secure Teach and his daughter, Ruby, before the crown could get to them. Because Ruby was somehow special and had something that everyone wanted. Captain Teach's capture at the hands of the Reeve and the navy. The three companions' escape from Wisdom Rool. Hunted through the streets of Philadelphi. And further, and further, until Athena found her tale at the foot of this very hill and she and Cram hanging sausages from the trees.

When she finished, Wayland Teach was yawning, Henry was listening, eyes half lidded, dawn was creeping through the window, and Cram and Cubbins were wound together, sleeping on the floor like two wolf cubs.

Winnifred Pleasant Black, however, perched on the edge of her rocker.

Black turned to the captain. "And this is your little girl?"

The captain looked as if he might crow or cry. "Well, not so little."

Black turned to Athena. "And the three of you," she said, "you, Cram, and this Henry, without you they both—Teach and his girl—would be locked away right now."

Warmth crept up Athena's spine, and she sat a little straighter. "I suppose that's true."

The room was quiet, just the hiss of the ashes and the squeak of the rocking chair.

Black refilled her pipe and set it alight. "May I see the diary?"

Athena glanced at Henry. He stared into the hearth. Ever since the captain had given him the sacred journal, he had become a hermit indeed, locking himself away at all hours, refusing anyone access, mumbling under his breath about algorithms and temperate fluctuations. He reached into his coat and unlocked it with the button hanging around his neck, the button Ruby's mother had left for her. He held the journal out in the dawn light, shadows playing across his chemystry-scarred hand.

Black took it and paged through the procession of inscrutable equations. "What does it say?"

Henry's nose twitched. "There is a place over the mountains where three rivers meet. A city. That is all I have deciphered so far."

Winnifred Pleasant Black blew out three perfect smoke rings. "I know it."

She stood up and slung the sleeping Cubbins over her back like a rucksack. The boy blinked awake and giggled. Black said, "A friend in danger, hmm? And noble deeds? And peril in the lands beyond? Well then, you have yourself a guide."

"Excellent," Teach said with a grin. "Shall we leave tomorrow? Or the next day, if you need to gather supplies?"

Winnifred Pleasant Black walked to the heavy fur "door" that hung over the cave mouth. "Oh, no, Captain Teach." She slung the fur aside, and the cold morning blew in on a swirl of snow. "There is no going into the mountains until winter has passed. No matter how deeply it stings, you must hunker down. We leave after the heavy snows are gone, but not until then."

"Winnifred—" Teach started.

"You heard me. I know it hurts, but so does a musket ball when it needs to come out. If that boy tries to hoof it, he won't make it to the bottom of this hill, let alone into the high places. He needs to heal; you know it and I know it, even if he don't. And if you go out there in deep winter, even with me, you will die, and then what will happen to your daughter?"

A quarter of a year, she was saying? All her life Athena had moved with purpose. Under her own power, teeth to the wind. Was she cursed, somehow?

And what of Ruby? Athena's heart clenched. What terror would the Reeve put her through before they even began their journey? What devilish experiments? Was she even alive?

Athena smiled.

It was the only way to stop from pulling her own ears off. Patience was not her strong suit, never had been, but if it must be, it must be. "Cards, anyone? Apparently we have a little time."

CHAPTER 10

A man is the sum of his actions.
—Halvard de Anjou, *Bastionado*

Ruby grabbed the palisade wall, steadying her perch to look out over her shoulder and down into the valley. A midday flurry had sprinkled the trees with snow, and the wind kept up its endless assault. Islands of red and gold leaves struggled to stay afloat in a creeping sea of brown and white. Directly below her the trees washed up against the cliff face like a motionless tide. A gust of wind ruffled Ruby's thick coat, and she steadied the pail on the thin plank that was her only seat. Just two weeks at the fort, and winter was already coming on hard. She stuck out her tongue to catch a few flakes, savoring the brief, clean coolness. Too brief, before the vinegar funk crept back into her nose from the pail. She dipped her rag into it, taking care to keep her hands clear, and spread more of the varnish onto the wall.

"Up!" she yelled.

Above, Levi Curtsie's white head stuck out over the pointed top of the palisade, and then he gave an angry wave. Ruby had never thought that such a harmless gesture could be filled with rage, but that boy pulled it off. The ropes holding the plank in place creaked, and the whole getup began to rise. The huge shafts of timbers, sanded smooth by unknown Tinkers, rolled past until it stopped: a fresh patch of gray wood ready for a strengthening bath. The chemystrally hardened wood needed priming every six months. She rolled her eyes. Tinkers. Making more work for the rest of the world for a hundred years.

She dipped her rag in and began again. Her eyes watered, and her stomach rumbled. Why did chemystry always smell so terrible? Couldn't the Tinkers use their almighty skills to make their concoctions smell like rhubarb pie?

Of course the new girl drew the plank duty. Hanging from a stick and two pieces of twine hundreds of feet high. You'd think they would protect her precious blood a bit more, even if they didn't care about her. But Ruby didn't mind. She liked it. It kept her away from the taxing pokings and proddings of the Swede. It was at least a few moments' rest from Avid Wake's endless badgering. Wake had named Ruby Sweetling—because she wasn't an orphan—and the name had stuck. What could she do but keep her head down and try to stay out of their way? Ruby had sand, but she wasn't in a hurry to catch another beating from some lanky giraffe with an ax to grind.

Orphans. All of them. She had to hand it to the Reeve. What's the best way to train a fierce, loyal, relentless crew? Fish up the ones without parents, with ties to nothing except you.

"Up!" Ruby yelled again, and the plank rose, almost cresting the freshly sharpened points of the palisade.

Hoofbeats hammered the road below. The plank was its own little crow's nest, and Ruby had a clear view of the winding, narrow track that made its way up to the gate. A single horse and rider struggled up it, scattering puffs of fresh snow in their wake. The horse slowed, lathered and heaving, but the rider flicked the reins, urging it forward. It was Ward Dove, the pale, pockmarked reeve from the carriage ride.

She disappeared into the gate, and only a few moments later the whole fort shook. Levi Curtsie popped his head over the palisade with a scowl. "That's the summons. They want everyone." He reached a hand down the wall.

Ruby gave him the pail. He took it and wrinkled his nose.

"Go on. I'm right behind you," she said.

Levi scowled but disappeared.

Ruby climbed up over the palisade. The walls and yard buzzed with reeves and cadets, all moving with purpose. The whole of the fort crowded restlessly below one of the staircases. On the stairs' first landing stood Ward Dove and Wisdom Rool.

Rool raised his scarred hand, and all went silent.

"Sisters and brothers, the crown has need of you." He scanned the crowd. "Ismail?"

Ward Cole raised his hand. "Lord Captain?"

"Ready all the traveling packs and horses we have for long journeys. Cadets, you will aid Ward Cole. All reeves with me to the library."

The yard burst into activity, Ismail Cole shouting orders and cadets running to and fro, while the clump of reeves headed into the main fort.

What did the crown need? Why were the Reeve on the move? Finally a chance to discover something useful. Ruby grabbed a sack of turnips from the wagon and hurried toward the keep. She waded into the crowd of cadets in the kitchens, all of them stuffing cheese, hardtack, and vegetables into an orderly line of traveling packs. Ruby dropped the turnips in the pile and then lost herself in the crowd, sliding over toward a side door.

"Teach!"

Ruby schooled her face: intent and hardworking. She turned to see Ward Cole standing in the other doorway, five packs across each shoulder. "Where are you headed?"

"Summoned, Ward. Hale said the doctor needed me urgently."

He stared at her for a moment, then nodded. "Off you go then." He turned away, shouting, "Someone take these packs to the stables!"

Ruby slid out of the kitchen and into the empty passage down to the lab. As soon as she was certain no one followed her, she changed course for her true destination: the library. Scratch that: two reeves stood guard outside the door. She had to find a new spot, and quick. The roof! No time to double back for the climbing harness. She risked a trip back down to the kitchen and nicked a coil of rope from the traveling supplies. From there she hustled up the stairs and through the trap. The hall was built into the outer wall, and the palisade spikes were taller here, giving the roof a little fence of its own. She shucked her boots, tied off the rope on one of the spikes, and lowered herself to a spot right next to the open window of the library. She did not look down.

Ruby rested her feet against the timber wall and edged herself as close as she dared. A jumble of black-clad elbows and shoulders and heads jammed the window, all facing inward. Someone was speaking, and it was impossible to mistake the deep gravel of its owner: Wisdom Rool.

"Edwina, the door, please. This is no news for cadets."

Ward Corson said, "Yes, Lord Captain." A door latched.

Wisdom Rool let out a long sigh. "I will be brief, because you all must be on your way. Dove has brought fresh orders for every one of us, as well as difficult news. Boston is burning."

A chorus of questions competed for one another, along with calls for "quiet!"

Rool said, "Ward Dove?"

Dove took over. "Several chemystral incendiaries were set off in close timing throughout the city, including one inside the Reeve town house on Back Street." She took a breath. "I was the only survivor. The chemystral fires have proved difficult to extinguish, and when I left, parts of the city still burned. The governor is contemplating evacuation."

Ward Corson said, "Do we have any idea who executed it?"

"We do not," said Rool. "But rumors are flying in the coffeehouses that orders written in French were found at one of the sites. Some of you will be traveling with me to Boston to look into it. The rest of you have been ordered into the countryside. Reports of militia activity and brigands are blossoming like mushrooms, far more quickly than they can be investigated by our cadre in the field."

"Then Scoria will be defenseless, will it not?" It was Corson again.

Wisdom Rool chuckled. "Edwina, you and Wards Cole and Burk will be staying to supervise the cadets' training. Between the three of you and this fortress itself, I have very little worry for their safety. Doctor Swedenborg will also be staying behind, and I am certain his chemystral aid will be invaluable."

An uneasy murmur passed through the room. It wasn't only Ruby whose skin crawled when the Swede was near.

"That is all. Prepare yourselves for travel. Dove will bring you your orders by dawn. Read them, commit them to memory, and burn them. "

The meeting broke up. The door opened, and the sounds of bodies shifting and receding commenced.

The wind ruffled Ruby's hair. A bomb. Bombs. And chemystral to boot. Boston on fire. Uninvited, the overturned tinker's carriage popped into her mind, the foiled robbery where she had first met Athena. Did that street even exist now? Was it burned to bits, like the rest of her former life?

A shaggy head popped out of the window.

"Yah!" Ruby cursed under her breath.

Wisdom Rool looked up at the rooftop. He looked down at the river below. Then he looked at Ruby. "My faith in you is well placed, Ruby Teach. Your initiative never ceases to impress me."

She got control of her breathing. "It's here, isn't it? The war. You said a war was coming. And you needed me to win it."

"So I did." He shrugged. "You are correct. Of some concern to me is that I do not know who is waging this war. I must away for a while to put some work into that. I will return when I can." He leaned even farther out the window and added in a whisper, "Study hard, Ruby Teach. I need you at your fighting weight. How fares your research?"

"The Swede has said that it will provide unparalleled fuel for invention, creation, and destruction. Also, that he has that information from the highest levels of the crown. Oh, and one more thing."

"Yes?"

"He is impossibly creepy."

"That is all you have?"

"Yes, but—"

"I have no time for your buts."

Her frustration warred with her anger. "But what *is* the secret? Do you at least know something of it?"

"I have been told that you carry something that could transform the function of this world."

Anger won out. "The same as the Swede. Could you be any more vague?"

"I could, if you like."

"No. No." She clenched her hands around the rope, wishing it were his neck.

"Do what you are best at, Ruby Teach. Sneak and

find. Sneak and find." He patted her knee and looked down. "Off with you now. We don't want you to catch your death." Then he was gone.

Ruby scaled the wall as quickly and quietly as she could, mind afire and stomach at sea. At the top a folded note lay tucked into the knot of rope.

She opened it. It read, "Be careful."

She crumpled up the paper and tossed it into the canyon.

CHAPTER 11

Doubt is not a pleasant condition,
but certainty is absurd.
—Voltaire

Emmanuel Swedenborg held Ruby's earlobe as if it were a dead butterfly, delicately and with mild distaste. He murmured a little tune as he peered through a magnifying lens at the apparently fascinating goo inside her ear. Without looking up he said, "So you continue to deny any knowledge of the gift you carry?"

Whatever his chemystral power, he couldn't interrogate his way out of a piecrust. "To deny it would imply that I know the secret and I refuse to give it to you."

He tugged the ear a little harder. "You have not answered my question."

"Ow. No, Doctor, I don't know the first thing about it. To be honest, I hope you'll be able to discover it." Charming him into telling her the secret was a long game, but one of her only plays at the moment.

"I hope so, as well, Ruby. I hope so, as well. Hm. Your ears are splendid. Pity." He pulled back from the lens and stared off into space.

Ruby used the moment to take in the laboratory. There had to be something useful. Journal on the far table. Cages all about. Racks of tools, all neat and tidy. Blast. "What's our next step, Doctor?"

He cocked his head at her. "Excellent question. I believe we shall look into your interior. Mr. Hale, will you bring me that little octopoid, please?"

Evram wheeled over a metal cart. On top of it, amid a scatter of probes, tubes, and vials, sat a water-filled case at the bottom of which lay a sad-looking squid. The creature had a small tube attached to it, running out of the case and into a coil on the cart. At the end of the tube was a little metal cup. The doctor moved to place the cup on Ruby's neck.

She pulled back. "What are you doing?"

Swedenborg's breathing rang through the mesh at his neck. "It is not dangerous. We are merely employing this little apparatus to ask more questions. Please observe." He placed the cup on her neck. It was warm as flesh.

Evram flicked a switch on the case, and the squid quivered. Suddenly its slick skin changed color to a deep crimson.

"Focus, Mr. Hale."

On the red canvas of the squid's body, shapes began to resolve.

"What—what is that?"

"Why, that is you, Ruby," Swedenborg purred, gaze rapt on the little octopus. "Your internal fluids, to be precise. These creatures have astonishing mimicking properties, and our device here creates a sonic resonance that—well, suffice to say that for a short time I can look inside you."

Hairs rose on the back of Ruby's neck. Every fiber of her wanted to run away, and it took all her will to stay still. This was what she wanted to know, wasn't it? She schooled her voice to sound excited. "What do you see?"

He ignored her. The squid's body rippled, as if someone had thrown a stone into a pond, and then all at once it was clear. Something was moving around in there. "Evram, my journal. Now."

The boy hustled the journal and quill over.

"What is it?" Ruby said. "What's happening?" Were those animals? Ruby fought down a wave of bile at the thought. No, they weren't animals. They were moving too regularly, in formation, like squadrons of ships floating inside her.

Symbols.

Swedenborg's pen flew across the page, but the symbols would not stand still, pulsing and weaving in and out of the frame. There were hundreds of them, thousands even.

"Blast. They're moving too quickly. I can't see anything," said Swedenborg.

"Doctor," Evram said, "it can't—"

"I know, Evram, but I need more—"

Ridges marched across the body of the squid for a

moment, obscuring the symbols, and then it quivered one last time before it went completely still. It was dead.

Swedenborg turned back to Ruby, eyes gleaming. "Alas. He has passed on to the happy sea where squids go for eternity. He was our only specimen, but our plucky little companion has served us well."

Ruby's mouth was dry. "How?" She didn't need to pretend to be flabbergasted. "What?"

Swedenborg grinned. "Well, Ruby, it seems we are gaining ground on our elusive quarry."

"What do you mean? What happened?"

"Did you see those equations?"

Equations. Like in her mother's journal? "Yes, Doctor."

"Fascinating, isn't it?" He sat himself up as if announcing someone's birthday. "Here is my hypothesis. Your blood itself is carrying your secret!"

"But I've told you I don't know what it is."

"That is what makes this so exciting! I no longer need to converse with you at all! It is your tissue and your corpus that will show us the way."

Two sessions? He had discovered that much in two

sessions? It had taken the magician Fermat—the greatest chemyst she knew—days to even suspect that the secret lay in her blood. She had to do something. Events were moving far too quickly. The little squid floated up near the top of the tank unmoving, a grim reminder of just what might happen if he got to the answer first.

Swedenborg closed and locked his journal and was already bustling about the laboratory as if Ruby and Evram were not even there.

On her way off of the chair, Ruby stumbled into the cart with a clatter.

Evram helped her up, but not before she had lifted two of the probes from the cart and secured them up her sleeve.

"Thanks, Evram."

"You should be more careful, Ruby."

"I will." And I hope you don't find those two probes missing.

Just as she made it to the door, the Swede called out, "Oh, and before you depart, Miss Teach?"

"Yes?"

"I shall need some of your blood."

CHAPTER 12

Inaction is the devil's plaything. Doubly so is Action.
—Aquila Rose,
adventurer and ne'er-do-well

The stars shone later that night. Ruby sat in her windowsill, clouds of breath steaming in the chill mountain air. It was not enough to quiz the Swede and hope he dropped some key piece of information. He was far too clever for that. For more than a fortnight she had sat on her hands. She had been waiting for something to happen for far too long.

For what, she knew not. Athena, Henry, Cram, her father, and the crew to storm the fort in a great tunneling automaton, digging up out of a hole in the middle of the yard, spitting streams of fire at the Reeve? The picture made her smile, but did they even know where she was?

And what of Gwath? She chided herself. Her guardian had to be dead, killed by Rool on the *Thrift* long ago. Didn't he? Even Gwath could not escape the man. Besides, they were all of them in the way of her focus. Ward Corson had said, up on the roof, that the Reeve had no attachments, that it helped them. If she was to seek out the truth of her secret and learn the ways of the Reeve, she had to let them go. Their ghosts crept in through the cellar of her heart or the attic of her mind, and she could not let that pass. No, she was a crew of one, and the storm was rising. Somebody had to climb the mast to reef in the sail.

Ruby Maxim Four: "No One Rescues Princesses but Themselves."

From the hall outside came the call "Reeves in, lights ooot!" Ward Burk was walking the halls tonight. Her Irish lilt rang out, ordering the cadets to sleep. If they caught Ruby out of her room, they might clap her in irons or worse, but she could think of no way that could be worse than Swedenborg's examination table.

Ruby secured her improvised picks and kept still at the door for an hour after Burk's calls ended before she finally eased the door open. The hallway was dark and empty, without even a sconce or tinker's lamp alight. Small comfort. Ruby had to use her other senses. No one was about, only the faint moan of the wind creeping in through the windows along dim streams of moonlight. Ruby kept to the small passages and out-of-the-way rooms on her way down into the belly of the fort. The fear of punishment faded in the face of the thrill of taking action. A faint red light bled into the storeroom down the hallway from the kitchens. A voice called out in the quiet. Ruby froze. No one came down the hall; somebody told a joke about a honey cake. She moved on.

Fresh herbs and air braced her as she rounded a corner into the sand room. The neatly raked lines shone in the moonlight streaming through the open windows. The cold wind nipped at her bare toes as she crept around the outer ledge of the sand bath. The lock on the stout door fell easily to her makeshift picks, crude as they were. Stone and iodine pushed peppermint and soapwort out of her nose as she descended into the realm of the Swede.

The harsh white of Swedenborg's tinker's lamps were muted, turned down for the evening. The laboratory lay through an arch at the end of the hall. Light crept under one of the two doors at the far end of the hallway. The near two doors were dark. In one of these four rooms there had to be some record, some clue to the Swede's experiments. Or at least she hoped so.

She had never been through any of the other doors. Ruby had no idea what hours Swedenborg kept, nor where he slept (if he even did sleep). She knelt down next to the first portal on her right and listened. It was faint, but there it was: the slow, silvery tinkle of his breathing through the mesh on his neck. She froze. He mumbled in his sleep and then cried out, softly. She could not hear the words, but after that he sobbed.

Silence. Emptiness. Strange that something so difficult to find in the day came like an old friend at night.

She eased away from the door and across the hallway. No sound beyond this one.

She slipped the lock. Inside, it was as dark as the innards of a burlap sack at the bottom of a well. Ruby hesitated. Gwath had taught her how to feel the size of a room with her skin and her breath. It felt close, like a large closet, and dust tickled her nose. She reached out her hand, then pulled it back. Not the wisest notion to paw about in the lair of a master Tinker. There would be stickers and burnies and scaldies and who knew what else. Inside, she cursed. She needed light. She withdrew for the moment.

She padded down the hall to the next door. Not snoring but a different sort of sound crept with the light from the other side.

It was singing.

Ruby put her face down on the cold stone. Evram Hale's painstakingly polished buckled shoes kicked back and forth in rhythm with an old nursery lullaby. He didn't really have a sense of pitch, but he was very committed.

She needed light, and there was light in that room. Could she trust Evram? Or sharp him, at the least? Nothing to do but cast the dice. Very, very softly Ruby knocked.

The singing stopped.

"I'm sorry, Doctor Swedenborg. I did not mean to wake you," Evram said from the other side of the door.

A brief flame of an image sprang into Ruby's mind. Using her Changer powers, she transformed into the form of Swedenborg and ordered Hale around, discovering everything she needed to know. After that, in Swedenborg's posh carriage, stocked with victuals, she made her way back to Philadelphi and her friends in triumph.

That didn't happen.

Instead, Ruby knocked again.

Silence on the other side of the door.

It opened just a bit, and the light blinded her. Evram Hale peered out from the other side of the crack, puzzlement in his pale olive eyes.

He blinked. "Ruby Teach, you are supposed to be in your room," he whispered. Evram was about her size and about her age, but he carried himself all wrong. As if he were afraid of breaking or were consciously thinking about moving every arm and leg piece by piece. He was wearing smoky quartz lenses and a scorched leather apron, and he held a smoking vial in his hand.

He didn't run yelling for the Swede or shoot some Tinker concoction in her face. Score one. Project Hale was moving forward. She did not like thinking about it this way, but he was what Gwath would call a prime mark, gullible and friendless. About the fort Hale was a bit of an outcast himself. He was Swedenborg's apprentice, damning enough. He didn't train with the cadets, either, and they respected strength and courage, not attention and smarts. He was quiet, sure. But quiet like a deep pool. Henry Collins quiet. He *watched*.

And he was watching her now, waiting for her to respond.

"I'm sorry, Evram," Ruby whispered. "Can I come in?"

Evram blinked again. "Why are you out of your room?"

Ruby blinked right back. Quick, girl. She fanned the possibilities like playing cards. Feeling ill? He would wake the Swede. Afraid of the dark? Why come down into the dark? Barnacles, there was no good reason. She had to leap straight for sympathy and hope it blocked everything else out. Evram was an outcast. Use that. "I'm hiding from Avid, and I need help."

His eyes went saucery. He glanced down the hall and then stepped aside, motioning her in.

It was a wide chamber. A ragged old sheet hung down from a rod on the ceiling. Hale looked down at his shoes.

"Would you like to see my horse?"

It was not what Ruby expected to hear.

If he had said, "You can't be here, Ruby Teach." Certainly.

Or "How can I help you hide from Avid?" Possibly.

But "Would you like to see my horse?"

Ruby punted. "Yes?"

He moved the iron stool and grabbed the edge of the sheet, a weed doctor ready for the big reveal. His face split into a wide grin. "This," he said, "is Sleipnir." He said it like *slayp-neer*.

He whooshed the sheet aside. Behind it stood a miracle.

The horse was tall, as high at the shoulder as Ruby atop Evram, and it was like a gearbeast, except its alloyed bones and gears gleamed burnished copper in the light. Eight legs, not four, came down from its deep barrel chest and muscled hindquarters, standing sturdily on the stone floor of the workroom. Where the gearbeasts were menacing, this automaton somehow conveyed a calm, a safety, that fairly hummed. So beautiful it hurt her heart.

When Ruby could speak, she asked, "Where are the eyes?"

Evram kept looking back and forth, between her and the big horse, and he launched into speech. "Doctor Swedenborg has not let me put the eyes in yet. He says that the organic affinity of animal eyes will twist the spirit of the thing into madness, as with the gearbeasts." Ruby shuddered and nodded. Hale pushed on. "So *I* am wondering if there is not some way to craft eyes that will speak to Sleipnir in a way that will not drive her mad and will allow the tendency of the alloy to inform her disposition in a more useful manner."

"She is . . . beautiful," Ruby said. The word did not suffice, but it was the one she had.

He blushed. "It is my apprentice project to make journeyman," he said. "Doctor Swedenborg says that he works only with the best. He says I am a prodigy." He said it with no pride, only a relation of fact. "He says that it must be perfect before we attempt to activate it. I am working nights to perfect her." He stroked the flank of the metal steed.

"Why does she have eight legs?" Ruby asked.

"I found a picture in a book of myths in Doctor Swedenborg's library. She is Odin's horse."

"Who is Odin?"

"A one-eyed god from the north. He is very wise."

Evram seemed perfectly content chatting about the intricacies of his project until the whole building woke up, but Ruby did not have that kind of time. So she fell back on sharping. The boy was gullible to a fault. She painted on a scared look. "Evram, I'm sorry to interrupt, but I have to ask you something."

"What's that?"

"Can you help me?"

His hand stopped moving. "With what?"

Ruby took a breath. Ruby Maxim Five: "Never Drop the Mask." "Would any of these other doors lead back to my room? I fear that Avid and her friends will find me if I take the main passages."

Evram frowned, working a puzzle. "Not through the doctor's bedroom. Or his library."

His library. That was the other room, the dark one.

Perfect. She smiled ruefully. "Very well. Can you lend me a light at least? I was almost lost in the dark on my way down."

He frowned again and grew very still. Ruby held her fear in with her breath. Had she exhausted his patience? Would he call for the Swede? He scuttled back to a worktable behind Sleipnir. While he rummaged through a mess of flasks, burners, tongs, and scales, he said, "I cannot give you one of the doctor's lamps, but I can give you something I made. It is mine to give. Here." He held out a scarred wooden box, about the size of his hand.

She took it.

"Open the slat," he said.

One side of the box looked as if it might move. Ruby slid it open. Green light shot out, right into her eyes. "Ow. Thanks, Evram."

"I am sorry," he said. "But here, look." She blinked her eyes until they adjusted. In the box lay a green glass marble, no larger than her thumb. The light rolled off it, like sun on a lake.

"It is a marble," Evram said.

". . . Yes," Ruby said.

"I like marbles. I made it myself, so that means I can give it to you."

There was no guile in him. It made her sad. "Thank you, Evram. This is a fine gift."

He nodded. "Do you want to hear about its efflorescent properties and the affinities of the illuminated oil I applied to it?"

Ruby smiled. "Perhaps another time."

He thought about that for a moment. "All right."

She slid the slat closed over the light. Here was the hard part. "Evram, do the rules say you need to tell Doctor Swedenborg about this?"

He thought for quite a long moment this time. He looked at her, and he blushed. "I do not think so. You have disobeyed none of the doctor's rules, so there is no need to tell him. He has told me many times that I volunteer too much information, so he would most likely not want to hear about your visit."

Ruby nodded and turned to ease open the door.

"Ruby Teach?"

"Yes, Evram?"

The boy was blushing again. "Do you want to come back sometime? To help me with Sleipnir?"

Ruby breathed out very slowly. "Of course, Evram. I would love to."

The library door sealed Ruby in the darkness with a hiss and a pop. She slid open the panel on the marble box, and clear green light rolled out.

It was a low room, like a ship's cabin, but encircled floor to ceiling with bookshelves. Ancient, moldering volumes and birchbark scrolls crammed together, threatening to fall to the patterned rugs under her feet. In the corner sat the Swede's desk. It was brass-bound maple, the pale wood stained corpsey in the marble's light. A roll top covered the entire front, secured by a lock where the roll met the base.

She slid the probes out of her pocket. She would be through a cute little desk lock before her fingers even knew she was picking.

Wait.

She barely stopped herself in time. Ruby crouched down

with the marble, and indeed, a nearly transparent trip wire, barely glistening in the marble's light, ran athwart the room. She had to slow down. Underestimating Swedenborg would be her undoing. He was too devious and too dangerous.

She eased herself over the wire and fell into the lengthy, painstaking dance Gwath had taught her for such situations. Two more trip wires, one at chest level, one at her waist, crisscrossed the room. A careful examination of the desk lock revealed a clever little needle trap that would assuredly have poisoned her or turned her to stone or set her on fire. The thin probes were not ideal, but Ruby managed to deactivate the trap. The lock opened with a faint click.

Thankfully the Swede kept his office neat, and the rolltop was well oiled. It opened silently. A stack of papers lay on the left, his journal on the right.

"Blast," Ruby whispered. The journal boasted an intricate little lock. The probes were far too blunt for such a delicate task, and there just wasn't enough time. The clock in her head read, "TOO SLOW," and Ruby agreed. Sunrise must have been right around the corner. She would have to come back. She riffled quickly through the papers, searching for anything that might refer to her. Letters to other Tinkers and orders for materials mostly. One caught her eye. It was a short note, but its broken wax seal bore the lion of England.

> You must preserve the carrier until you have extracted the necessary information.
>
> Once you have obtained and tested the complete schematics, I am certain that we need not tell you that any other copy, even the original, is a threat to our interests. Please make certain that it will not fall into other hands. Full authority is yours in this matter.
>
> By order of His Majesty I am,
> Sincerely,
> James Stanhope, Lord High Intelligencer

"Carrier," she whispered. It was Ruby. *A threat.* "Not fall into other hands." Swedenborg was going to kill her. After he discovered what she carried, he would make her as dead as that squid in his laboratory. Blood pounded in her ears. She willed her hands to stop shaking. After a few moments, they did. She stowed the knowledge down deep, in the box in her belly. It would not serve her now.

Ruby forced herself to take as great care leaving as she had when she arrived. She returned the paper to its spot, made certain that all was as it had been before she opened it, reset the trap and the lock, threaded back through the trip wires and out the door.

She barely made it back to her room in time. She tore a hole in the bottom of the mattress and hid the probes and the marble box deep inside. It would have to do.

The faintest light hid behind the hills across the river. Dawn was coming, and another day. She collapsed into her bed, but before she even closed her eyes, there was a call from the hall.

"Reeves up, feet oooooout!" Burk again, making the morning rounds. Ruby sprang up and began doing her stretches. She hadn't slept a wink, but she felt fresher than she had for a very long time.

Ruby Maxim Six: "There Is Nothing So Refreshing to the Spirits as Mortal Danger."

CHAPTER 13

The application of force is the Art of the Soldier. It is the application of strategy that is the Art of the Reeve.
—Training manual, Reeve of England

Evram Hale opened the little compartment on the gearbeast's flank. The chemystral "dog" picked up and put down its paws woozily, as if it had just woken up, though its mad, living eyes still rolled about, moving from Ruby to Hale to the walls of the stable and back in a constant loop. The last time Ruby had been this close to a gearbeast, it had been trying to flay her and Cram for dinner. Without the barking and gnashing, the slowing *tocktocktock* of its insides rang loud in the silence. Somehow helping Swedenborg's assistant with Sleipnir, the gearhorse, had transformed into helping Evram with many of his tasks. She didn't mind. The closer she could get to him, the closer she could get to the Swede's experiments. Two more weeks had passed, however, and she had nothing new to show for it. Several midnight trips to the office had gathered her only two things: frustration at the excellence of the locking mechanism of the Swede's journal and, through the pile of letters, an annoyingly comprehensive understanding of the Swede's difficult relationship with his greataunt and her large stable of cats. So she spent as much time as she could with Evram.

As the little cadet fished about in the gearbeast's insides, the *tocktocktock* slowed even further. He did not seem to notice, olive eyes staring upward as if he were trying to fish a lost necklace out of a well. "Almost . . . I have it."

There was a faint click, and he pulled something hand-size out of the beast. The gears and pistons wound down to a stop. The eyes, too, staring into a fixed nothing.

Ruby whistled. "What is that?"

Evram carried the little metal disk the size of a

chicken egg over to a table crowded with beakers and tinker gear. "Sparkstone" was all he said as he picked up a small pitcher full of red metallic powder and carefully poured it into a hole in the top of the disk. He held the circle out. "Will you hold this for me, please?"

Ruby took it. It was surprisingly light in her hand, cool and smooth to the touch. "What does it do?" she asked.

Hale put both his hands over hers. "Wait, please," he said.

"Evram—"

"Wait, please, Ruby." He closed his eyes for a moment, then twisted his head just so, and *something* happened. Where before, the disk was cool, now it was warm. Hale wobbled. Was he fainting? Ruby grabbed his elbow.

He took the sparkstone out of her hand and hurried back to the gearbeast, hand back into its innards. He fished about again, and a few moments later another click, and then the gears *tock . . . tock . . . tocktocktock* wound back up. Evram closed the little door, and the gearbeast gave a whine and shook its head like a puppy.

It turned its eyes on him, and Hale looked back. Ruby

got the shivers all over again.

"Saunter," Evram said.

With a snap, the beast was up on all fours and trotted out the stable door.

"Are you all right?" Ruby asked to cover her interest. The word had to be a command of some kind. Did it work only for Evram? She filed it away.

"I apologize for my abruptness," he said, "but the charging of the sparkstone had to be done quickly, else the lack of energy might have damaged Arcas there."

"Arcas?" Ruby snorted. "Fancy name. Why not just call them all Grinder or Crusher or what have you?"

Evram eased himself down onto a stool. He took a spotted handkerchief out of his vest pocket and patted the sweat from his forehead. Ruby smiled. He was like the youngest little old man she had ever seen. "Arcas was a member of Actaeon's hunting pack. It seemed a fitting name, you know, considering—"

"Ah, interesting!" Ruby was in no mood for one of Evram's mythological story sessions. He would go all night if you let him. Information is what she needed. "Are you the only one here who can recharge a stone like that? Must be an awful passel of work."

"Doctor Swedenborg is a very skilled chemyst, so I suppose he could if he desired. He says it is good for my discipline, however, so it is my job. It was much more tiring when the stable was full."

When Ruby had arrived at Fort Scoria, the "stable" had been chock-full of gearbeasts, the little stalls complete with strange hoses hanging from the ceilings and the workbench equipped with all manner of odd tools, but it was a ghost town now, with only old Arcas left to stand patrol. Since the gearbeasts and all save three reeves had left, Ruby had to admit she was breathing a bit easier.

Ward Corson stalked into the stable, red hair pulled back under a black hood.

So much for breathing easier.

The reeve scanned the empty stalls. "Where is Arcas?"

Evram struggled to his feet. "On patrol, Ward."

"Fetch her and place her on the wall walk, please, Hale. We may have need of her." Evram nodded and hurried out. The ward's eyes flicked over to Ruby, as green and flinty as her jade fingers. "Up to the walls, Teach. We have visitors, and I need everybody on the palisade."

"Yes, Ward." Ruby hurried off toward one of the staircases. Corson deserved her respect.

That was why Ruby gave her an extra ten yards head start before turning around and tailing her through the shadows toward the main gate.

From the dark underneath a set of stairs, Ruby watched Ward Corson open a small door set in the corner of the much larger gate. It clacked shut behind her. Up on the wall, Avid Wake stood guard, scanning the darkness, but she was looking out, not in. Ruby, heart in her throat, slipped through the little door and closed it with the faintest of clicks.

She was outside. For a moment she considered running, but just for a moment. They were in the middle of nowhere. She was on foot. The wards would track her down. Besides, her secret was tied to the fort.

Still, it was brilliant to be out of the walls. Ruby made her way down the curving trail cut in the stone to the open hillsides above the gorge. The bitter cold night cooperated with her, thick clouds hugging the bright moon, casting slivers of light and shadow across the plain. The ground advanced away from the fort like an avenue, bordered by more cliffs on the left and the deep canyon on the right. No sign of Corson, but it was easy to see where she had been headed. On the other end of the plain, at the edge of the forest, a large fire burned.

Ruby stayed in the shadows, edging along the cliff face toward the fire, until she settled behind a large boulder. It was the closest she could sneak without alerting the sentry lurking in the shadows of a tree. Beyond him Ruby counted a mix of women and men in stained and well-used buckskins, some New French, some Iroquois, all huddled about the fire to ward off the wind. Several of them wore the floppy cap of the voyageur: trappers down from New France. They fairly bristled with guns and hatchets. A fat buck, spitted and roasting, hung over the fire.

Not ten feet from the far side of the circle, Ward Corson stepped out of the forest.

Somehow she had made her way past the entire

camp, sentries and all. Aside from a few muffled curses, the people around the fire held themselves together well. Muskets and clocklocks appeared, accompanied by hatchets and knives. A rail-thin man with a peaked beard looked up from his whittling, a half-finished bear. He cleared his throat. "Welcome to our fire," he said with a heavy French accent. He gestured to an empty spot on the ground. "Would you join us? Some food?"

Edwina Corson shook her head. "No, thank you."

The man narrowed his eyes. "Ah. Well then. How can we help you on this cold, clear night?"

"I have a request," said Corson.

"We are happy to hear it," said the man.

"I would like to request that you leave this particular stretch of land, as it is occupied."

"We are just hunting. Traveling with the wind. We are sure to be gone in the morning. You are from the fort, up on the cliffs?"

"Yes." Corson shifted her feet. The ten hunters all shifted in response. "I think you are not simple hunters," she said.

"Oh, yes?"

"Yes. I think you are New France militia, or perhaps even French Army, sent here to test this area."

The man laughed, short and sharp. "Well, and if we were, I do not envy you your position, mademoiselle."

Corson's face went still. "And why is that?"

"Well, we are ten, and you are one." He stopped whittling and held up the knife, a sharp warning the length of Ruby's arm. "And if we were those folk that you say, we would be remiss in our duty if we did not take you back to answer some questions." He jerked the knife down once, a signal, and the group around the fire, as one, surged toward the reeve.

Corson sucked in her breath, and then she screamed. But not in terror. It *was* terror. It was a roar from the belly of hell itself. It knocked Ruby onto the ground, and when she scrambled up, what she saw turned her stomach. Ward Corson towered over the French, somehow feet taller than before. Scars crisscrossed her face and hands. Metal mesh crawled up her neck. Ruby held on to the boulder for dear life. No words passed through her mind, no thoughts even, just a growing howl of horror. Corson roared again, and the quivering, gibbering voyageurs ran into the night, leaving their equipment, their guns, and one half-whittled bear.

A moan escaped Ruby's lips. A little one.

The Corson Thing fixed Ruby with its terrible gaze. Raw, red rage lay there, and the certainty that if Ruby did not run, she would be consumed by the beast that stood before her. It stopped her heart.

Darkness.

Ruby opened her eyes to a rock wall. Where was she? She turned her head. Edwina Corson sat cross-legged in the dying grass, framed by a gray winter morning sky.

"Welcome back," Corson said.

Back? Back from where? The beast. The memories flooded back, and Ruby rolled, quick as she could, to sit up with her back to the rock wall.

"What did you do?"

Corson smiled tightly. "What do you mean?"

Was she playing with her? "You know I saw it. You

changed yourself into a beast, a terror that drove away those French."

Corson shook her head. "It was a Work of Spirit. We do call it the Roar of the Beast. If you hear it, you see your deepest fears. Your own mind supplies them. Whatever they saw, I think they will be running back up north with stories of a monstrosity that guards this pass." She leaned forward. "And what of you, Cadet Teach?"

"What do you mean?" Ruby had fainted. But she never fainted. Except once, in the alchemyst Fermat's tower. When she had turned herself into a barrel. Was that— "Oh."

"Yes. Oh. How did you manage that?"

Manage what? Her pulse raced. She had obviously changed, the strange condition that manifested only when she was terrified. But what had she changed into? A barrel, like the last time? Something else? She had to keep her cards close to her vest. "It's something that I do when I am afraid."

"Why don't you do it when Wake is beating the stuffing out of you?"

"You know her. She would have just kept kicking me,

no matter what I turned into." Ruby Maxim Seven: "A Sliver of Truth Makes the Best Lie." The real answer was that Ruby had no idea when or why it happened. She could control changing as much as she could control the weather.

Corson stared at her. "Why are you lying to me?"

Her stomach fell. "What? I'm not." Brass it out.

Corson pulled Ruby up by her arm. "Very well. I do not appreciate your games. Perhaps the Swede will enjoy them more."

"No! Wait!" She pulled against the iron grip. "Please don't tell him."

Corson knelt and looked her in the eyes. "Speak then, Ruby. I owe no allegiance to Swedenborg. He is not of the Reeve, nor do I approve of his methods. But I cannot help you if you lie to me. Speak your truth."

"Ward—"

"We train spies and fighters, Teach, so a certain amount of disrespect for authority is part of the job." She leaned in very close. "If you lie to me again, however, I will be done with you and give you to that man without hesitation."

Sweat coursed down her back. The Swede couldn't

know. Wouldn't this knowledge just get him closer to the answer he sought? She flexed her fingers. The ward was by far the lesser of two evils. "All right. I— I can't control it. It just happens."

"Do you know what you change into?" Barnacles, she was quick.

Ruby blew out her breath. "No." She bulled on before the ward could interrupt. "Can we leave it to the lord captain? On his return?"

Corson looked at her for a long time. She nodded her head. "All right then. We'll wait. But you must do something for me."

"What? Anything."

"Train harder."

Ruby's cheeks warmed. She still could not do a Work to save her skin. She cursed herself for blushing. The Reeve were her enemies. Why did she feel shame for not living up to their precious standards? She looked away. "I—"

Corson grabbed her face and held it fast. "Think on this. We train here to master the flesh and the spirit. I have not seen the like of what you did last night, but do you not think that Reeve training could help you with this shape-shifting?"

"I was captured. You don't really want me here. You said that the first day. I am a prisoner, not a cadet."

Corson inhaled once, sharply, and then clenched her teeth as if she were about to bite something off. "Shape-shifter. Reeve. Call yourself what you will. If you are a blade, I will sharpen you. I choose my students, and I think you are worthy." She raised her eyebrow. "You are more than just a pumpkin."

The wind whistled through the gorge.

Ruby blinked. "A pumpkin? I changed into a pumpkin?"

The ward nodded.

Ruby winced. "That, at the very least, should tell you that I can't control it."

Corson smiled. "Indeed."

CHAPTER 14

The world is a jewel box brimming with the most delicate of
secrets. One cannot access them with hammer and axe.

—Dr. James Sutherland

Every day they stole more of her blood.

Evram rolled up Ruby's sleeve and carefully lined up
the little point to a new spot amid the dense field of pin
marks on her forearm. "Almost there," he said. At least
he knew his business. The point slid smoothly under her
skin, and the glass bulb atop it began to fill.

At least today she had company.

Avid Wake perched on the chair next to her, board

stiff and pouring sweat, her own bulb of blood almost full.

She leaned over to Avid and whispered, "Don't worry. I'm sure their plans for you are harmless."

Avid's nostrils flared, and she looked away. Avid was scared of something? Anything?

"Would you like to have a look at my blood, Avid?" Ruby stretched on the chair like a cat, as Athena might have.

"Hold your arm still, please." Evram blinked his pale olive eyes.

The older girl met Ruby's gaze, a taut grin twisting her face. "I would, Teach, I would. The first time I saw it was my favorite, mixed up with the mud of the yard. Tell me, how do you do that?"

"Do what?"

"Make your body pump out a normal girl's blood, red as a cherry. When I know it has to be blue. Posh girl like you. Sweetling. Do you make it red for the boy there, just before it comes out?"

Ruby cocked her head. "It's a secret."

"Hold your arm still, please, Ruby Teach," Evram said.

"Yes, please stay still, Miss Teach." Doctor Swedenborg chuckled as he rolled a cart into the laboratory. "We want to put on our best face for Cadet Wake here. I'm certain you don't want me to strap you down again. Do you?"

"No, thank you, Doctor," Ruby said.

The Swede smiled at Avid. "So good to see you again, Cadet Wake!" Somehow she twitched even stiffer.

The cart rolled to a stop in front of them. On it sat a tall glass cylinder, mounted on a circular base packed with intricate machinery. Evram began tinkering with it. "Please don't be fearful, Cadet Wake. You are here purely to provide us with a control element of a new experiment. I suppose you should be thankful. Miss Teach here is occupying my time these days, so I no longer require you and the other cadets' . . . assistance." Avid licked her lips and stared straight ahead. Swedenborg knelt down next to Avid and extracted her bulb, now filled with blood. "Evram?"

"Almost ready, Doctor."

The Swede watched Avid's blood swish around in the bulb, a faint smile on his face. You never knew what he was thinking. The anticipation exhausted Ruby, as if his delicate iron-strong fingers were always poised to close about her neck. "While we wait, are you certain you don't want to do some more work on Avid? She has difficulty managing her anger. Don't you, Avid?"

The other girl's jaw tightened, but she said nothing. Was she shaking?

Swedenborg's reptilian eyes flicked back and forth between Ruby and Avid. "You have her blood racing. That is certain."

Evram straightened his shirt. "Ready, Doctor."

The Swede handed him Avid's blood. "Excellent. Begin, please. Remember, even progression of your Source."

The little chemyst inserted the bulb into the top of the cylinder. Red dripped into the clear liquid, and a cloud bloomed gauzily downward with each drip. Evram placed both his hands on the base and cocked his head, beads of sweat collecting on his forehead. The cloud *solidified,* sucking in on itself until all that remained was a delicate sculpture, a perfect spiral that ran the height of the cylinder.

The Swede nodded. "Well done, Evram."

The boy smiled shyly and then quickly produced all manner of calipers and instruments, rushing through an intense measurement of the blood spiral. After a few moments, with a *plork*, the spiral contracted into a single solid rock, floating in the center of the cylinder.

"Thank you, Cadet Wake. That will be all," said Swedenborg.

Avid gave Ruby a venomous look and then scurried out of the room as if her feet had been lit on fire.

Swedenborg tittered. "Oh, she *likes* you, Miss Teach."

"We're going to start a sewing circle next week." His titter turned into a laugh. The self-satisfaction just oozed out of him. Could she catch him off guard? Evram fished out Avid's blood rock with a long net thing, and Ruby nodded at the cylinder. "This is amazing."

The Swede smiled. "It is fascinating, is it not?"

"Oh, indeed. It looks like a brilliant device. Did you construct it yourself?"

His eyes narrowed. "Flatterer." His eyes traced Avid's path out the door. "You don't really have anyone to talk to you, do you? Except Evram and me." He leaned in and smiled. "Very well. I'll share it with you. We are, after all, in this together."

Chill fear climbed up her legs. She tried to keep it from her face. "Tell me."

"I'll show you instead."

The Swede inserted the bulb of her blood in the machine, and another cloud descended into the cylinder, drip by drip. He touched the base with an index finger and clicked his tongue. The process happened much more quickly this time, but what formed was not remotely an orderly spiral. It was a riot of symbols. A thicket of whorls and lines exploding in three dimensions, accompanied by an equally deep thicket of intricate symbols, equations, and strings of numbers.

"Oh, my," said Swedenborg.

"You were right, Doctor," said Evram, voice tinged with awe.

"Evram, quickly, my journal." The boy rushed it

over with pen and ink, and Swedenborg scribbled in it furiously.

That . . . was her. Ruby did not need to manufacture the fascination in her voice. "What is it?"

The doctor's breath clouded the glass, like a child's to a sweets shop window. "They're brilliant, Miss Teach. Whoever did this to you." Her mother. "Your blood seems to have some kind of quality that allows it to be imprinted with information. It is changeable somehow. And someone used that quality to store a schematic. This piece is only a small part of it, I think, but this machine, whatever it is, must be built. I will—"

The shape collapsed all at once, leaving nothing behind but a floating red lump.

"Poof!" The Swede wiggled his fingers and closed the journal as if performing a magic trick. "We shall have to spend many more sessions together, Ruby, but we have made huge strides today!" He turned his hungry eyes on her, and the silver tinkling of his breathing accelerated. "You are a walking codebook, my girl, and I cannot wait to decipher you. My skill, your blood. Oh, what wonders we shall make."

She stumbled down the hall from the laboratory, stomach roiling, mind racing. What kind of machine? How much blood? Why had her mother done this to her? And what use was any of this information if Wisdom Rool was not even here to tell it to?

She ripped open the door to the sand room, shutters closed against the cold night. The fresh-raked lines cast fluttering shadows in the light of the chem pots.

Something struck her on the head. She fell to the ground and struggled to her knees.

Avid Wake stood in the doorway. "You were funny back there. Let's see some more of that blood, Sweetling."

Ruby put up her fists. At least this was something she could control.

CHAPTER 15

Emptiness is only the beginning. But it is the Only Beginning.
—Training manual, Reeve of England

Ruby picked up one bare foot after the other on the slick, cold grass. The mist coming from the lake mingled with the steam from the cadets' mouths as they clumped together at dawn. Ismail Cole had rousted them out of their beds in the dark and led them down to the walled meadow that took up the rest of the outcropping. Why did this sort of training always need to happen before the sun came up or at darkest midnight? Ruby yawned and immediately regretted it. The beating she had gotten from Avid Wake the night before had even crept up her neck into her jaw. Avid was in the crowd, too, up front, desperate to be seen in the lead.

"Awake?" Ward Cole smiled. He was never not smiling, and his eyes always opened just a little too wide, as if he'd smelled something surprising. He was dressed, as they all were, in a sleeveless muslin shirt and knee-length breeches. They hung from his thin frame like becalmed sails. The man was nothing but sinew and bone.

"Well, if they are not, they will be soon," said Ward Corson, as she pulled herself out of the lake behind him. Where Cole was thin, she was thick as a tree trunk, and knotty as well. Her dripping red hair lay flat on her head, framing her flat, severe face.

Behind her, a line of square boards stretched out for fifteen yards or so into the lake. They floated very closely together, connected to one another by a thin cord that ran under the center of each. Ward Burk was treading water at the end of the line of boards, holding it straight.

"Right," Corson said. She turned to Cole. "Show them."

Cole turned toward the lake and went still as a stone.

He shook his arms out. His hands struck his legs with a clap.

Then he sprinted down the shore. Providence, he was fast.

He didn't stop at the edge of the water. He gave a joyful whoop, and his bare feet slapped the boards as he ran high-stepping across, arms out like a wire walker. At the last board he teetered off to the side, tucked his feet, and sliced into the water with a perfect dive. The boards behind sloshed up and down like ships in a storm, and Cole swam to a point halfway down the line. Cadets murmured all around Ruby.

"Quiet," Ward Corson said.

The murmuring stopped.

"A reeve needs quiet," she continued. "Not necessarily about you. That may well be impossible. You will be surrounded by noise all your life. Clocklocks firing. Citizens screaming. Foes threatening. Children, machines, animals." She flashed her two jade fingers in the half-light. "Torturers."

A fish splashed, somewhere out on the lake.

"We are the arm of the crown when the army will not do, yet neither will diplomats. Our work is in the shadows, in silent studies and secluded forests, in alleys and on rooftops. So we must create quiet. In ourselves. If there is a fracas inside, you will not arrive at your destination. A Work of Flesh—for example, lightening yourself as Ward Cole just did—requires deep quiet inside you." She stepped aside, leaving the path to the boards open. "Who will be first?"

"I will," Ruby said. She stepped out of the crowd.

Ruby Maxim Eight said, "If They Cast You Out, Make Them Respect the Outcast." So she ran at the boards with a wild yell of her own. Her feet pounded on the grass, and she almost slipped twice before she got to the shore. She reached down inside of her for that quiet. In a flash she knew what Corson was talking about. It had become a habit when she was working locks with Gwath. *He* had been a Changer. Had he been teaching her already? Had the years of lessons not just been for thievery but to unlock this birthright? She could do this. She would do this. She found a kernel of fire in her belly. She grabbed it and lifted herself high with all her might. She would carry herself across.

She got to the second board.

The lake was warm, at least. Hot springs feeding it.

As she swam back, Corson called out: "Good, Teach. You're reaching for something." Ruby pulled herself out of the water, and Corson squatted down next to her. "You know the problem?"

"What is it?" Ruby said, water streaming from her nose.

"You're reaching for something."

Ruby swallowed the selection of curses that came to mind and nodded as if she knew what Corson was talking about.

She tried two more times, with Corson giving her less and less advice each attempt. Ruby didn't even get to the second board either time. She could barely contain her fury. It wasn't that she didn't believe that she could do it. It was failing. Failing in front of this group of cods-heads. They hated her, and that just made her want to stick it in their collective eye. She was more than just some package. She was. Their stares bored into the back of her head.

"All right, Teach. That's enough for you. Let's give someone else a chance," called Corson. "Into the drink with you, and monitor the boards halfway down." Ruby gladly dunked her head back in the lake; it was warmer than the chilly air. The smelly water from the springs crept into her nose as she swam out to replace Ward Cole. As the morning warmed, she didn't know whether to be angry or pleased that few of the cadets did much better than she. Levi Curtsie went completely silent and made it to the third board before falling in. His sister, Never, jumped up and down, whooping much as Cole had done, but she never made it past the first board. Elvina Moats did a strange little high-stepping dance, complete with an off-color shanty, but she went in the drink as well.

None of them called to her or even spoke to her when they landed in the water. Not even Levi or Never. Ruby splashed her hand gently. Ripples cast out from her palm back toward the shore. She did not mind the isolation. She had much to think about.

Avid Wake stepped down to the water, preparing to race onto the boards. There were many more things than just the beatings that irked Ruby about Avid, but one of the most irksome was this: she was *talented*. In the exhausting sparring sessions in the practice yards, in the strange, painful postures they shoehorned them into day after day. The point—or so the reeves said—was that occasionally, in the absolute exhaustion, pushed past all endurance, one of the cadets would feel it. The Void, the emptiness, the nothing inside them that could fuel them on to astonishing things. Not only were the Reeve a disciplined fighting force, but they had unleashed in themselves a kind of chemystry of the body, and Avid, more than any of the rest, seemed close to unlocking it.

Avid had run back up the hill a bit and sprinted toward the water. As her foot hit the first board, she opened her mouth to holler like the others, but no sound came out. Instead, she looked mildly surprised, as if she had walked around a street corner and seen a dancing dolphin.

She stepped onto the next board.

And the next.

It was all very fast, one foot for each board, and before you knew it, she was coming up on Ruby halfway across the spring. The cadets on the shore began to cheer.

It was a beautiful thing to see.

Which may have been why right before Avid reached her, Ruby tugged, in the slightest way possible, the edge of the board. Avid's foot slapped against water, not wood, and she careened off of the trail and sailed headfirst past Ruby into the lake. Avid's face shifted from peaceful surprise to a mask of anger. Ruby saw, too late, the large rock that lurked under the surface, and Avid's upper body snapped back as she slammed facefirst into the rock.

Avid's arms whipped out in a strange parody of Ismail Cole's, and then she was still and senseless in the water, blood seeping from the deep gash on her forehead. She began to sink.

Ruby was the only person remotely close enough to do anything. She grabbed at Avid and tried to keep her from sinking, but the bigger girl was dead weight. Ruby stuck her head into Avid's back and her hands in the other girl's armpits, and her feet got purchase on the rock for a hopeful moment but then slipped out from under her. She slammed back onto the rock itself, and the wind went out from her. She struggled, unsure which way was up. Her hands got tangled in the cloud of Wake's hair, and Ruby floundered more frantically as the pair of them sank further.

She needed to breathe.

She was seeing stars.

A pair of hands grabbed her from below.

Had Gwath finally come for her?

But no, the hands were from above. She was moving up. And then her feet and then her head broke the surface, wrapped though it was in Wake's jerkin. She caught a brief blink of a network of thick scars, all over the girl's back; but then Ruby was free and gulping in great gouts of air. She got her feet under her and rested them on the rock, arms moving in the warm water to keep her steady.

Ward Burk had somehow arrived there from the other end of the lake, and she was treading water and supporting Wake. As the other two wards swam out to help, she smiled at her. "Well done, Teach. That was a near thing."

Ruby tried to control her breathing, and all she could do was nod. It *had* been a near thing. Ruby had almost killed Avid, and herself in the bargain. The worst part? She didn't feel scared.

Or sad.

Or sorry.

What was she changing into?

CHAPTER 16

Loyalty not to women or men.
Nor to power.
Loyalty to an ideal.
—Training manual, Reeve of England

Evram held two sapphires in his hand. The jewels twinkled brightly under the harsh white light of the tinker's lamps.

Ruby sat on the stool in the corner of his workroom, one foot tucked under her leg.

"I am glad you are here, Ruby."

"I am, too, Evram. Why are there two gemstones in your hand?"

He bobbed from one foot to the other. "Because! The doctor has finally approved my plan for Sleipnir! I can activate her!"

"Really?" The eight-legged horse automaton stood behind them, shining in the light. And he had made that. Evram was not charming or strong, but making a thing like this: that was something altogether more special. He had a feel for automatons. Even the gearbeasts seemed more . . . present when they were around him. It gave her a pang. She looked about the workroom, tools scattered everywhere, a half-eaten plate of bread and jam forgotten on the table. He was in his place, doing a thing that he loved. And that thing was extraordinary. Ruby, on the other hand: what was she?

"Will you help me?"

"Sorry?" The question pulled her out of her daydream.

He stood on a table on the other side of Sleipnir's muzzle, at eye level. Ruby pulled over a stool and stood on the other side. He handed her one of the blue gems.

"Where did you even get these?" she asked.

"They were tucked in my crib, left with me on the doorstep of the town hall."

"Oh."

Evram stroked the braided brass mane. "They need to be put in the sockets at the same time. Their presence should complete the circuit, and that should wake her up."

"Should? Should the doctor be here, so he can see?" And perhaps let slip something more about me?

"He is sleeping, and I want to make certain that she functions properly before I show him." Evram blushed. "Besides, I thought you might want to see it."

"I do!" Ruby kicked herself. He was so nice, and she was using him. It was terrible, but she had to if she was to survive. Her heart did beat quickly at the thought of seeing Sleipnir awakened.

"On the count of three." Evram's hand shook a little. "One. Two."

"Three," Ruby said. The sapphires fitted into the sockets as if they had been made to house them. Which, of course, they were.

Nothing happened.

Ruby leaned in and whispered. She had no idea why she was whispering. "Evram, what is supposed to—"

Sleipnir snorted.

The shock sent them both backward, Evram into the wall and Ruby all the way off her stool. Sleipnir chuffed, a deep metal but ever so *horsey* sound. Ruby couldn't move. Suddenly this thing, this statue: it seemed very much alive.

Evram laughed. He never laughed.

The sound shocked the gearhorse, and it backed up a step, burnished hooves sounding on the stone. How was it that metal could look startled? Evram moved forward, ever so slowly. "Easy, girl. Easy." All trace of hesitation was gone. He was sure of hand and tone. He stroked Sleipnir on her muscular neck, and she moved forward tentatively. "That's right." Evram turned to Ruby. The look on his face was hard to describe. Ruby settled on "profound peace." "Would you like to?" he asked her.

Ruby walked forward carefully, and the gearhorse watched her out of the corner of its eye. She put her hand out slowly and then finally her palm on its neck. It didn't feel like fur. But it didn't feel like hard metal, either. Evram had done something to it that made it fall somewhere in between. It was wonderful. She took her hand off to look at Evram, but Sleipnir wasn't having any of that. She butted Ruby softly on the arm.

"She wants more," Evram said. "She likes you."

They cared for the gearhorse that night. As they rubbed her skin down with a kind of curry comb that applied oil and buffed it at the same time, Evram said, "The form of the metal lends itself to behavior. Gearbeasts are crafted savage, so they act that way. But if something is alive, it needs reminders of its intended nature. I hope things like this will help Sleipnir."

Ruby hoped so, too. It felt right to be helping someone with something good. So much lying. Lying to Evram. Corson. Swedenborg. But what choice did she have? If she did not lie, this place would carve her up. She put another squirt of oil on the brush and tried not to think about it.

"Ruby?"

"Yes, Evram?"

"Sleipnir has words. They will let you take control of her, aside from any other orders from the Reeve."

Why would he tell her that? "Why would you tell me that?"

"Because she likes you." Evram set his teeth. "And because I do not like what they are doing to you, and this is mine to give."

"Tell me," she said.

"Sea and Sky."

That night Ruby put her bare foot upon the wall of her cell. She wobbled. Her other leg could barely hold her up. It was a Work of Flesh she tried, to connect herself to the wall, to stand upon it like a floor, as Ward Burk had on Ruby's first day at the fort.

Her knees were skinned, and she tried again. Seeing Evram make such an amazing thing drove her on. She told the people in her heart to go farther away. They finally obliged, walking away down the halls of her memory to the quiet places, slipping out the doors of her heart as she unlocked them one by one.

The last ones to go were Athena and Henry. They looked at each other, then bowed as one.

Inside her all was as quiet as snow at dawn.

She launched her foot up next to the other.

Pain seared through her foot, and then she fell to the ground in the moonlight. Had she twisted it? Or broken it? She held her leg up, and it was easy to see. All five of her toes were the color of storm clouds, with whorls and grain running through them, made entirely of gray wood.

It was not a Work, not by any stretch of the imagination. But it was something else, something better. The Void, the key to the power of the Reeve, had unlocked something unexpected in her. Something she had never been able to accomplish on her own. She had changed.

CHAPTER 17

*I have heard of French trappers who made some Deal with the
Devil for a flying canoe, for the purpose of Visiting their
Sweethearts back home. We are not so lucky.*
—Nestor Graham, lead trapper, Rupert's Bay Company

"Careful there." Winnie Black held out a calloused
hand, and Athena grabbed it, grateful for the help off
the ferry. The river, swollen with spring melt, had bucked
and roiled as if it were as happy as any of them to finally
be on their way.

It had been a long winter in the cabin above
Harris's Ferry, which had all the amusements and lovely
qualities of an abandoned small town on the edge of

the wilderness. That is to say, nothing.

Cram popped up from a stand of bushes across the field, a rooty mass in his hand. "Miss Winnie!" he called. "Look! I found some turtlehead!"

Cram and the woodswoman had struck up an odd friendship, wandering the hills together, digging in the snow for strange herbs, and staring sagely at rabbit droppings. Still, at least he had been doing something. While they had ranged the hills, Wayland Teach made a second profession of staring moodily into the fire, Henry had eyes only for his journal, and Athena? Well, she fought herself. She spent hours a day in front of the walls of the little barn, parrying, thrusting, working tempo and form against that most tireless of opponents: her shadow. It galled her to wait. Ever since she was a child. That terrible feeling that while she was doing absolutely nothing, great events sparked and fired all over the world, leaving her behind in the dust. Ruby Teach needed to be saved, and that saving was Athena's business.

The captain stood next to one of the stocky pack mules, patting it with exaggerated care. He was a different man on the land: uncertain, jagged.

Henry Collins glanced up briefly, and their eyes met. He ducked his head back down into the journal. Over the winter the leather-bound book had grown fins and wings of parchment paper, sticking out from all angles, and the young Tinker had worn out twenty grease pencils scribbling notes everywhere. Winnifred Black said his leg had healed as well as it would, but it would never be as it had been. He had rarely set foot outside the cave. He had a wild look about him, his hair unkempt and matted, and he was always tapping the pencils or chewing on them, muttering under his breath. They had not spoken much since the escape from the *Grail*, but she often caught him looking at her.

Cram trotted back to the rest of them, his ridiculous tailed fur cap bobbing atop his head. Apparently there was some manner of rat's cousin called a raccoon. He produced from somewhere a pigeon leg and gnawed on it as he sorted through his rucksack with the other hand. The white mule called Constance, the one with red eyes, peered over his shoulder.

Winnifred Pleasant Black crouched on one knee, checking the cinches on the saddle of her enormous black mountain goat, Peaches, a beast that had quickly set out its own boundaries by nearly biting Athena's hand clean off. The only people it would suffer near it were Winnifred and her cub, who crawled all over it and hung from its horns as if it were a statue in Tinkers Square. The woodswoman had supervised their kit, courtesy of an abandoned dry goods store down in the deserted town. She had loaded up the four of them with a seemingly endless selection of spikes, hammers, flint, steel, tents, snowshoes, and pemmican. So much pemmican. The greasy concoction of fat, dried meat, and acidic berries made Athena's stomach turn just thinking about it.

And that was their company.

But where was Ruby Teach?

Athena still caught herself, turning to see Ruby's face when Cram said something ridiculous or Henry said something pompous. Infuriating as she might be, the little rogue could at least be counted on to provide amusing conversation. She had known Ruby for such a short time. Why did it ache so deeply?

So she put her armor on, to keep the hurt at bay. She donned the impenetrable smile, the one that she had worn since she was six, the one she had worn since her father had told her that if he had no male heir, then she would just have to do.

They set out across the little field toward a solid wall of trees, stretching to the horizons. Athena gazed back over the river. Somewhere back that way lay Philadelphi. And London. Cobblestones, coffeehouses, libraries. Civilization really. Everything she had ever known. This journey was madness. Would they ever return?

Winnie Black tapped her on the shoulder. Athena jumped. Where had she come from? Eerily quiet, that one. And perceptive. Four months in close quarters had made it certain that Black knew Athena wasn't "Athen," but she kept on as if she had never noticed. That suited Athena just fine.

Black waggled her eyebrows. "No lords of the manor here."

"What do you mean? Isn't this land claimed by the

crown? You mean, we're passing into French land?"

Black gave her a long look. "No, young sir. I mean this land is claimed by no one. It is its own thing. Beyond those trees lay more trees. Trees, trees, trees. Mountains, yes. But those mountains are covered in trees. All the way to the cracking huge lakes in the north and the ocean in the south. We shall take old paths, now abandoned by the ones who used to walk them." She took a huge, smiling breath through her nose. "Smell that?"

Athena sniffed. "Peaches?"

"No. Freedom. No law in that forest but instinct, no mercy there but a quick kill." Athena did not, she absolutely did not like the look of the mad smile that wound its way onto Black's face. "Home," the woodswoman said. She clucked at Peaches, and the great goat set out after the others.

"Brilliant." Athena did her best to seem excited and then realized that no one was paying her any mind. She kicked a stone into the river and then set out after the others.

CHAPTER 18

BUMBLEBUFFLE:	*What do you mean, "we are betrothed"?*
CATHERINE:	*It is not an incomprehensible sentence.*
BUMBLEBUFFLE:	*Oho, then! You must be most pleased to be my fiancé! I am, after all, rich, charming, and intelligent.*
CATHERINE:	*You have an adventuresome approach to your vocabulary.*
BUMBLEBUFFLE:	*Which?*
CATHERINE:	*Oh, well. "Charming." "Intelligent." (coughs) "Pleased."*

—Marion Coatesworth-Hay, *A Game of Vials and Vapors,* Act III, sc. i

Down in the valley the sun peeked up over the trees, and that's when Cram had to sit down. The orange, pink, red, and yellow piled on top of one another like melted sugar candy, and the air was so clear he felt as if he could reach down and touch the treetops and the glittering creek below. Like tinker's chemystry, but a thousand times better. A little flame of joy lit down in his belly.

He stoked the fire. The morning chill lingered, and

while his body still ached like old roof beams in the morning, change had weaseled its way into his eyes and ears. And his noggin, mayhaps. The first night he had lain down, every crack of a stick was a beast, sidling into camp to make a meal of him. The ground stabbed him with rocks through the night, and *everything* itched.

Last night, though, they had staggered into the clearing Miss Winnie had found them, nestled halfway up the side of a hill, and after his chores Cram had fallen to sleep as quickly as he pulled up his blanket. He had dreamed of Peaches, of all things, and riding her across a great plain of tall grass, hurrooing on an old hunting horn, the way they did in the stories.

He leaned down to sniff a cluster of fine little white flowers, a riot of yellow inside each of them.

"What are those?" a voice behind him asked.

"Bloodroot," Cram answered. "The Algonkin say you can use those to catch the heart of your ladylove."

"Can she eat it, your ladylove?"

"Not if she wants to keep down her breakfast," he said. "But she could use a paste made from the root to take a wart off her fingers."

Winnifred Pleasant Black sat down beside him.

He offered her a piece of jerky. She took it. They looked at the sunrise awhile.

"If you had to get back down there, how would you go?" Black pointed down into the valley.

Cram scanned the hillside. "Little gully over that way, by the big maple."

"Looks steep. What about that scree field instead?"

"Only if you wanted the rocks to deliver you to the bottom with a broken leg or worse. Mam didn't raise no dimwits."

She chuckled. "You've a knack for this, boy. One last question."

Cram gritted his teeth and prayed to Providence.

"Which way is Philadelphi?"

This was the nubbin. Trees? They seemed to line up and call out their names to him. Animals? He had a keen eye for this three-toed paw or that spread of cat scat. But bearings? He stroked his chin, trying to look wise and to buy more time. The sun was coming up there, but moss on that side of the tree, except on the leeward . . . He stuck a shy finger back over her shoulder, pointing, he hoped, to Philadelphi.

Miss Winnie took his wrist in her hand and moved it exactly the opposite way. She gave him a tight smile. "We'll keeping working on that. Good?"

He didn't answer her. Movement flashed down in the valley. "That smoke?"

She clucked her tongue. "It is."

They woke the rest and gathered them on their bellies, peering over the edge of the hill.

Lady Athena rubbed the sleep from her eyes. "What is it?"

"Someone had to light a fire to dry their clothes after crossing the river this morning. There's smoke down there," Black said.

"Smoke?" Henry asked. "Who is it?"

Black spat. "One way to find out." She eased up, taking care to keep the big oak between her and the fire.

"You're going down there?" Athena asked.

"Could be something, could be nothing, but my sense

is you don't want someone following you, wherever it is you're going."

"Here."

Wayland Teach held out what looked to be a gold monocle, ringed by clear glass filled with a bright green liquid. Cram knew it. Ruby had used it like a spyglass when they had been trying to get off the *Thrift*. "You can see as far as you want with that, and belay the bickering."

Athena took it from him. She snuck her head up over the edge of the hill and put the monocle to her eye. She whistled. "Take a look. Anyone know them?" Neither the captain nor the woodswoman did. When Cram took his turn, he almost fell off the hill. The view swooped and swooshed with the faint sloshing of the chem inside the monocle, and the forest rushed up at him. It took him a few moments, but with Lady A.'s help he focused in on a campsite in a clearing much like theirs, but near the bank of the river. He went cold. There were hard men and women down there, at least ten of them, and they were armed: hunting spears, swords, clocklock pistols, even a few long guns. He handed the trinket to Henry.

"That don't look like a hunting party," Cram said.

"Oh, I disagree," Henry said as he looked through the monocle. "Two girls down there are the ones from the King's Bum back in StiltTown. The ones who were after the journal." He handed the monocle back to the captain. "They are a hunting party. They're hunting us."

They loaded the mules quickly and as quietly as they could, and the whispers flew so fast Cram's head was spinning.

"But who is it?" Athena tossed a saddlebag over Constance's flank. "Reeve? Tinkers? Bluestockings? And how did they find us again?"

The professor grabbed the bag from the other side and helped cinch it down. "Why don't you go down and ask nicely? Or perhaps they'd like to come up for a cup of tea?"

Black cut them off. "Fighting ten of them with half that number is not my reckoning of a garden party, no matter how stealthy we are. We split up."

"What?" said the others.

"My aim is to take the mule train, cut another path

from the bottom of this hill, and lead them astray." She nodded at the captain. "Barrel Guts here moves quiet and does what I tell him. I need him and his big feet to make a likely trail."

"What about us?" Henry asked.

"You need to preserve the journal and find my Ruby's mother," Teach said. "Ruby is in your hands."

"But what if you do not return?" Henry tapped at the journal. "'The meeting of three rivers,' it said. Only you know where that is."

Black blinked at him. "Well, it is the meeting of three rivers, yes?"

"Yes," Henry said.

She waved her hand vaguely to the west. "Then head that way, until you find yourself a river. After that, follow it until you find two more."

"What?" they all said again.

The woodswoman shrugged. "Easiest thing in the world. If you run into any Algonkin, be especially polite."

Henry waved it away. "But right now you are talking about leaving us and then somehow finding us again in this forsaken wilderness!" Crackers, he was truly angry.

Winnifred cinched the strap on Peaches's saddle. The goat's bleat rumbled in Cram's feet. "I have in mind a certain stratagem."

It all was coming to a head now, like the worst of stews or pies gone wrong. Cram could see the figures on the slate even before Winnie Black turned to him.

"Tell me true, Cram. Can you guide Henry and milord to that ridge?" She pointed over her shoulder to a flat-topped butte on the other side of the forest, barely visible on the horizon.

"Me?" He wished he hadn't squeaked just then.

They were looking at him. He flipped and flopped the question over in his head. He had been learning. It was a solid three or four days to that butte, weather and terrain depending. The professor's leg had not healed correct and would slow them down, so maybe five days. Six? It stood out on the landscape, though; you could not miss it. But listen to him! Like some puffed-up sheepherd, full of himself and trying to impress the ladies.

"Cram?" Athena said.

They all were still looking at him. "Yes?"

"Can you do it?"

Cram was no leader. He followed. He was, officially, a follower of Lady Athena. He didn't mind being a follower. In fact, he rather cottoned to it. Let others make the big choices, the ones that mattered. He would be there for a knock on the noggin with his churn or a clever twist to pull their fat out of the fire.

"I'll try."

Who had said that? His best guess was that he had. Sounded like him. Came from the general area of his mouth. He put his hand over his lips, so nothing else would come out.

"You can do it." Miss Winnie clapped him on the shoulder. "Besides, you must."

"What if I had said no?"

"You would have had to do it no matter. But now you chose it." Black leaned over and whispered into his ear, "They'll respect you more for that." The words barely reached him through all the wind rushing through his ears. Leading. Him.

Winnifred Pleasant Black surveyed the three of them, hangdog and fearful. She turned to her boy. "Cubbins, when I set you loose in the forest, how many days did it take you to get back to the house?"

The little boy gnawed intently on a clump of sedge grass. Without looking up, he held up four fingers.

"That's right. Four days. And what birthday did we celebrate when you got home?"

Cubbins shifted the grass in his mouth, a fuzzy green pipe. He held up his hand, five fingers standing tall.

Black nodded. "Five years old." She turned back to them. "You are more than twice his age. Stay alive twice the days he did, and we will do our best to get back to you."

They divided up the supplies. Most of the gear stayed on the mules, and all of the tents. Black and Teach would be building fires at night and setting up a camp the same size as before. Athena, Cram, and Henry had goodly portions of pemmican in their packs, enough for a week or more. Cram wondered briefly what they would do if the food ran out and they had still not been found. Mam always said, "Give me a rock, some hot water, and a shoe, and here I have some soup," but he wasn't sure this was what she had in mind.

Miss Winnie hauled herself onto Peaches's back, Cubbins already perched between the goat's horns. "No fires, neither. We want them to see us, not you. Huddle for warmth under your blankets. You'll be fine."

"Raw pemmican. Capital," Athena muttered.

Wayland Teach gave each of them a big bear hug. He saved Athena for last. "You'll never stop trying to get Ruby back. Promise me," he said.

Surprise shadowed her face. "How can I promise that? We don't know where we are going. We don't even know what we are looking for. If we do find Ruby's mother, then we have to find Ruby and—"

He held up a hand, as if warding off evil. "You must believe you can succeed. It is the only way to fight the fear. Act as if you will get her back until you fail. If you fail, then find another way. If you fail again, find another way. That is the promise I ask."

"I promise," she said so softly Cram could barely hear.

The captain squeezed her arm and looked deep into her eyes with the faintest of smiles. He moved over to Constance. They had tied the mules in the line, and the white one was the lead.

"My best guess is seven days' time, if all goes well," Black said. "We will see you on that rise after leading them a merry chase, and then we'll tell tall tales of our travels. I'm certain of it."

"And if we don't see you?" Henry asked.

"Ten days. If we haven't made it then, we're not coming." She *tch*ed at Peaches's reins, and the goat gave Cram one last mournful nibble before they turned and trotted off down the slope. Teach took them all in for a long moment before raising his hand in farewell and trotting off on Constance, the other mules in line behind.

A bird dropped something on Cram's hat.

Athena raised her eyebrows. "Whither away, O Mighty Hunter?"

Cram thought of Ruby, and what she might have said, but decided against it. He turned and headed up the slope.

CHAPTER 19

Revenge is the ugliest of businesses. Uglier even than lawyering.
—Aquila Rose, adventurer and ne'er-do-well

The thirteenth thicket crouched below, waiting to pounce on Henry. The thickets might as well have been conscious. They were sneaky beasts, deceptively quiet and apparently benign, but Henry had learned over the past few days that they hated him with all of their thorny hearts. He eased himself down onto a flat patch at the top of the hill, his leg awkwardly in front of him. The blood in it pulsed with his heartbeat, but the steady ache was a vast relief over the pain that jangled from his ankle up his leg whenever he put his weight upon it. Wintering in Winnifred Black's cabin had given it time to heal, but the woodswoman said the bones hadn't set exactly right. He would limp for a long time, perhaps for his life. Better to think on the wind.

A cool breeze fluttered at his collar and wrists. The air refused to follow them down into the hollows, and he leaned back, letting it wash over his face. By Science, it was hot. Spring was in full bloom, but the friendly green was as deceptive as the flowers decorating the briars below.

Cram flopped down with a grunt, his bag clattering beside him. Boyle eyed the ground but leaned against a big sprawling tree instead. Cram could probably have told them what manner of tree it was and even whether you could brew its leaves for tea, but Henry didn't need a cup of bark right now. Three days of the boy's leadership had taken them up and down the winding, densely forested hills with very little evidence of rhyme or reason. Occasionally the flat-topped hill would heave into view, neither nearer nor farther as far as Henry could see, and then they would plunge back down into the close, fuggy bottoms. It was hard work, and Henry had stopped counting the scrapes, bruises, and stab wounds when he started counting the thickets instead.

But that was beside the point.

He worked his ankle in the stout moccasins, and pain flared up almost to his waist. This was the point. His stomach churned with worry. Could he keep up?

"Just give me a moment," Henry said.

Cram nodded and handed him a waterskin. It was warm and tasted of leather, but when it hit his throat, it was all he could do not to just dump the entire thing on his head.

"How much farther?" Boyle asked. Cram grimaced and looked across the little valley.

This was her game. It irked Henry. "I imagine we have eaten up the leagues since the last time you asked," he said. "A quarter of an hour can make miracles."

She pasted on that stuffed-cat grin. "I am merely curious as to our progression across the landscape."

Cram stabbed at the dirt with a stick. "I don't know, milady." He hunched his shoulders. "What I mean to say is it could be we made another half mile."

"Toward or away from our goal?"

"It pains me to say it ain't that simple."

"Again, I think we'd do much better staying on the ridgetops, where we can keep our goal in sight," Athena said.

Cram shook his head. "Miss Black taught me that the ridges lie acrost our path. If we stay on top of 'em, we go sidewise to our goal. The only way is to cut straight through. Never mention that we stand out like a boil on a pig's bottom up here."

"The valleys, however, are steep and awash with patches of thorn and briar," Boyle said. "I fear that because of the difficulty of the terrain, we are moving with less . . . speed than before." She studiously did not glance at Henry.

"Finally," Henry said, and pulled himself up on a low-hanging branch.

"Finally?" Boyle said.

How could she pretend that she did not know what he meant? "Finally we speak of the thing that is stuck in your craw."

"And that is?"

"I am slowing you down," Henry said.

"What of it?"

"What do you mean, 'What of it?'?" Henry couldn't breathe. The throbbing in his leg had moved up into his chest. "I cannot go faster. I am trying, but I cannot."

"I did not claim that you could go faster. Nor did I claim that it was in any way personal," Boyle said with care, and that care galled him even more.

"No, neither did you claim any of the responsibility!"

She looked at him as if he were a sick puppy. "Responsibility?"

"Responsibility for . . . this." He could not name it. He waved his hand over his leg.

Athena laughed. "Is that what this is about? The stairs?"

Her laughter pulled his fingers into a fist. "How could it not be about that?"

"Henry, that was a long time ago," she said. In the silence that followed, she blew out her breath. "Fine. What more can I say? I did not know you. You were keeping us from our goal. I had to make a flash decision, and so I did. I pushed you. I would do the same again."

"I am glad to know how we stand then."

Boyle opened her mouth. She shut it. Then she began again. "Henry Collins. I consider you a comrade. I will fight beside you. I will even defend you. I see that you are hurt, and I take responsibility for that hurt. But I will not coddle you. Now, I have a ridiculous valley to cross."

True to her word, she started down the hill. And Henry watched her go through a haze of rage. He was perfectly positioned to see something launch itself from the tree above and plummet toward her.

Time slowed, almost to a standstill.

Father Friel had often said that he was the quickest thinker in the Jesuit school in Port Royal, but Henry disagreed with that description. It was not that he thought quickly. A more accurate description of the phenomenon would be that at occasional moments not of his choosing, his experience of the passage of time slowed drastically. This slowing gave him an opportunity to examine problems or questions at a leisurely pace. This was one of those moments.

The cat was about Athena's size and thicker, weight 150 pounds or so. It was neither a bobcat nor a lion of the mountains. It was heavily muscled, especially on its squat hind legs. Its fur, various shades of green and brown. Its paws stretched outward, each with an enlarged hooklike claw that looked sharp enough to shred muscle. Two flaps of skin extended from its chest to its forelegs, creating wings of a sort. Its elongated prehensile tail ended in a wicked-looking ball of ridged bone, about the size of two fists put together. Henry had read of ball-tailed cats, the mythical predators of the western forests, but he had never imagined he would ever see one.

Without waiting for Henry to finish his inspection, time sped back up.

The cat pulled its forepaws in and twisted in the air so that the ball of bone was now plummeting at Athena's head. Henry grabbed a vial from his pouch, but the beast was too close. He yelled, "Boyle!"

Athena spun, just barely pulling her head from the path of the tail. The creature screeched and opened its flaps, and the ball slammed into her shoulder. The girl cried out and went down.

Another yowl sounded behind him. He whirled to see a second of the creatures crouching on a limb, directly above Cram. It bunched its hindquarters, and this time Henry did not hesitate. As it leaped, he reached inside of himself for his Source and thréw the vial. It hit the oak tree with a clink and puffed into a cloud of black powder, covering the tree and the cat. Henry *pushed* with his Source.

The black powder turned blue. It exploded in a gout of fire just as the cat leaped. Fire might signal their presence to trackers, but that was the wager: some fire or no Cram.

The flaming thing hurtled out of the tree, yowling, and headed straight at the serving boy. Cram threw himself in the only direction possible, down the hill. He tumbled, rolling, but if he made any sound, it was drowned out by the burning animal before Henry. Its eyes glimmered, and it spun, tail swinging around like a flail. The ball struck Henry full in the belly, knocking the air out of him. He was flying for a long moment, then slammed into a tree trunk. Bright spots flickered across his vision. The flaming cat screamed in rage, awash in chemystral fire that burned far more hungrily and fiercely than a normal one, and it leaped, hook claws outstretched. Henry threw himself facefirst to the ground. Heat licked at his neck, but the cat, mad from burning and fear, landed just past him. Three steps away, it fell to the ground, twitching and mewling.

Henry pushed himself up. The smell was terrible. He leaned on a tree and retched. Pain lanced through his stomach with every move. It would have been easy to stop. It would have been easy just to sit down and hope Athena Boyle and Cram could handle the other one. But he could not.

He stumbled to the top of the slope.

Below, in the clearing, Cram lay unmoving. Athena stood with her back to a tree, facing not one but two cats. Her sword moved back and forth between one and the other. One bled from its foreleg. The other spun, and Athena danced around the tree. The ball smashed into the bark, just where her knees had been. Her sword licked out. The creature sprang out of the way, tail raised for another strike.

Her skill, her balance, her anticipation: it was breathtaking. And ridiculously, in a low, singsong voice, she was talking to the cats.

"That's right, pretties. I'm the one who will give you some sport." The injured one turned to Cram and hissed. Athena lashed out with her sword at its flank. "Not that one. I know you only want to play with conscious mice." The ball of the other swung at her, and she ducked behind another tree. Bark flew. Athena darted to the other side to strike again, but the cat was there, anticipating her attack. It lashed out with its forefoot, and Athena twisted desperately aside. She gasped and stumbled back, the other cat circling. But she had nowhere to go. The briars formed a solid wall of thorn behind her. The cats closed in, tails whipping back and forth in anticipation.

Henry found he could not move. On the stairs in Philadelphi, she had left him for dead.

Athena saw him. "Henry!"

He looked down the slope at her. Then he turned away.

CHAPTER 20

That palisade is too danged low. Nain't you never
seen a ball-tail jump?

—Ernesta Coolidge, huntrix

Henry Collins turned and walked away. His thoughtful
face and ragged hair disappeared over the lip of the hill.

"No," Athena said under her breath. She could not
believe it. For Cram's sake at least. She knew where she
stood with Henry, but she had always thought there was
a fellow feeling between him and the other boy. Nor did
the chemyst strike her as a coward. She thought that at
least, when they finally had it out, it would be face-to-

face. Well, she would not give him the satisfaction of calling after him.

The cats closed in. How absurd to die in this forsaken wilderness, with no one to witness and no reputation to be gained. She kicked out and caught the wounded one in the face. It yowled and raked its keen claws at her. She whipped her leg back into the tearing thorns of the brake, but her blood was up so high she barely felt them. The paw lashed in again, and she tried to parry it; the madly strong thing batted the blade away as if it were a Christmas bauble. The sword spun through the air and fell to the ground just a few feet away. It might as well have been miles.

Too quiet on her other side.

Only by instinct did she duck, and the ball of bone at the end of the other cat's tail smashed into the briar, just where her chest had been. The beast screamed and twisted, lashing out at her neck. Only one direction left. She hunched her shoulders, closed her eyes, and pushed back with all her might, iron-hard thorns raking across her back, her arms, and her face, into the hole made by the ball. She drove her feet against the earth until the thorns were too thick for her to move, and then she opened her eyes.

The branches had sprung back into place behind her, like a curtain, and a good two feet of briar stood between her and the cats. Her tricorne, quirked at a jaunty angle, hung midway between her and the outside. The wounded cat launched itself after her but then scrambled back, yowling in pain and frustration. The other one just stared at Athena. They were intelligent, these things, not just cunning. Pack tactics for hunting, diversion, isolating the wounded. The staring one was the larger of the two, with grizzled whiskers and a blaze of white fur on its shoulder, surrounding a wicked-looking scar that trailed down its back. It hissed at Athena.

It turned toward Cram. The boy was still lying on his side, moaning, only half awake after his tumble down the hill. She cursed. How had she left him so defenseless?

"No," Athena whispered.

The big cat stalked toward Cram, tail whipping back and forth.

"No! Cram! Wake up! Move, you daft butler!" Athena yelled. No response. But what could she do? The other one stood sentry, planted between her and the sword, licking the wound on its leg. If Athena pushed her way out of the brake, they would be on her in seconds, and what would that do for Cram? Once she fell, they would have him for dessert. And what help then for Ruby Teach?

She yelled, "Oi! Whitey! Here! Come for me, you motherless tabby! Come on!"

The big cat just looked over its shoulder at Athena, and she could swear that the thing smiled at her. It turned back, and its powerful legs bunched to spring. Athena could not watch, but she had to. She owed Cram that much.

Fire came over the hill. Blue fire blazed from the torches in both of Henry Collins's hands. Screaming like a mournful banshee and limping like an angry grandfather, he hobbled down the slope. The torches burned like daylight in the shadows of the hollow. Both cats hissed and yowled, backing away from Henry, who stood over Cram like Leonidas at Thermopylae. Then he *advanced* on them, swinging the torches as if he wanted to fly. Henry edged toward the wounded one and singed its fur. It howled and launched itself away over the hill. Henry speared one torch into the ground at Cram's feet, grabbed the other with both hands, and then came toward the big ball-tail, stabbing the torch forward like a spear, and yelling, "Ha! Hie thee! Felidae! Back to the dark with your brothers! I singed one of yours to death, and I will not hesitate to singe you as well! Beware of the singe-er!"

He truly needed to work on his taunts.

With the last "Hai!" the big cat had had enough and bared its fangs at Athena one last time. It turned, leaped up over the hill, and was gone.

Henry Collins doused the tree limb torch and hobbled over to the briars. "You in there, Boyle?"

"I am. I am indeed. Thank you, Henry, for coming back for us. That fire was well thought, though I do wonder if we may have given ourselves away."

He pried at the branches with the branch. "Fire put the fear into them. They would have feasted on us otherwise. No thanks necessary. It was Cram I came back for. Let's unravel how to get you out of those thorns."

He would not let it go, that moment on the steps. "Hail, and well met to you, too. By the way—"

"I do not have time for pleasantries, Boyle. Now that those things have our scent, they'll keep hunting us."

"I do not think that will be a problem."

"Why not?"

She could see it plain as day, hovering over his shoulder like some kind of halo. "Because I think you've lit the forest on fire."

The cats did not return. Nor did any other animals, as they seemed to be much more preoccupied with the preservation of their pelts.

Athena emptied the contents of Cram's sack on the ground.

The boy looked up in woozy horror. "Milady, nooooo."

She ignored him and tore through the meager remains of her supplies. Henry did the same right next to her. "Henry, do you have anything that could put out the fire?"

He looked up. The blue chemystral blaze was spreading quickly along the ridgetop. "No," he said, pawing through a worryingly small collection of flasks and powders. "I could make some of it change color. Possibly." He turned to Athena as he scooped it all back into his pouch. "You?"

"Nothing." She nodded her head upslope. "That is far too large for my powers." She jiggled a flask of colorless liquid. "I could cover us all in breathable water for at most half a minute." Her minor training in chemystry was useless compared with something like this. She piled the reagents into his pouch. "Here, just take all of it."

It was no small thing to give another chemyst your reagents, and Henry recoiled. "What? No."

"Just take them. No time to argue. Save that wind for running." She reclaimed her sword and their packs, they got Cram on his feet, and they lit out. The serving boy was groggy but able to stand with their help. The crackle of the fire grew to a rumble, and little flames peeked out of the undergrowth at the top of the hill.

"Come on!" she shouted. They scrambled to the top of the next hill supporting one another, a drunken six-legged crab, and stopped to take their bearings.

"Oh, my," said Henry. He was looking back the way they had come. Beyond their little hollow, the fire spread across the landscape, a curtain of blue flame that widened as they watched. The hungry thing wanted the whole forest.

"I do not know about you two, but I have no desire to end my life a fricassee," Athena said. Bravado was her only weapon against the creeping fear. "I invoke Captain Wayland Teach! We run until we drop, and then we pick ourselves up and run some more."

Each of the next two hills was steeper than the last. Athena tasted charcoal, and the smoke was getting thicker. A corset of iron cinched across her chest, and each breath was a battle. Cram kept looking left and right, as if for a trapdoor out of the forest. Henry's face lay frozen in a mask of concentration, teeth bared and clenched like the big cat's. He was lagging. Cram was supporting him, and Athena was supporting Cram. How long could she keep going without someone to pull her?

Henry cried out. Her shoulder wrenched. He was lying on the ground, clutching at his leg. The mask of concentration was gone, replaced by pain, frustration, and fear.

Athena saved the breath she might have cursed with and scrambled to his side. Cram was there on the other.

"No!" Henry yelled. His voice barely carried against the thunder of the fire. "I am slowing you! I will burn us all." He wrestled in his coat for something, and he pulled it out. It was the journal and its button key. "Take it!"

A copse of trees burst into flame barely fifty feet away.

"Go!" he screamed.

Cram looked to her, pleading. For what, she did not know. To go? To stay? To sprout wings and fly them to safety?

Henry was slowing them. But had they all not pledged themselves to Ruby? And who would even be able to translate the thing?

"Lady Athena!" It was Cram.

The ground moved beneath them like a landslide. Athena caught a glimpse of horns and hooves, and then all she could do was to grab Cram by the collar and throw them both sideways to the earth in a heap. A huge buck galloped past, right through where Cram used to be, so close Athena could see its black nose glistening. It paid no mind to them, and neither did the stream of deer that followed. The hooves churned up the ground of the hollow like fresh farm soil only a foot from their prone bodies.

Cram was already on his knees. "That way!" he shouted, pointing after the deer.

It looked like more fire there, not less. "Are you certain?"

Wild eyes. "Go!"

She crawled over to Henry and put her face next to his. "You get up, Henry Collins! If you lie here in the earth, bemoaning your fate, then so will we! We all will die here, and you take that weight to whatever scholar's Hades you'll be going to." She tapped the journal. "This is yours to bear! You are the only one who can unlock it!"

He shook his head, eyes down. "Damnation, Henry! You know what this means! If the journal goes unlocked, then Ruby goes unfound!"

Henry looked at her, and something brittle flickered there. But he moved.

He gathered his hands under him and pushed. Athena and Cram grabbed him, and they were off.

The three of them lit out after the deer. The smoke bit at Athena's eyes and nose, and she could barely see the tracks ahead of them. She dared not look back. The heat licked at her neck, and there was no room for anything but holding on to Henry and putting one foot in front of the other.

Step.

Step.

Slosh.

It was a puddle. No, it was a pond. No, it was a lake. The smoke cleared for a moment, revealing a great mound of fallen trees, apparently floating on the surface at the center.

"There!" Cram yelled, but Athena needed no urging.

She forged forward into the water, legs, waist, chest, as the icy cool rushed over her. Shapes in the smoke stood in the shallows. Deer, a fox, a family of rabbits. Her next step found no purchase as the shore dropped off. She flailed backward into the other two.

"Too deep past here!" she yelled. The island of fallen trees was still off in the distance. Cold crept in through her leathers.

"We can't stop!" Cram yelled back. "Water's too cold. Can't stay in it for too long!"

"But it's too deep!"

"This way! We have to go under!" Cram turned and pulled a hand from each of them onto his shoulders.

Athena pulled her hand back. "Under? Cram, I cannot swim!"

Henry pulled his hand back as well. "Nor can I!"

Cram panned back and forth between the two of them, a mad look on his face. He pushed his oilskin bag over to Henry. "Wait here!" And with that he dropped below the surface.

"Cram!" she called, and lunged forward, flailing at

the water. She ducked under, trying to see him in the dark. She grabbed forward at nothing, muddy swirls in front of her. One foot slipped free of the mud, and then the other. She wanted to scream but knew that she couldn't. Strong hands grabbed her just as she began to sink. She found her footing again, and her head came up into the air. She held on to her savior as if her life depended on it. It was Henry. "What do we do?"

Henry Collins's mouth hung open. He shook his head, wide-eyed.

The fire had reached the shore, and groups of other animals had crept deeper into the lake. A curtain of blue flame raged at its edge, and even this far into the lake, the heat warmed Athena's face like the summer sun. From below, the cold crept in, and shudders began running up her legs. She tried to quiet them but couldn't. She could feel Henry's shivering as well.

It seemed like a year they stood there, trapped between the fire and the cold.

Cram's head popped up, splashing water everywhere. He sucked in great gouts of air. "I found it!"

"What?" Athena had never been so happy to see anyone in her life.

"No time! We have to get. . . . out . . . water!" His teeth were chattering. "Grab on, you have to trust me! Push with your feet. Keep your mouths closed."

Henry and Athena looked at each other. "He seems to know what he's about," he said.

A laugh came out of her: a wild, terrible thing. She grabbed Cram's shoulder.

Henry grabbed the other shoulder. "Breathe deep!"

She did, and lucky thing, because just then Cram pulled them under.

CHAPTER 21

Cold-bathings is a great advantage to health.
—John Wesley, *Primitive Physick*

The cold of the water ate into Henry's bones. The roar of the fire barely penetrated under the surface in the silty brown. It was nothing compared with the sound of his heart. He kept his eyes open. If he lived through this and got withered and aged, with children and grandchildren and then great-grandchildren all sitting about his knees in a nice little house near the shore in Port Royal, he would have quite the story to tell. His fist ached, it was so tight on Cram's shirt, and he did what he could with his other arm, moving it in a vaguely paddle-esque motion. It didn't do much, however, and the water offered a delightful ease, a cool laziness leading to a long, well-earned sleep. So he stopped paddling.

A hand on his chest shook him. Rude. He was ready for bed. He needed to clear the humors and let out the big sigh that he always sighed as he was curling up for sleep. But he was not supposed to sigh. Someone had told him that. The rude person shook him again and then pried his hands out of the blankets and placed it on something. Sharp, wood. It was the edge of a hole. But he could barely feel it. His hands seemed . . . separate somehow.

Water.

Henry was underwater and nearly out of air, and Cram was trying to get him through a hole in a jumbled wall of muddy, slick wood. It was a wide hole, a shadow tunnel taller than he was, made from branches. His pulse banged in his ears, and he could not really feel his legs, but he hauled himself up through the protruding spikes. Breath clawed at his throat, like an animal trying to get free. He kept on pulling, and the air slipped out, bubbles playing about his face. Then his head broke the surface. There was no light, but there was air. Earth, rot, and sweet, sweet air. And there was a shore, he felt it underneath him, an earthy, muddy slope, and he kept pulling, and pushing with his knees, and he dragged himself right out of the water onto the bank.

So good to finally be back in bed. It was so cold in the house, and so warm here.

"Wake up, sir! You have to stay awake!" It was the serving boy Cram. For some reason he was stripped down to his underthings, ribs sticking out like handles on a market day basket. Henry shrugged off the hand and put his head back on the pillow.

Not pillow, mud. He opened his eyes, and all he saw was still water and then a faintly lit wall of sticks, mud, and moss. He turned his head, and behind him rose a sloped island of earth. This was in the lake. The fire.

The journal!

He wrenched it from the coat pocket, fearing the worst. However, the journal's author was beyond clever: the cover had grown chemystrally on contact with the lake, sealing itself against the water. It would not open. His reagents, however, had not fared so well. The powders had blended into a mass of useless goo, and all that remained were the two sealed flasks Athena had given him.

He found he was shaking all over again.

"Cram?" he chattered.

"Come on, sir, this way, we need to get you warm."

A merry fire burned at the top of the slope, leaking light, and Henry knew in his bones that he had to get to it. Athena was there as well, chewing on some jerky. Her back was to the fire, and she held her arms tight around her knees. She had very little clothing on, either, and her shoulders and arms were slim and very pale. A circular red scar lay on her lower back, a souvenir from a clockshot wound she received the day Henry and she met. She looked over her shoulder at him through a curtain of wet black hair. "Please do not look at me," she said in a quiet way. Pained.

He averted his eyes. "I'm sorry. I didn't—"

"Got to get them togs off, Professor, and quick," Cram said, and he began pulling off Henry's overshirt. "The cold of the water's still in 'em."

His fingers began to move. This was no time for propriety. When was the last time propriety had been appropriate? He couldn't rightly remember. His buckskins came off, and the warmth started to leach into his bones.

Cram pushed on him. "Come on then. Miss Black said if you ain't got blankets for warmth, all you got is each other. Can't be thinking about what's proper."

"That's not what I—" Athena knitted her brows. "I don't want you to see . . . *this* me."

The way she said it hit Henry. Not combative, not forceful. Careful.

Cram looked down. "It's the only way we last through the night, Lady."

"What about back to back then?" Henry turned his own back toward the fire as an offering. Athena did not respond; but she did move, and then two sets of shoulders were against his.

And so they huddled together, and indeed, it was warmer. The smoke crept up into a dark hole in the ceiling, the only opening in a riotous crisscross of logs, sticks, sod, and who knew what else?

"How did you start a fire?" Henry asked.

Cram nodded at a small clay pot lying on the ground. "Flicker pot. Miss Winnie told me about 'em. 'Taint chemystry, just some hot coals from out there. Sealed with mud. Cadged the pot from you while you was fainted."

Clever. Henry shivered. "Where are we?"

"Beaver lodge," Cram muttered, attacking another piece of pemmican.

The ceiling soared above them, at least twenty feet in the air.

"What kind of beaver made this?" Henry asked.

"Giant beaver, I surmise."

"Oh, good then," Henry said, and his head hit Athena's shoulder and he promptly fell asleep.

A splashing spluttering exploded from the shadows below, and a few moments later Cram emerged into the firelight. He shook himself off like a dog, and lake water sprayed in a fine mist over Henry and Athena. He plopped down on the dirt, pushed his wet hair out of his eyes, and helped himself to a hunk of raw, gooey pemmican. Henry and

Athena said nothing as he chewed through a number of bites, moaning and licking his lips. He looked up.

"Still burning," Cram said.

Henry leaned back against the makeshift chair of logs and sticks. "Two days. It has been burning for two days."

"Powerful chem there, Doctor." Athena got up and began to go through her daily stretching routine. They had been traveling for weeks together, but since the lodge had become their whole world, new features had popped out. For example, neither Cram nor the Boyle girl could sit still. The serving boy had been back and forth through the underwater passage so many times Henry had lost count. And Boyle? She fought with shadows. Hour after hour, sheathed in sweat, tearing through sequence after sequence, slashing the air apart with her sword so Henry sometimes felt sorry for it. Henry supposed he was no different, only his obsession was made from paper. He paged through the diary in the dim light from the hole above. The watertight seal had released when the journal had dried, but open or closed, it was still a mystery to him. The cipher of the first section, the one with the description of the city of three rivers, had been difficult.

It had taken up a good third of the pages, cramped, clear equations and proofs leading to nowhere in themselves, but this new portion . . . There was something different about it. The code was more dense, more complex, if that was at all possible, and hinting at even more glorious secrets. It scared him frankly, but he could not put it away and kept coming back to it like, well, a beaver to its lodge.

Athena stopped fencing. She turned. "Why did you come back?"

The question hit him in the stomach. "What do you mean?"

"For us, to scare away the cats. Why did you return?"

He had asked himself that question many times. Why save your nemesis? Why not leave her to die? Was it Cram who had brought him back? "I do not know."

"Well," Athena said. She began fencing again.

The silence grated.

"How do we know the landlord of this flat will not return to collect our rent by chomping us with its protruding teeth?" Henry asked, of no one in particular.

Cram stopped chewing for a moment. "We don't," he

said through a mouthful of pemmican.

"Do you not fear that this great beast will come splashing out of the dark, ferocious and angry that we have invaded its home?"

Cram moved the pemmican around in his mouth. "No, sir, I do not."

Henry folded the diary in his lap. "And why not?"

"Well, Professor, there are two reasons, as far as I can see." He picked up a twig. "Reason the first, I refer you to the raging devil fire outside. I reckon that a little bunny rabbit could not forge a path through it, let alone a beast that might have made this." He pointed at the roof, high above them.

"Fair." Henry could not help smiling.

"Reason the second, Miss Winnie mentioned to me that beavers are as restless as a boiling egg. If they have not come back yet, mayhap they have moved on."

"They?" Boyle paused in her air stabbing. "There may be more than one?"

Cram chewed for a moment on an errant piece of pemmican. "They mate for life. Have little ones. Mam always said you ain't safe until you got someone to watch your back and someone else to watch the one watching your back, beggin' your pardon."

Boyle stared for a moment and then went back to her stabbing, with some cutting and flourishing thrown in.

Henry nodded. "So, you think we may be safe."

Cram nodded.

"Then why go back and forth between here and the outside so many times?"

"Well, Professor, I need to check the fire."

"Because . . ."

"If it don't go out soon, we are going to be late to meet the captain and Miss Winnie."

"Indeed."

"Also, if it goes out, the beavers might come back."

"Ah."

"Yes."

The little fire crackled.

"You know, Cram . . ."

"Yes, Professor?"

"You are quite the capital serving man."

Cram smiled and looked away. "Thanks, Professor."

CHAPTER 22

Protect and nurture your brothers and sisters. They are your only shield against the uncaring world.

—Training manual, Reeve of England

Walking around on wooden toes was stupid. Ruby had not been able to change them back immediately or even after a few hours.

After four nights of focus, slow as molasses, painful as acid on a rope burn, there they were. Five infuriating and completely un-Ruby-colored toes stared back at her. She had changed them, but now they had scales like a dragon's and glowed green as grass in the chem pot light.

What good was changing if she could not change back? Or if it took a week to give yourself a different color of hair? Or forever? She had to be careful. If the Swede saw any of this, he would cut her toes off for research.

How had Gwath done it? Noses, hair, skin, in less time than it took him to fry an egg. And always in secret. Thirteen years of training. Ever since she was a baby, Gwath had been her teacher. She could remember, clear as day, balancing as a toddler, trying to keep one foot on his beefy thigh as he waggled it back and forth until she fell. He caught her every time before she hit the deck. And yet he had never taught her this.

Had he known she was a Changer? Fermat had said once that it passed through families but sometimes skipped generations or hopped around. Gwath was a Changer. Ruby was a Changer. It couldn't just be coincidence. What did that make Gwath to her? Her father's brother? Why would they have not told her? Her mother's brother? Something . . . else? It pained her to think about it, but it floated just out of reach. A sweet, sad kind of pain that she could not locate in her toes, or in her mind, or even in her heart.

It was a thought that in times before, she would have shut away in the iron box in her belly, where she kept everything locked up. But somehow she didn't want to. The box was right full anyway. Locking things up there had always kept her moving forward. That heavy box, full of feelings and fondness and bonds and frustrations: Was it holding her down? Or keeping her stuck? After all, it certainly made her the opposite of empty.

The nights were so quiet. The cadets on watch did not call to one another. The silence gave her time to think. She climbed up into the windowsill. The river below shone silver in the night.

The biting chill of winter gave way to the promise of a Pennswood spring. But as the days warmed, so did Ruby's frustration. She took to roaming the halls, searching for she knew not what. The Swede's journal remained locked. Wisdom Rool had taken her lockpicks, and with them sitting in his saddlebags in Savannah or Acadia or on the moon, she had no hope of opening it. The Swede had an endless appetite for her blood, and Evram was so obsessed with Sleipnir that he barely talked of anything else.

So Ruby kept working at changing.

One night she couldn't bear to stay in her room a moment longer. Night after night of working changes. She dreamed of doing something, anything else, but because they were where the changing had begun, she kept hammering at the toes. From scales to bunions, from doughy white to weathered clay, and then finally, after a brief holiday of red fur, she had finally gotten them back to almost matching her own skin. The pain burning up her leg every time she tried to change became a constant companion. Could she create a nose, though? Or a larger jaw? Nothing. What was she missing? Two times—into a barrel at Fermat's tower and into a pumpkin during the Corson incident—she had completely transformed her shape. But she couldn't when she was actually trying.

She needed air.

The roof was the only other place she could find to

be alone. Ruby climbed up the ladder and then pushed the trapdoor open.

Avid Wake stood there, a sprinkle of rain in her hair. The tall girl leaned against one of the railings. "Here for the view?"

"Yes," Ruby said, because "I've come up here to clear my mind so I can change into furniture" might not go over so well. She kept her distance and moved to the other side of the roof.

They stared at the view. Ruby sneaked a few glances at Avid. The bruises on her face had healed. She seemed calm, less ferocious than down in the yard. A scar on her cheek gave her a constant . . . well, not a grin, but a smirk? She was waiting for something. An appeal? An apology? Ruby was skilled at both.

But she would give neither.

Time passed.

Avid laughed.

"What?" Ruby said.

"They give you so much notice," Wake said.

"Who?"

"Who else? Lord Captain Rool. Ward Corson. Cole and Burk. The Swede. You're like their little chickadee. They have to hold you close inside their pockets to keep the cats from you."

There it was. "So you wish you were me, do you? Even though I'm a prisoner and all."

Avid laughed again, but it was the tiniest bit hollow. "You have your own room. You do as you please, Teach. We have to prove ourselves every day, on the bodies of our brothers and sisters. If I don't measure up here, they send me back." Something terrible passed across her face, but scorn quickly masked it. "And you say you're a prisoner."

Across the river a spark lit up. Avid saw it, too. "Fires," she said. "I think they're burning farms."

"Who?"

"Does it matter?"

Ruby cocked her head. "Well, of course it matters."

Wake turned to her. "Not to me. If someone burns a farm, you stop them. No matter who they are."

Ruby shook her head. "That's not what I—"

"I saw what you did."

Ruby gripped her toes in her boots. "Avid—"

"I saw you tip the board down at the spring. At the turn of the year."

The wind whipped across the roof. The glow of the distant fire grew.

"I didn't—"

Avid rolled her eyes. "Just own it, Sweetling. You tipped me over because you couldn't stand that I could do it and you couldn't. It galled you, so you almost killed me."

Ruby shook her head. "I didn't mean to."

"What? Kill me? No, I know. You just meant to take something special away from me."

It had been wrong. And Avid was right. "I don't know why I did it, Avid. I—" Was she going to cry? She was not going to cry. Not in front of this one. Ruby clamped down. "I'm sorry." Ruby looked down at Avid's fist. "We going to fight now?"

Avid gave her a look. "Burk told me."

"What?"

"You saved me, too."

"So?"

Avid's brows furrowed. "I—I do not understand you."

Ruby chuckled low and without humor. "There is a club. I believe they are having patches made."

Wake kept her eyes on Ruby as she crossed to the trap, as if she were some kind of hunting cat. She went down without a word.

The moon crept out from behind the bank of clouds: a white disk under a gray blanket.

Ruby tried to turn herself into a ladder.

It didn't work.

CHAPTER 23

Make the Wilderness a Garden? Are you mad? The flora and fauna of this land are rich beyond measure. Full of wild, heated life we have not yet seen. Explore it? Absolutely. Live in it, revel in it. But if you try to tame it, you will kill it.
—Dr. James Sutherland, fellow, Royal Society

Ash gets in your breeches.

Cram shook out his leg to try to coax the ash out, but the shaking just drove it all deeper. It was everywhere: in his hair, in his nose, in his armpits, and let us not forget the breeches, including parts that Mam said never to talk about in polite company. Lady Athena and the professor looked like ancient warriors from the homeland Mam had told stories on, covered head to toe, except it weren't blue dye they were wearing. It was gray-black, like they had taken baths in a charcoal pit.

And it itched. Oh, Providence, it itched.

He tore his scarf from his face. "I can't take it," he said. "Milady, please."

"Cram, I said no."

"I beg of you, mistress of mine, I will do for you whatever you desire, I will slay demons, I will carry mountains, I will float you on my back across the River of Hell itself if you only, for goodness' sake, and for the respect of my childrens and grandchildrens, and because I know you are at heart a goodly person, if you only scratch this little place below my shoulders." He turned to her, hoping that his pose of helplessness might stir some tiny little fire in her stern and iron heart.

"No."

"But—"

Athena stopped on the slope and turned around, kicking up a small puff of ash and debris. She pulled down the handkerchief covering her mouth and spat. "Cram, please. If I scratch that place, you will simply itch worse. Henry Collins is your warning. Look there."

The professor was bringing up the rear, and he did indeed have his long arm out of its sleeve and was scratching his back as if it were a fiddle at a barn raising. When he noticed them watching, he stopped. "What?"

"I see your point," said Cram.

They forged on. Behind him Henry cursed under his breath in very unscholarlike tones.

The fire had burned for three days, and when they finally could cut loose from the beaver lodge, they had emerged into a blasted world: grass, trees, bushes, even animals scraped from it like the icing from a cake. Only blackened trunks, the bones of the hills, and ash, ash, ash lay underneath. In an odd way it made the journey easier. The thorn brakes and switchbacks were gone, and their path to the hilltop lay bare in front of them.

Course, the toad in the pudding was what happened to them others. Winnie Black and the captain had more sand and more sense than most folk Cram'd ever met, but worry tugged at him nevertheless. Had they been burned? Had they been caught? He tried to soothe the little voice inside him that ranted on such things, but it kept telling tales of roastings and battles until he had to pinch himself to stop it even for a moment.

Two days had passed since they left the lodge. It was a lifeless trek. The animals were the smart ones, and they had skinned out but good. There were still scattered fires everywhere, so they risked a fire one night, and he had tried to make rubaboo, but it tasted more like boiled pitch than Miss Winnie's magical pemmican stew.

It was climbing all day long, sometimes knee deep in ash drifts.

Up ahead Athena topped a slope and stopped for a moment.

She gave a whoop and disappeared.

"Professor!" Cram called back to Henry, and started running, and then he started coughing while he was running, but he had to keep going. Fire was in his lungs by the time he got to the top, and he saw what evil had taken his mistress.

It was a little pond in a meadow full of tall grass and big yellow flowers. Lady Athena stood neck deep in it, shooting up a jet of water out of her mouth like a whale. It lay on the middle of a wide plain where the fire seemed to have finally, blessedly burned itself out. Cram let out his own yawp and then shucked his buckskins as if they were burning, down to his drawers. He lit out down the burned-out slope, across the ashy field, into the green spring grass, then into the air, spinning down into the water. Oh, it was cold. He yelled as he came up for air, and then he had to duck again as Henry Collins, gimpy leg and all, barreled in behind him. They splashed and laughed like wee children. Cram hadn't laughed like this in a long, long time.

The flat hilltop loomed above. They had arrived.

The sun still rode high in the sky, so after they had washed themselves, they scrubbed their leathers within an inch of their leathery lives and hung them up to dry in a big maple tree. The pond was fed by a creek at one end and then drained by a creek at the other, and it stayed clear as Sunday morning.

Henry Collins lifted Cram off his feet with a huge hug. "You did it, Cram!" He dropped him and turned to

Athena. "The finest guide in all the land, Boyle! Double this man's wages this instant!"

Lady Athena was chewing on a long blade of grass like some farmer. "Brilliant, Cram." She clapped him on the shoulder.

Cram grinned so hard he feared his face would fall off. He had brought them there. He, and no other. Cram had got them to the lake in the fire. Cram had got them in the beaver dam. Something wriggled in his belly, but it wasn't like when you had too much pemmican for supper. It was warm and strong. For the first time in his life he felt—what was the word for it? Equal. "Thank you, milady, Professor." On the grass before him their shadows mixed with one another, hanging together, not apart. That made Cram even happier.

A voice boomed down above. "Shut your yaps, children! This is a peaceful meadow!"

As one the three of them looked back up the hillside. A dark figure stood there, carrying a staff. All other detail was blocked out by the glare of the setting sun. "When you are finished mawking and chattering, and after you have returned to your clothing, come up to the summit for tea." The figure turned majestically and perambulated up the path. It was a grand effect, spoiled somewhat when the shape tripped and fell out of sight with a squawk.

Cram licked his lips. "That weren't Miss Winnie or the captain."

Lady A. drew her sword. "Apparently someone lives here."

"Someone clumsy enough to trip over his own feet." The professor folded his arms. "Is that all you ever do? Draw your sword? Does this strike you as a dangerous moment?"

"All moments are dangerous if you give them enough time," she said.

He blinked. "What does that even mean?"

"It means that someone needs to protect us."

"Oh, really? And why is that?"

"Because the world is dangerous."

Henry looked significantly at her sword. "Have you ever thought, milady, that perhaps the world is dangerous to you because you are preemptively dangerous to *it*?"

"*Pipe down.*" A flock of birds erupted from one of the trees. The head of whoever it was had popped back into view. When they did not continue, it popped back down again.

Cram cleared his throat. "I think this may be a parley for another time."

"Fine," Athena said, loud-like, and then, after Cram had jabbed her in the ribs, whispered, "Fine. But we must be on our guard, yes? We have not come through all this to be simply cursed or hexed by some savage shaman." She sheathed her blade.

Henry whispered, "I believe curse and hex may be the same thing. And why does it have to be a savage shaman? Have you ever met one of these savages you keep referring to? I'll have you know that the people of this land that I have met in Philadelphi—"

"Quiet. Please," Cram hissed, and thrust his arms down at his side. They both looked at him as if he had grown four more arms. Someone had to make sense, and it would be neither of these two. But they stopped talking, so he turned and marched toward the hill before they could start up again.

The path trailed across the meadow and then up and around, and just before it reached the summit, a little hollow was cut into the side of the hill. A cave yawned back into the earth, but on a patch of ground in front of it sat the largest rocking chair Cram had ever seen. It was rough-hewn from what appeared to be the trunks of small trees, held together with wire, thick rope, and in one spot a pair of underbreeches. In the rocking chair rocked the strangest of beasts: covered in gray, white, and black hair and vaguely man shaped. Two fangs thrust up from its lower jaw, and inside its marbled brown eyes lurked a strange intelligence. In one massive paw lay a tiny corncob pipe, and a wisp of smoke curled up from it.

Henry said, "Very well, draw the sword."

Lady Athena's hand flashed toward the hilt.

"I wouldn't do that if I were you, laddie," rumbled the creature. Cram's brainpan was busy exploding, but he was fair certain that the whatever it was spoke with a deep, burry Scots brogue.

Athena kept her hands out, palms up. "We come in peace."

The creaks of the rocking chair vibrated in Cram's feet. "Very well, and a fine welcome to all three of you." The creature stood up, towering over them, eight feet tall at least, and bowed.

They stared at one another.

"Em, pardon me for asking, but who are you?" asked Henry.

Its head-size fist flashed toward them. Cram flinched and closed his eyes. This was the end. The professor soon to be headless, and Cram not far behind. When he opened his eyes, the hand was still there, hanging in front of Henry. "Doctor James Sutherland, pleased to meet you," it said.

The professor gingerly placed his hand into the mitt, and they shook. "Henry Collins, a pleasure," he stuttered out. Cram thought that would be an appropriate time to faint.

CHAPTER 24

If you travel from me, still I will give you enough.
Enough dates and figs for the journey,
Enough water to reach the next well.

—Taki, Ottoman poet, 1696

Athena sat in the moonlight and committed murder. She killed, with great ferocity, a honey and acorn butter sandwich. Cram, Henry, and she were tearing through sandwiches, and there seemed to be an infinite supply. "Doctor Sutherland" puffed on his pipe and did not eat. Occasionally he licked at the back of his hand with a big black tongue.

"How is your sandwich?" Doctor Sutherland asked.

"Excellent, thank you," she said. The claws on the beast could have torn her to ribbons, but he seemed delighted to experience their company.

Athena shivered.

"Perhaps you would prefer a fire, my dear?" The beast frowned. "I am so terribly sorry. Ever since, well, I acquired this fur, I have completely forgotten about the chills that take one in the night."

"No, thank you," she said. Both Henry and Cram were looking at her, curiosity burning in their faces. Brashness did have its benefits. "Doctor Sutherland?"

"Please, call me James."

"Very well, um, James." She searched for the words. "I wish to cause you no offense, but I cannot help noticing that even though you have been incredibly hospitable to us, and even though your speech is that of a gentleman, and a highly educated one at that—"

"Yes?"

"Well, to put it plainly, your body seems to be that of some kind of furry savage creature."

"Not that we are offended in any way," Henry added.

"No, indeed, sir!" Cram said through a mouthful of acorn butter. "Thankful and verily unoffended!"

"The word you are searching for is *yeti*, my dear."

"Yeti?"

"Indeed. Well, the Algonkin call them stone giants, or *Ge no sgwa*, but I am more partial to the Himalayan *yeti*. Rolls off the tongue, don't you know. Let me explain." He puffed on his pipe.

"Well." He puffed again and let out the smoke in a slow sigh around his massive fangs. "I can say this no other way. This yeti"—he clapped his paw on his chest—"ate Doctor James Sutherland."

Athena decided the best response would be to remain very still. "You ate him."

"Right up. Chomped straight through his skull and gobbled up his brain." He tapped a fang. "This mouth is intolerably powerful, you see."

With a sheepish smile that revealed the whole of his impressive catalog of fangs, the yeti went on. "Well, Doctor Sutherland . . . or now me, I suppose, was a brilliant man. I blush to say it, but it is important, I think, for the story. A groundbreaking natural philosopher, he had traveled to the colonies from his native Scotland. He set up here in the woods, in this very cave, undertook some cracking research regarding the local flora, and then the yeti discovered him one stormy night and ate him. And somehow, Doctor Sutherland's, well, self moved along with his more meaty parcels into this body. The yeti—I—changed. I collected acorns. I began to cultivate bees. And tobacco." He held up his pipe. "I have a little garden plot down the way, you know. This landscape is absolutely rife with strange and exotic plants. It is why I decided to live here in the first place." He placed a fond paw on the arm of the rocking chair. "I also built this." The wood popped off with a crunch. "I am still perfecting my handicrafts."

Cram piped up. "Forgive me, sir, but . . . you ate him. That seems hardly fair play to me."

The great shaggy head nodded slowly. "I have thought on this long and hard, young master. When I ate Doctor Sutherland, I was doing what yetis do. Now, with my faculties and a robust helping of Doctor Sutherland's particular philosophy, I am mortified and ashamed. Except . . . I am also the yeti, am I not?" He held up his paw, and sharp ebon talons eased out of it, shining in the moonlight. "Because I have these claws, should I therefore roar, beat my chest, slice you into morsels, and wolf you right down, you who are my new friends?"

"We would prefer you did not." Henry Collins chewed his lip.

Athena didn't answer. In her way she, too, wore a different skin.

Silence fell. The doctor looked back and forth among the three of them and cleared his throat. "What about the lot of you then? What brings you travelers to this out-of-the-way place?"

Athena smiled. This territory at least felt familiar. "We are meeting some friends here. Wayland Teach and Winnifred Pleasant Black."

He took a long pull on his pipe. "The woodswoman! Winnie is a fine lady. She must have sent you to me. You are welcome to all my hospitality until these friends of yours arrive."

They rested for five days on the hilltop. The doctor helped them resupply their food stores with acorn hard bread, flavored with berries and honey. It was a magnificent change after what Athena privately thought of as the Great Pemmican Death March. Sutherland and Cram went on long walks during which he apparently told Cram about mushrooms and edible plants and such. Cram seemed absolutely undisturbed that he was undertaking day trips with a man-eating creature. Sutherland did seem a yeti of his word, however, and made no sudden movements to consume them. Could the three of them have stopped him if they'd wanted to, powerful as he was? The helplessness offered Athena a strange kind of comfort. She slept well for the first time since they had left on their trip, and Cram and Henry looked fresher and more alive than they had since StiltTown.

On the fifth day, two days past when the others were due, Athena went looking for Henry.

He sprawled in the sun on the bank of the pond down in the meadow. One thing all that arm and leg was good for was sprawling. His boots lay on the grass, and he had shucked his buckskin overshirt in the midday heat, the collar of his cloth shirt open to the breeze. She stood by the trunk of the willow and watched him for a while. He had the journal out, and if a herd of elk had galumphed by, he would not have raised his head. She rolled her shoulders. She had come here for a reason.

She sat down near him on the bank. After a moment he marked his page with care and sat up. He had a clumsy grace about him, like a yearling, still learning to walk.

"Henry," she said.

"Boyle," he said.

"Will you not call me Athen?"

He chewed his lip. "Very well."

Why was this hard? "I kicked you from the stairs."

He frowned. "Yes. Yes, you did."

She had to tell the truth. "I would do it again."

"So you have told me before. Thank you for dropping by to make certain I understood that."

"Wait. Henry— That is not—" She pulled some grass out of the ground.

He opened his book back up, then closed it. "Boyle."

"Athen."

He made an *mmf* sound. "We do not need to be friends. We share a common mission, to rescue Ruby. You did what you felt needed to be done."

She cut in. "If you were in my position—"

"I—" He bit back something angry. "Who knows?"

Just then an animal, covered in ash so thick it was unidentifiable, came out of the waste beyond the creek. It dived into the lake without a moment's thought of them. It splashed about, spit water, then got out. It shook the water from its coat, along with some more ash, then headed out through the grass.

"What was that?" Athena asked.

"Fox, I think. Have to ask Cram, I suppose." A wisp of a smile fluttered.

She would have preferred to face a pack of ball-tails than this. "You saved my life, you know. With the cats. Even if you say you didn't. I owe you a debt." He started to protest, but she cut him off. "Let me finish, please. I am sorry about your leg. I would do it again, but I ask your forgiveness."

"How can I forgive you if you would do it again?"

"I don't know, but that is what I have."

"Well."

"I like you, Henry. You are strong, and you are brave, and you are smarter than I will ever be, and, well." She straightened her shoulders. "And you are honorable. I think you are a better person than I, sometimes by far. I have never had many friends. Save Cram, and Ruby perhaps, at one time, I have never had any friends. And Cram is my servant, and Ruby is my responsibility, and I am not certain if that matters or—" She was dancing, feinting. She had to extend to strike. "If you could find it in yourself to forgive me, I would like to try to be your friend."

He did not answer. He looked down at the journal and flipped through several pages. He showed her one. It was forested with equations and symbols, so thick you could barely see the page. The symbols were all in one knifelike, cramped hand. Over it Henry had scrawled emendations and partial bits and pieces in looping letters. "Here," he said.

"What is it?" Athena said.

"I think I have discovered it, the question of the journal. I believe Ruby's blood carries some manner of cipher or code."

"Her blood? How? What is it?"

"I think it is the plans for some kind of artifice or mechanism."

"An engine of some kind? Or an automaton? What does it do?"

"I don't know yet."

He looked at her for a moment, about to say something? But then the Henry door closed. He went back to the book. It was his way. Going back to the book, closing out the world. This time she did not accept it.

"Why are you doing this?" she said.

"What?"

"The whole thing. The journey. The code." Anger, a strange anger, flared inside her. "Burned, trapped, ball-tailed. You have nearly died three times, to my knowledge. You bang your head on that book until your brains must be bruised and bloody. Why are you doing all this? What is Ruby Teach to you?"

He cocked his head at her. "She saved my life."

The force of it stopped her in the street.

"She saved my life, Boyle. And so did you, down in that brig on the *Grail*. If you three had not found me and taken me out of there, they would have hanged me from the yardarm for a traitor."

"But you saved my life, and Cram's, twice even. Once at Fen's and the other—"

"With the cats, yes, and then I lit the forest on fire—"

She laughed.

The humor left his face, and an ancient sage remained. "And so we are bound, the four of us. We are bound together by fire and blood." He looked down at the journal. "But I would be lying to you if I did not say that this"—he tapped it with one long finger—"*this* has bound me, too. It is a work of genius, I think, and it contains something bigger perhaps than all of us. I want, I need, to solve it." He looked about, as if there might be other reasons in the meadow. "That is why I am on this mission."

They sat for a while, and she tried to think of something else to say. "Thank you." She stood up slowly, uncertain of the terrain. "Henry?"

"Yes?"

"The other thing?"

He looked at her, much as she imagined she had looked at the fox or at one of the ball-tails, trying to decide what to make of it. "I do not know, Boyle. I do not know if I can forgive you. I will try."

It was something. She went to go.

"Boyle?"

"Yes, Henry?"

"Why are you on this quest?"

She thought for a while. "I honestly don't know." She did know. But she could not say it. If she named it, it would make it real.

CHAPTER 25

*The rules be different up in them mountains. You hain't seen what
I seen. And I hope you never do.*
—Jimmy Two Hands, tracker

The sun was creeping behind a wall of pink and orange,
and they built a fire. The doctor broke out a crock of
aged honey, flavored with elderflower. The flower part
tasted funny, but Cram liked it enough that he kept on
slathering it all over an acre of acorn hard bread.

"More honey, Cram?" Dr. Sutherland asked.

"Yes, please!"

Dr. Sutherland was a right kindly host, and it hadn't

taken Cram long to ken that he didn't mean them no harm. If he had, well, they'd a been in his furry belly by now. He shrugged and snuggled up next to the fire. Like Mam always said, "Worry about tomorrow when tomorrow sneaks up behind you in the morning and pushes you out the window."

Lady Athena stood up. "They're late."

The professor looked up from the diary. He had run out of paper days back, and now it sprouted so many bark bookmarks it looked as if it might walk away on barky spider legs at any moment. "Your point?"

"They are late!" Lady Athena repeated. "More than a week now. We have put this off for too long. We need to go."

Henry closed the journal. "Athena, what can we do? We have to wait for them. Without Winnie Black, we will never make it to the river valley."

She closed her eyes for a moment. It was her "lend-me-patience-so-I-do-not-skewer-this-chemyst-with-my-sword" look. "Henry, time is wasting. We cannot be certain that they even survived."

That didn't sit well. You had to believe folk were still alive. Cram's other voice wondered to him if that believing might be what kept someone among the living, even if all hope was lost. That's why he kept that candle flame of hope alive for old Gwath. And that's why he had to speak up now. "Here now, milady. Miss Winnie could navigate her way through a tunnel at midnight with Cubbins lying across her eyes!"

"I know that, Cram, but they might have run afoul of extenuating circumstances."

"Such as?" Henry said.

Athena whirled on him. "Such as a massive sheet of horizon-to-horizon chemystral fire. For example."

"Aha, so this is my fault!"

"I am not saying that. Winnie Black absolutely is a masterful tracker. And Wayland Teach absolutely is a masterful man." She clenched her fists. "And if they were able to, they absolutely would have made their way here by now!"

Her voice lowered to a whisper. "Ruby Teach is in some unknown danger, and we cannot drag our feet any longer. I feel I am going mad. We must finish this fool's errand and salvage whatever strange goal is at the end of it. The sooner we accomplish that, the sooner we get on to our real business." She gripped her sword hilt. "We should leave tomorrow."

Henry chewed on his lip and held her gaze. "We have no guidance. I will wait."

"A pox on your waiting!" Athena stalked into the night.

Cram found her on top of the hill, perched on a large rock. The rolling land spread out in a forested carpet below to the . . . West? East? Hang it. "Philadelphi ain't nearby, that's for certain."

"Not nearly so far as England."

He sat down on a smaller rock next to the big one, and they stayed like that for quite a while. She had to breathe, she had to simmer; that much he knew from the months he had spent in her company. He had to time it just right. Too soon, and she would blow up again. Too late, and she would be lost to stony silence. There it was, a tiny shift in the set of her shoulders. He made a prayer to Providence and jumped in. "Milady . . ."

She let out a big breath. "Yes, Cram?"

"I don't mean to intrude, but—"

"But I am a horse's ass?"

"Only occasionally and with great legitimacy."

Her profile was lost in shadow, but he could hear the strain. "This adventure, this— It is useless. We stumble ever deeper into this forsaken wasteland, searching for something impossible, guided by folly and whimsy."

Cram licked his lips. "Yes, milady. Am I folly or whimsy?"

She laughed a moment, but then the laugh broke off in the dark. "You are a brave companion, my friend, and I am lucky to have you. Never forget that." Cram's chest swelled. "But the whole of this thing is a fool's errand, taking us ever farther away from the main chance: to save Ruby!" She threw a rock over the edge of the hill. After a few moments there was a far-off clatter.

Her voice went all soft. Not moony. Just not steel, as it mostly was. "You know, a few days ago . . ."

"Yes, milady?"

"Henry Collins asked me why I was on this journey."

"And what did you say?"

"I didn't."

Cram waited.

"I do not have the words for it. It is concrete in my body, like my pulse or my tears. It is this: I cannot rest until Ruby Teach is safe. And to that end I have cast my lot in this venture, and I am desperately uncertain of it."

It hurt him to see her like this. "Should we go, miss?"

"Where, Cram? Where could we go?"

"Well, back to Philadelphi? Start the search there? The trail might be a wee bit cold, but mayhap we could get back with the Bluestockings, or Mr. Fermat—"

"No, no. I defied their orders; I deserted them. Those doors are closed to me. I have cast my lot with this . . ."

"Adventure? Heroic journey? Tale of great doings?"

She sighed. "As you say. I am certain there are orders from my father for my return in every Grocer safe house from here to the kingdom of Sweden. I cannot go back in disgrace. We must go forward into madness."

"At least we go together, milady."

"Together with Henry, who hates me."

"Well—"

"Cram."

That was her signal for his silence, but this time he would not be silent. He could not. "Milady, I think you may be mistook." She moved to speak, but he soldiered on. "But even if you ain't, are you going to let that stop you? You going to lie down on this hilltop and watch the stars circle around until you grow roots? No, you ain't. Because you are my lady, and you're one part leather and two parts steel, and you don't lie down for no one."

She said nothing. He had overstepped; he knew it. His other voice was tanning him something fierce right now. Mam always said, "Tell the high folks what they want to hear, not what they need. 'Cause if you tell 'em what they need, they gonna decide they don't need you."

She turned to him, a shadow in the starlight. "You are not an excellent servant, Cram," she said. "But you are a good friend." She took his hand and shook it. He felt lucky it was dark because the size of his grin was unseemly. "I think I'll stay up here for a while longer. Will you sit with me?"

"Of course, milady."

"But not talk?"

"Of course, milady. I am most excellent at not talking. Why, once Mam said—"

"Cram."

"Yes, milady."

The stars spun about, and Cram got lost in their stories.

CHAPTER 26

Our ancient Greek brothers and sisters had a word: Dynamis.
Dynamis is your heart, your spirit, your will to victory. Is there a
link between your dynamis and your ability to access the Source?
Ask me instead, "Does the basket shape the apples?"
—Pierre de Fermat, lecture to the Acadamie Philosophie, 1677

The sun woke Ruby in her windowsill, creeping in over the top of her scratchy sheet. A little bird had landed on the sill and sang her a sweet song. Birds made her nervous. They were pretty, but their eyes were dead. She shooed it away and rubbed the sleep from her eyes. She had spent the whole of the previous night trying to grow a sixth toe. She looked down. Still five toes. Another failure. She turned just slightly and groaned. The bruises from training the day before had melded into a single winding track of pain across her entire body. Body pounded into mush, and no progress on the Works front, either. She was certain that she was the worst reeve in the colonies.

It took a few minutes to unkink enough to get a foot down onto the floor. Slipping on her boots was a heroic feat. She had to rest for a few moments after that. The blood was flowing by then, however, and she could at least stand up straight as she headed out through the door.

Ruby Maxim Nine: "Never Show Them Your Pain."

The sand baths were mostly empty. A few stragglers were scrubbing themselves vigorously. The sand was just as good as water for cleaning, and the wards claimed that it toughened your skin. Thank Providence Evram did something tinkery with herbs and powders to freshen it each night. The tall storm shutters were thrown wide, and a warm wind was pushing the first hints of summer into the room from across the canyon.

Ward Edwina Corson perched on the windowsill: a jaguar on a branch. The wind ruffled her shaggy red hair. "Clean up and then meet me in the changing room, Teach."

Ruby hesitated: "I'm near late now for Assembly, Ward. Should I—"

"You are with me today," Corson said, and walked out. No footprints followed her across the sand.

Ruby started scrubbing. Rubbing the sand into the bruises across her back and belly was a special kind of awful, but she knew it would be worse tomorrow if she didn't. The herbs and such added to the sand worked wonders.

Ward Corson stood in the changing room, a tiny book cradled in her hand. She trailed her jade fingers over the lines as she read. She favored the long, divided skirts worn by many of the women in the Reeve, and her vest and tunic were spotted with yesterday evening's meal, goat and beets. The ward had an arm's-length relationship with neatness.

Ruby dressed, and Corson read her book. It took Ruby a while, though she counted it a great victory that she did not groan once. But what was Corson doing here?

As soon as Ruby was dressed, Corson said, "Walk with me, Teach," and stalked down the hallway. A back stairway changed from stone to rough-hewn wood several flights up, and then Corson led her out onto the walkway on top of the palisade. The trees in the valley beyond the river shimmered in the humid April air.

In the courtyard the cadets were already at Stairs, a sinuous line of tortured bodies, walking on hands and toes. From a press-up position, head first, you walked up the stairs, then back down. Keep your back like a plank, or start over again.

Corson caught Ruby's glance. "You don't like crawling stairs?"

Ruby shook her head. "No, Ward."

"Neither did I." She stopped at a corner of the palisade.

Corson tapped her jade fingers on the grayed wood of the wall. "I hated Stairs. I trained here, you know, one of the first. Younger than you. Fifteen years ago. My ma died in a fire in our hayloft, and lucky for me she took my pa with her. So I came with the first shipment when the Reeve took this place. Oh, I hated Stairs. The pain in your forearms, yes? Like tiny spears." Ruby nodded. Corson looked down at her crystal digits. "So you know what I did?"

"No, Ward," Ruby said.

Corson numbered on her fingers. "I finished all the tasks. I mastered all the tests. I took the Oath. And then I never did Stairs again." She gently prodded Ruby's shoulder. "You're running out of time, Ruby."

Ruby's mouth went dry. Did Corson have Rool's confidence? Did she know of the Swede's progress? Did she know about her spying? Possibly, but what if she did not? Ruby would be admitting to sabotage and worse. "Ward, I am working at the training," Ruby said.

"And the other thing?"

Cautiously Ruby said, "The changing?"

"The changing. Have you made any progress?"

"Very little." It galled her to say it.

Corson nodded. "Something holds you back. Something is in the way. I see it. Do you not feel that? Perhaps you must give yourself fully to the Works or the changing. Perhaps they will not accept divided loyalty."

"Loyalty to those who beat me?"

Corson snaked her head, side to side. "Chart your own course. They will continue to beat you, I'm sure. Until you finish the tasks. Until you master the tests. Until you take the Oath. Or until the Swede gets what he wants from you. Or the lord captain." She turned and walked on. "Come. We're late."

Corson led Ruby over the gates along the palisade. Below them the narrow, winding road, almost a tunnel— the same one Ruby had trailed Corson down months ago—cut deep into the rock and wound steeply down from the gates around the side of the bluff to the plain. An enclosed bridge stretched over the road to another crag and a smaller building. The close, warm interior of the bridge was dark, lit by only a few arrow slits and slots in the wall. Ruby peeked through one, and the road lay directly below, in easy spitting range. Or shooting range. Or hot oil range. She did not envy anyone who might try to storm this place, even when manned by a skeleton crew of cadets.

"Keep up, Teach," Corson said. She had already reached a door on the other side. Ruby hurried through and gasped.

A wide circular room opened in front of her, tall as well, and domed at the top. Windows marched all the way around, or doors more like: the frames extended down to the floor. Nothing but air lay beyond. The thick storm shutters had been opened, and fresh, clean wind whipped through them, cutting through the heat of the day. In the room's center crouched a riot of cranks and gears, all supporting a massive telescope. Ruby had seen many telescopes in her time on the sea, but this one was the size and girth of a tinker's carriage. It peeked out through a wide slot in the domed ceiling. In its sizable shadow, staring out of one of the floor-to-ceiling openings, stood a heavy cat of a man with a haystack of blond hair.

Wisdom Rool turned to greet her, empty eyes full of nothing. He smiled. "Hello, Ruby Teach. I have missed you."

Ruby bowed correctly, as she had been taught. "Lord Captain."

Rool sighed. "I see you have been inducted into the habits of our fellowship. I have never understood the scraping and the bowing and the flourishing. We are hammers and saws. No need for formality." He turned to Corson. "Thank you, Edwina. I should like to speak to this one alone, if you don't mind guarding the door?"

"Of course, Lord Captain. I will protect you from the dangerous cadets." Corson bowed and left, shutting the door behind her.

Rool pursed his lips. "I see where the bows and scrapes come from. Edwina and I came up together. She was quite the joker then. She has . . . hardened." He traced the trail of scars that ran over his neck. "I suppose we all have. Well." He sat on the floor, stuck his legs over the edge, and patted the polished floor next to him. "Come speak with me, Ruby Teach."

What had her world come to when she was relieved to see her old enemy? She eased herself down next to him, favoring the bruises.

He watched her out of the corner of his eye. "Training going well, I see."

"Ah, yes, O Lord Captain. I am being molded into the image of a reeve. The molder uses her fists, her feet, and once, in the pantry, a meat tenderizer."

"Avid Wake."

"Yes."

"The Reeve recruit only children without family. England *is* our family, and you"—he raised an eyebrow—"your loyalty is to a different kin."

"And what about you? You have me sneaking about behind everyone's back, pursuing some sort of secret agenda. . . . Ward Corson will roast me over the spit if she catches me lying again, let alone—" She caught herself right before she spilled the grog. Rool didn't know about—

"Your transformation?" Barnacles. "Edwina told me about it. And I daresay it makes you ever more interesting to me, my apprentice."

The heat drained from her face. "Don't you dare call me that."

He raised his eyebrows, all sham surprise. "But you are, are you not? You are my agent inside my own house, hunting hidden Swedish rats."

"No, I am not."

"So you have made no progress in your search for the good doctor's research?"

He was moving too fast, dancing from point to point. "No. I mean, yes, I have, but—" Her hand curled into a fist. "My blood is a blueprint. He is making a machine from it, down in the laboratory." She swallowed. "When it's finished, I think he's going to kill me."

"What will the machine do?"

"I don't know. I can get to his notes, but they are in a chemystrally locked journal."

"But you pick locks for breakfast, do you not?"

"I could pick it before you woke up to start *making* breakfast, Lord Captain, but not with two blasted stolen probes. It's like using a ham hock to do needlepoint."

"I can get you a ham hock, if you like."

"That's not what I—"

"I know it. I know it." He chuckled and then sighed.

He stared out over the valley. It was easily five hundred feet down to the river below. A hawk flew by under their feet. How would it feel to fall all that way? Flying like a bird. Of course the flight would be quick, and the ending less pleasant. She looked over at Rool. Gray shot through the blond at his temples, and bags hung under his eyes. He looked exhausted, and she momentarily terrified herself by trying to imagine what could possibly exhaust him.

"What is happening out there? We have no news."

"It is as I feared, Ruby. The incendiaries in Boston were only the beginning. Out on the frontier it has already begun. English militia burning French settlements. French militia tearing up English farmsteads."

"War."

"Yes, and both countries are sending their armies to defend their territory. Colonial leaders—Van Huffridge of the Rupert's Bay Company, Governor Keith—howl that we do nothing to protect them. But Ruby, riddle me this." He narrowed his eyes. "I spoke with some gentlemen of an English militia company, and they claimed to have no knowledge of these actions."

"Were they lying?"

He showed his teeth. "They spoke under a great deal

of duress, so I have a deal of faith in their truthfulness."

Ruby shuddered. "Very well."

"Further, I came upon the . . . remains of a French militia unit, but, and I find this quite fascinating, they bore weapons marked with the sign of an English arms merchant, and their brand-new uniforms were crafted from a fine strain of wool found only in East Anglia, in the heart of England. What do you make of that?"

She momentarily forgot her anger. "They are all fakes."

He winked. "And where does that knowledge take you?"

It was dead clever. "Someone else is starting this war."

"And?"

"Someone not the English or the French." She whistled in admiration. "Do you know who it is?"

"I do not, Ruby Teach, and the skill with which the puppeteer's hand has been hidden has caused me no end of vexation." He snapped his scarred fingers. "That was some high-order thinking, my apprentice."

"Don't call me that!"

"As you say." The wind ruffled through his hair. "But I hope you can see that given the currents of skulduggery in the waters all around us, it is difficult for me to trust anyone, even my sister and brother reeves."

Division in the ranks? Could she use this to her advantage somehow? But why tell her this? "Is that why you asked me here?"

"Indeed, Ruby Teach. I find myself in an intriguing position where one of the few people I can trust . . ."

"Is me."

"Is you."

"Well, that's quite a pickle, Lord Captain."

"You have no idea."

She looked at him, staring at her. She could not read him. She had never been able to read him, and a thought struck her. That emptiness she had been searching for? He was the embodiment of it. No regret, no fear, no uncertainty. She found herself admiring it. Just a little.

"Here is what I propose. Soon you will be presented with a mission. I would ask that you agree to it and pursue it to its end with your typical ferocity."

"In exchange?"

He laughed. "Well, you'll still have your life. But second, I will say that if you do me this favor, you will likely become closer to the denizens of the fort and thus more able to spy for me."

"How?"

"I will finish. Thirdly"—he stood—"I will offer you my full protection from the good doctor. If he plans to do you in as soon as he understands the secret you bear, then it might benefit you if I was standing between you and him."

"I have your word?"

He laughed. "If you wish. But if I am lying, you are doomed in any case. You need me more than I need you, Ruby. I need you for information, but you need me to survive. Will you do this thing for me?"

"What is it?"

"Yes or no?"

He was right. It made her teeth ache, but she had to do as he asked. Whatever that was. "Yes."

"Good. Thank you. Someone will come to you.

Do not speak of this conversation to anyone. Do you understand?"

"Yes, Lord Captain."

He gestured in the direction of the door and turned back to his vista. "See yourself out."

Well, good-bye and thank you to you, too.

"Ruby, you'll need these."

She turned on instinct to pull out of the air what he had thrown at her.

Her lockpicks. The weight in her hand, it made her feel something that she hadn't in months: she felt whole.

CHAPTER 27

Hypothesis: The pressure exerted by a given mass of a gas is inversely proportional to the volume it occupies. Correlations to sentient gases?

—Robert Boyle, Sc.D., FRS, fellow,
Royal Society and Invisible College, London

Henry could not take it anymore.

He had been traveling at the front of the group, with Cram, but there was something coming out of the serving boy. A combination of sulfur and acid. A gaseous emission that no devil's chemystry might have created. Cram seemed not to notice or pretended not to, but Henry could not bear it a moment longer. Without really thinking about it, he drifted to his other companion, and took to forging through the closely packed underbrush with their rearguard, Athena Boyle.

She had stared at him when he fell into step beside her and given him a dulled-down version of her customary smirk, but she didn't complain. They walked on in silence together for most of the day, until he tripped over a hidden root and planted his face in a patch of clover. He cursed. He did not want her to see him on the ground. He went to scramble up, but a gloved hand hovered in his peripheral vision.

Without really thinking, he took it.

Athena helped him up onto his feet and turned back to the path without a word.

Henry kept up. Something had changed with her that night before they left. After their difficult talk down by the lake, she had blown up with rage around the fire, but the next morning she had drawn into herself. Without her constant pressure, it was only a few more days before Henry also came to accept that Winnifred Black and Captain Teach were not coming. They were on their own.

So they asked Sutherland for help. It didn't take long.

The yeti doctor turned about, squinted up at the early-morning sun, turned again, and pointed. "It's that way. The three rivers. Two valleys over, and you're right there. Can't miss it. Take care around the Algonkin. They enforce their privacy fiercely. With weapons."

And that was that.

It had been a strangely peaceful trek up until this point. Henry could not for the life of him understand why given this smooth passage, he had decided to take a whacking stick to a hornet's nest.

"Is the rear of our column to your liking?" he asked.

Athena ignored the question. But she said, "You're getting stronger."

"No thanks to you" was the response he swallowed. Instead, he said, "Yes." He left the twitching pain and the worry about whether he would ever walk without a hitch back among the clover. What was the use really?

"I'm glad," she said.

"I'm not slowing you down anymore?"

Her lips tightened, and she gave him a suspicious look.

"I can jest, too," he said.

That quieted her for another two ridges.

He did not speak of forgiveness. Something hard that had not dissolved still stuck in his chest: a fixed geode or a strain of hidden ore.

Eventually they stopped for a rest. Henry noticed several concerned glances cast their way from Cram; but he ignored them, and Cram kept his distance.

Athena handed him a waterskin. "You know I am a Grocer, yes?"

"Yes." The leather clothing kept much of the heat off, but the sun beat down. The water sloshed down his throat, and then its cooling threads crept all through his chest.

"Well, what are you then?"

"What am I?" said Henry.

"Yes. I am a journeyman sentinel in the Worshipful Order of Grocers. An ancient society that watches from the shadows, looking to bring balance to the world. This is privileged knowledge, known to only a very few, and you had it before you met us. That night at Grundwidge

Fen's after you saved us—you did save us, by the way—Cram said you told Ruby that you were part of a secret society that watched the Grocers."

He coughed. "I may have said that."

"Well?"

This was not a road he had expected to go down. It shook him. "It is secret."

"Do you trust me?"

That was a thorny question. Anger, yes. Frustration, yes. Fear, no. Respect, yes. Friendship, uncertain. But trust? "I do. I do trust you. Oddly."

She waved her hand about, encompassing the silent forest. "Well, I don't think anyone will overhear."

A dusting of freckles marched across her nose. He focused on that as she took a drink.

"The Pepper Clerks."

The water sprayed across a stretch of underbrush.

"Pepper Clerks?"

"Yes?"

"I did not think there could be a name less, well, imposing than Worshipful Order of Grocers."

Henry's back stiffened. "It is three chemysts; I do not even know the other two. Fermat said they came to an agreement that the watchers should be watched, and when they came to that agreement, they were . . ."

She raised her eyebrows.

"Well, they were snacking on peppers."

She nodded sagely. An honest smile, not that confounded smirk, played about her lips. It changed her face. "And your position?"

"Sometimes he would call me Stock Boy."

"Ah." She made a claw with her hand and grabbed her forehead, groaning. "They can't resist, can they? Old folks with their impossible claptrap." She snickered.

He could not help joining in.

"It does lack a certain, well, gravity."

"Oh, indeed?" she said, and then he could not stop laughing. Cram studiously avoided looking back at them.

The solid deposit in his chest loosened, just a bit. So he asked her, for the second time, "Why are you on this journey, Boyle?"

"I could tell you that it is for the Grocers, and it is

because of my duty. But honestly? I don't know that that's the case."

"You didn't answer my question."

She looked at him, tender and hard at once. "Ruby." She took a shuddering breath. "She is not safe, and that tears at me every waking moment."

Henry handed her the water skin. She drank. Finally he said, "You are a good friend."

A few hours later Athena and Henry rounded a bend up the slope, and Cram was hunkered down behind a stand of trees. He put a finger to his lips.

A structure loomed above them on a high hill, surrounded by grass shivering in the wind. It was made of timber, as far as Henry could see: a long, low, sturdy thing surrounded by sharpened wooden stakes. Shapes moved in and out of the shadows up there in the dusk. Henry swallowed. Anticipation sharpened his senses.

"That is a well-maintained sentry fort," Athena whispered. "See the way the hill is cleared of forest, and the land behind? If we pass within a half a mile of here, whoever is on that elevation will be able to see."

"What about farther along the hills?" Henry asked.

Athena shook her head. "With luck we can find a gap in the patrols." Just then four shapes set out from the fort. They strode down across the ridge, parallel to the watchers. "If I were coordinating this outpost, there would be many of them, just like that."

Cram led them back into the forest a ways, before squatting in a depression by a little pond. "Could we tickle through by night?" he asked.

"We could, but how do we hide in the daytime?" Athena said. "If it's more grassland beyond, we're easy targets."

"Could we just try diplomacy? Travelers from the east, here to pay our respects, that sort of thing?" said Henry.

"Miss Winnie said the Algonkin do not look kindly on colonials of any sort: Frenchies, English, whoever. These little forts are here to keep us out." Cram sucked on his teeth. "And don't forget about the weapons. Doctor Yeti said 'weapons.' "

"Why do they keep so close?" Henry asked. All he

knew was that the Algonkin and the other peoples beyond the mountains had pulled back behind the mountains years ago, ending trade and any kinds of relationships with colonials almost overnight. Entire villages had been abandoned.

"They say that the pox we brought with us killed legions of them afore they abandoned the coast. Mayhap they don't take kindly to dying," Cram said. Henry looked at his boots, and blood rushed to his face. Why could the Grocers or Pepper Clerks not have stopped *that*?

It took the better part of a day, but Cram sniffed out a steep little ravine that cut across the land in the direction they were going. After watching it for a day, Athena said that she had timed the patrols for their best chance. Under cover of darkness, accompanied by a shooting star, the three companions crossed the frontier into Algonkin lands.

CHAPTER 28

Privateers? I don't truck with the like, old son. You can't serve two masters. Never trust a man who pirates for a king.
　　　　　　　—Precious Nel, scourge of the Seven Seas

Ruby's shoulders gave up and ran away. She crashed facefirst to the ground. The earth of the yard tasted of failure. Her legs were still wound with Avid Wake's, shins across each other's hips, hands on the ground, holding up the chest and the rest of the body. The Reeve called it the Crab, and the two girls had been given it as a reward after yet another scuffle.

Wake's arms quivered. "Up!" she managed to say

through her gritted teeth. Ruby levered one hand back under her shoulder, then the other.

She pushed, and her elbows came up off the ground. Every part of her shoulders and her arms screamed.

Then she fell again. Dirt got in her windpipe. She started coughing.

"Up!" Avid grunted. Ruby shook her head into the ground. She couldn't. It was too hard. A week of sleepless nights, and even with her picks, the lock of the doctor's journal resisted her efforts.

"Up, Sweetling!"

The slight didn't make Ruby feel smaller or more vulnerable or scared. It emptied her out, the way a hole would a bucket.

She put her hands under her shoulders.

And it felt as if someone had grabbed the belt of her breeches and pulled. It wasn't a huge pull, more like a bird tugging. But it was enough. Sparks flared behind her eyes as she slowly, ever so slowly willed herself up. She and Avid set off across the yard, hand by hand, inch by inch. She heard grunting, and then she realized it came from her.

Ward Corson had drawn a line in the earth with her heel on the other side of the yard. Ruby might have aged twenty years by the time they reached it. But they did. She and Avid collapsed together, heaving.

Avid rolled onto her back, curls plastered to her scalp, arms flung out like a scarecrow.

Ward Corson blocked out the setting sun. "Wake, with me. Teach, to your room. Get your things, and then meet us in the sand chamber." The two set out across the yard without another word from the ward.

Was this some new drill? Ruby struggled up, hands on knees, and then stumbled up to her cell. Her "things"? She had no things. No books, no possessions, no nothing. Corson had to have meant the lockpicks. What did Corson know, however? Was she on Rool's side? The very idea of the Reeve arrayed against each other was so odd that it put her even more on edge than she already had been. If this was not the "favor" the lord captain had asked of her, she might have to say good-bye to the picks forever. So she tucked her real picks into the waistband of her breeches and brought the probes along in her hand. Ruby Maxim

Ten: "Let Them See What They Want To."

She headed down to the sand chamber. It was empty save for Corson and Avid. The cadet had just pulled on an old blue shift, with a patched pocket sewn in the front. She was the spitting image of a fresh-faced farm lass.

"Clean up," Corson said. Ruby managed to mask the sound of the picks with the two metal probes as she disrobed. She thought she saw the ward's eyes flick to the picks, but Corson said nothing. The two of them watched, silent, as Ruby scrubbed herself clean.

Corson nodded to a pile of old clothing. "Put that on." There was a shabby pair of brown breeches, a shabbier coat, and a hat whose brim had left it behind. It felt blessedly familiar. Both she and Avid had boots in various stages of disrepair.

The ward said, "Leave your cadet clothes in the basket in the changing room, and then follow me."

Avid headed to the basket, and Ruby took the moment to sneak her picks into the new getup. They followed Corson out a side door and down a dead-end hallway. She turned to them.

"You have been selected for a significant task." This was it. It absolutely seemed like Rool's mission. "I ask a boon of you. You must work together. Your differences must stop. There is no room in your undertaking for petty bickering. You are effectively reeves in this, and you must act as comrades, not foes." Her gaze flickered between them. Avid nodded, and after a moment so did Ruby. If she was to play this part, she must play it well. "Good," Corson said.

Corson pressed a few knots, and a hidden door opened. Ruby did her best to seem uninterested as she filed the knots away for the future. The ward led them down a narrow winding stair.

The stair ended in a low cavern, lit by a single chem pot exuding greasy smoke. Three other cadets, all dressed like Avid and Ruby, stood in the shadows. Avid's beefy minion, Gideon Stump, looked ridiculous in too-small leather breeches, a spattered cook's hat, and a tattered waistcoat embroidered with turtles. The group was rounded out by the Curtsies, the brother's and sister's white hair vivid in the half dark. Ruby still knew very little about them. The

Curtsies kept to themselves. They even had a language of their own, nonsense words and hand gestures. But they practiced their exercises with a singular anger, as though they were trying to smash something to bits every run on the stairs or out to the lake. Never, the girl, tugged at the filthiest dress Ruby had ever seen, a high-necked society number that looked as if it had been through a swamp on the back of a hyena. Her brother, Levi, wore something . . . It was— Ruby couldn't quite tell. He was gifted at standing in shadows. Ruby could never remember getting a good, straight-on look at him. Shadows clung to him.

Ismail Cole held the harness of the last member of their party.

Sleipnir.

The eight-legged gearhorse, equipped with a set of large saddlebags and a workmanlike saddle, stood motionless next to the reeve. The gleaming bronze had been toned down to a scuffed brown. She almost looked like a real horse. If there was any doubt that she was an automaton, however, her eyes ended the argument. They stared straight ahead without blinking, the sapphires identical, each caught in a web of spider silver.

The other cadets could not take their eyes off her.

Ruby imagined, just for a moment, the look on the Swede's face when he discovered that both she and his apprentice's prize project had been hijacked.

A voice, razor on slate, scraped from the shadows. "My little dumplings."

Wisdom Rool came into the light, teeth delicately slicing into a strawberry. The cadets bowed with varying degrees of formality. Rool sighed. "You have been chosen to proceed on a mission that must be kept secret from your companions upon your return. You were selected for your discretion, some for your progress in the ways of the Void and"—his empty eyes brushed over Ruby—"others for your particular skill sets. As you come closer to your destination, Ward Cole will inform you of your task. This is a very important responsibility. I have every confidence that you will exceed our expectations. Good hunting."

He stood there, staring at them, until he finished the strawberry. He wrapped the stem in a white handkerchief and stowed it in his vest pocket.

"Well?" he said. "Off you go."

They looked about at one another until Ismail Cole said, "You heard the man. On me." He smiled at Gideon in a conspiratorial way and said into the gearhorse's ear, "Gallivant." It was not the word Evram had told Ruby. Sleipnir gave a steely whicker and nuzzled Cole's ear. Ruby thought he looked shocked. Cole nodded to Rool as they passed. "Lord Captain."

"Ismail, take care of the kits," he said. "I put my trust in you."

Cole's smile widened. "Well placed, Lord Captain. We will return triumphant before you know it." He sparked up a dim chem pot version of a lantern and led them off.

Rool and Corson faded away into the shadows at the back of the cavern. Ruby walked next to the gearhorse. Its breathing had a metallic tinge that reminded her of Swedenborg, but it was deeper, like that of a metal bear. Heat rolled from it. It kept the chill of underground out.

She couldn't be certain in the dim, but she thought, just for a moment, that Sleipnir looked at her.

At the other end of the cavern a patch of lesser darkness

separated itself. The scent of honeysuckle washed the stink of the chem pots from Ruby's nose. It was a cave opening. Cole stopped right before the exit and gathered them up.

Cole's bald head glinted in the dim. Ruby felt his smile more than she saw it.

"The lord captain gives me the willies," he said. The cadets chuckled, and Ruby shook the tension out of her shoulders. "All right, friends, we are taking a little early-summer jaunt, to stretch our legs and perhaps get into a wee bit of trouble. As for our roles in this little mummer's play? I am an outlaw Tinker, Izzie Coleman, Sleipnir here is my beast of burden, and you are my orphan wards. Not so different from our lives, yes? Now we're traveling to find somewhere you hungry waifs can get a hot meal and some work, make a place for yourselves in this hard and wicked world. Keep mum; choose names; speak only when spoken to. Questions?"

"Ward Cole?" It was Never Curtsie.

"That's Izzie to you and me, girl. What do you call yourself?"

"Nell," she said without missing a beat. "All right,

Izzie?" Cole's shadow nodded in the dark. "What's all this about?"

"The short of it is that we have a lead on some bad people, and they've evaded us several times before. So the lord captain thought you lot might be a bit more . . . unexpected. I'll tell you more as we get closer."

Gideon Stump cleared his throat. "Ward?"

"Yes . . ."

"Er, Gabe, I guess." He studiously looked anywhere but at Ruby. "I thought Teach was a prisoner."

Cole raised an eyebrow. "Well, the lord captain saw fit to send—"

"Thatch. Robby."

"—with us, so who are you and I to judge? Anyone else? Excellent. Keep to the path; it's a long way down. I want to get a good start before daylight."

They followed him out into the night onto a narrow track that snaked down the side of the cliff. Spruce and fir clustered tall and tight all about them. The path on the right fell down into darkness. A shooting star streaked across the sky. Cole led them down the steep track, only wide enough for single file. Ruby put her hand on Sleipnir's haunch. Was it moving with the horse's metal breath? She wasn't quite sure.

It was so dark she could barely see one foot in front of the other.

She tripped over a branch.

It was a little branch, witness to how tired she was, but she lost her balance. She grabbed at the horse, but her fingers slithered over smooth metal. She teetered, one foot in the air.

A voice said, "Careful."

A hand locked on her arm from behind.

It jerked her back to the path.

From the dark, Avid Wake said, "We can't have you going over the edge, Sweetling. Not unless I decide I *want* to push you." Wake let go of her arm and patted Ruby's shoulder. "Besides, you're here for your skills. I want to see what you can do. Hope you don't muck it up."

CHAPTER 29

*The sickness travels with them, and it lays our people low. If we
trade, we fall sick. If we war, we fall sick. Our only recourse, then,
is that we must withdraw.*
—Mother Green Foot,
Exodus Council, Keepers of the Western Door, 1702

Athena heaved her leg up onto the thick branch of the
red oak tree. She changed her grip, and the scaly bark
poked through her filthy gloves. Climbing trees in the
morning before the others were up had been the only way
she could get a moment to herself. Up on the branch now,
she put her back to the tree and turned outward.

She almost fell off.

A valley opened up below, and three rivers glittered

in the dawn light. They were big, even from a hill so far away, and the forest below petered out into an orderly pattern of fields and houses stretching as far as the eye could see. The city was huge, larger than Philadelphi. It radiated out from a series of islands where the rivers met. Massive low earthen pyramids squatted in the midst of a maze of tracks and buildings. A long wooden palisade surrounded the inner core; but the city must have spilled out of it long ago, and scatterings of long wooden houses and farms dotted the landscape all the way up to the edge of the forest. One lay just a quarter mile or so away, and there were already people moving in the fields.

They were here.

She shimmied out of the tree and hurried back to the camp. Cram and Henry were up and packed, though they had out some acorn bread and honey. The camp was peaceful, reflecting the rhythm they had fallen into after leaving Sutherland's. It thrilled her a little bit that that was about to change. She nursed her knowledge just for a moment, not yet wanting to let it go.

"What did you see?" Henry Collins massaged his

ankle. He seemed to have gotten stronger as they had traveled; but the injury still bothered him, and he worked it every morning. "I wager I know what you spied in your lookout." He held his hand over his eyes like a mesmerist at a county fair. Then he looked about and fluttered his free hand, as if seeking knowledge from the spheres. He pulled his hand away with a flourish. "Trees!" He bowed from his seat to the imaginary crowd. "Thanks to you, ladies and gentlemen! For my next astonishing trick, I will miraculously tell you what is on the end of your noses!"

"It is the city," Athena said. "We are here."

The two of them whooped and danced, little boys chasing a sugar wagon.

"Quiet!" Athena said. "You forget we are intruders here." But she couldn't keep the grin from her face. Two months in the wild. They had finally reached their goal.

As one they fell silent. They stared at one another.

Cram finally spoke. "Now what?" He looked at Henry, and she could not help it, she did as well.

He looked as flummoxed as the two of them. He blinked. "I— I do not know."

Athena let out a long, low breath. She put a devil-may-care grin on her face. "Well then, I suppose we should reconnoiter."

"But for what?"

"Henry will know it when he sees it, I'm sure." She felt nothing of the kind.

Henry, however, nodded, relief plain on his face.

They followed Cram through the thick woods, circling the valley, to a little copse of trees. They crept forward on their bellies in the underbrush. He had found a perfect view.

The rivers cut the valley into roughly three parts, meeting in the center. The palisade ran all the way around the central part of the city, even over the water where the walls screened multilevel bridges. The rivers close to the junction were thick with boats and canoes, and the forks to the northeast and northwest were heavily trafficked. Wide tracks left the city to the west and to the south.

People were everywhere: busy ants on the spokes of a giant's pinwheel. "This is no savage village," Athena whispered. "This fortress would take an army weeks to conquer, and the plains surrounding it make it even more devilish. The rivers alone would be a nightmare to encircle and control. They are roads in and out for food, reinforcements, messages."

The tales that had come across the water had been of one-legged, one-eyed giants, howling for colonial scalps. None were to be found in the valley below. People, however? There were plenty of those. Too many. "Can we sneak through?" she said. "Or make contact?"

"None of us speak a word of Algonkin," said Henry.

A beaten-down longhouse sat a stone's throw from them across the grass, separate from the other outlying structures. Its fifty feet were smallish compared with others farther down the slope, and the curved roof was dully painted with strange symbols. A small patch of crops lay behind it. Cram pointed at it. "Miss Black said the crops are corn, squash, and beans. Three sisters, they call them." He blinked his way through a thought. "I have an idea. What if we—" More blinking. "Aha, yes. What if we saunter over there and ask if they seen Ruby's mam? I know we don't speak their language, but mebbe signs and gestures? Mayhap they could point us in the proper direction?" He avoided her eyes, as if he knew what she thought of the idea. Good thing, too. He instead turned to Henry. "Professor? What do you think?"

Henry was not looking at them. He had taken out the journal and was flipping through it madly.

"Henry, what is it?" Athena said.

He didn't look up. "A tug."

"A tug?"

"Yes, as soon as we crested this hill. I thought I was just imagining it, but it just happened again."

"From where, Professor?" Cram asked.

"From the journal! Here." He put his finger down onto a page toward the beginning. "This page. This page is different."

"How?"

Muttering, he ran his fingers over the tightly packed equations. Suddenly a dotted line marched down the page nearest the binding, as if sketched there by a fine fountain pen.

"Henry, is that writing *moving*?"

Henry looked up warily. "This may become— I'm not sure how dangerous—" He chewed his lip. "You might want to step back."

Athena said, "What—"

And then Cram said, "Don't have to tell me twice," and he hauled her back into the forest a few yards. Cram hunkered down behind a boulder, fingers in his ears and eyes closed.

Henry and Athena locked eyes. Then he scrunched up his face as if waiting for a blow, and he tore the page out of the book.

Nothing happened.

They hurried back to him. Henry wobbled. "That . . . was powerful," he said, and then passed out on the grass.

Athena could barely see straight, but whether it was from fear or fury she had no idea. "Henry. Henry!" She bent her ear down to his mouth. At least he was still breathing. "Of all the muddleheaded . . . Cram, help me with him, will you?"

"Milady, look."

The paper from the journal lay on the ground, fluttering in the breeze. No. It moved.

It moved, and not in a blown-off-into-the-air sort of way. It folded itself. A clean crease appeared on the long edge, and then it folded *itself* over.

"Get back!" she said, and they pulled Henry back from whatever chemystral apocalypse that was about to be unleashed.

It folded again. And again. It kept folding and adjusting and tucking and preening until in just a few moments what was standing in front of them was a little paper bird. It stood no more than a finger high. It had no eyes, but the manner in which its head was cocked gave Athena the distinct feeling that it was looking at them.

It fluttered into the air and flew straight toward them.

Cram yelped and dived into the underbrush. But Athena had a feeling. It made no sense to lure someone out into the middle of the wilderness and then to create a foldy weapon to slaughter them. The paper bird flew closer, and closer, and then flew *over* her and Henry to land a few yards off in the lower branches of an oak tree. It turned its little head over its shoulder back toward them.

"Cram," she said.

"Shhh! I don't think it sees me!"

"Cram, it's to help us, not hurt us."

"That's how they always draws you in!"

"Get over here now."

He stuck his head up from the bushes. A leafy branch had attached itself to his hat. "Don't say I didn't warn you."

Next to her, Henry groaned and sat up on a shoulder. "You may be correct, Athena. The journal page was somehow primed to change once we arrived in this valley, and if I'm not mistaken, that little bird artifact will take us where we want to go."

"To our deaths!" Cram moaned.

They both ignored him. Athena helped Henry to his feet. "About time to see where this leads, don't you think?"

CHAPTER 30

FARNSWORTH: *How fares milady's fiancé?*
CATHERINE: *Bumblebuffle? I'm afraid he fell from a dock into a locked crate in the hold of a ship headed for Svalbard. Oopsies.*
FARNSWORTH: *What is a three-year voyage between friends? And lovely dress, I must say.*
CATHERINE: *Thank you! Its waterproof qualities are perfect for my laboratory!*

—Marion Coatesworth-Hay,
A Game of Vials and Vapors, Act V, sc. ii

The bird led them through the forest as patiently and politely as the best of butlers in a high manor house. Cram still didn't trust the infernal thing, but the Heroes did, so who was he to judge? It took them south. Or . . . north. Well, whatever path of the compass it was, it was exactly away from the valley of the three rivers. Would the little demon lead them straight up to a Algonkin fort? He would just have to be ready to pull the fat out of the fire.

The moon was high, though, and whether by luck or bird savvy they came upon no patrols. It led them ever higher and higher into the foothills until it came to rest on the limb of a great hickory tree, perched right on the edge of a high cliff.

Lady Athena peered over the edge. "Nothing. Just a drop." She sighed.

The professor looked about, confounded. "But . . .surely one would not go to the incredibly difficult lengths involved in constructing this journal just for—"

"A jest?" Athena said, puzzled.

At that moment the bird, at the very edge of the tree limb that hung over the chasm, began to peck the air.

"Mad as a hatter, I tell you. Its thinker is busted," Cram said.

"No, wait. Look," said the professor.

And indeed, at the spot where the birdie pecked, a sliver seemed to be opening up in the air. It kept growing downward until it hit the ledge of the cliff. The line opened like a curtain to reveal, on the other side, what was most definitely not a bone-shattering drop.

It was a meadow.

"Ocular septum," the professor whispered in awe.

"What?" Cram said.

Henry blinked. "An illusion, Cram. So people who come up here don't see what lies beyond this doorway." And with that the paper bird burst into flame. The tear in the air began to close up.

"Oh, my," Athena said. Then she was moving. "Come on."

No time for woolgathering. The three of them tumbled through the curtain.

The moonlight shone down into a meadow out of a storybook. A little lake gleamed like polished mercury, and a huge willow dipped its branches into the water like a high lady's hair. Next to the willow sat a two-story cottage, but in the colonial style and equal parts wood and metal. Its fine circular windows reckoned Cram uncomfortably back to the ones on HMS *Grail*. A little stone path led from a dock on the lake through the grass to the door of the house, and at the door, limned in silver, stood Ruby Teach.

No. Cram shook off the shock. Not Ruby, but the woman was the spitting image of her: her stance, her face, the danger in her eye. Except this Ruby's skin glowed pale as ivory, and her hair shone corn yellow, not raven black. She wore a sensible frock, with a stained leather apron over it, and weathered boots.

She was also pointing something at them, a wicked-looking sliver of black iron.

"You're not Ruby," she said. And then she twitched the rod, and the ground turned to mud under their feet. All three of them sank in an instant. The rod twitched again, and the ground was solid again, except they were buried up to their waists in the ground. She strode toward them with purpose.

"Milady," Cram muttered under his breath.

"Yes, Cram?"

"I believe we should be most polite with this one," he said.

Athena cleared her throat. "Agreed."

And then the woman was there. Close up, there were crow's-feet around her eyes, but she still was a fair ringer for Ruby. She tapped the rod against her thigh.

"Where is Ruby?"

"Madam—" Henry began.

The woman pointed at the journal. "That is mine." She aimed the rod at him. "Give it to me."

"Of course." Henry handed it over, fairly bursting with scribblings, paper, and bark.

She grabbed it and immediately opened it and paged through it furiously, turning it this way and that. Seconds turned into minutes.

Athena cleared her throat.

The woman's head snapped up. She turned back to Henry. "These are your notations?"

The professor swallowed. "Yes."

She looked him over for a moment, like a prize heifer. "Good work."

The professor swelled in spite of himself.

"And she gave this to you?"

"Yes."

"Where is she?"

Aha. Time for a tale, Cram thought. An exciting

recounting of their adventures, pitched just right to convince this powerful woman to aid us in our hour of need! He said, "It all began on a street in Boston—"

"The Reeve have her," Athena said.

The woman's face fell. She looked back and forth among them. "Well then," she said, "my name is Marise Fermat, we should get you out of that dirt, and you had better come inside, hadn't you?"

The three of them, awkward, confused, covered in dirt, stood in the middle of a well-appointed sitting room. The windows sported frilly lace curtains, a nice warming touch. Cabinets filled with silver and china, comfy (but not overdone) furniture, a circular rug sporting pink cabbage roses. Lady Athena picked up a small needlepoint cushion, taking care not to dirty it. It read, "Half of science is putting forth the right questions," in badly hand-stitched letters. She looked up. "I thought it would be more . . ."

"Mad chemystish?" Henry supplied.

"Yes," she said. "And less . . ."

"Cozy?" Cram said.

"Indeed." She laid the pillow carefully back onto the velvet sofa.

All around them, a never-stopping whirlwind of motion, Marise Fermat strapped things down.

They looked at one another.

"Madam?"

"What is it?" the woman said as she maneuvered a heavy leather strap across the face of a cabinet. She didn't wait for an answer and hurried down the hall, whence the sound of buckling and clanking commenced.

Athena blinked several times. "Madam, do you wish us to tell you how—"

Marise's head popped back into the room from the hallway. "My daughter is taken, yes?"

"Yes," said Athena.

"By the Reeve?"

"Yes," said Cram.

She turned to Henry. "And they know that she carries the formula from this?" She held up the journal.

"It is quite possible," Henry said.

Passing through the sitting room and up a green metal circular staircase, she said, "Then we have no time to waste." Her feet disappeared upstairs before she finished her sentence.

Athena looked between Cram and the professor. "I think I like this woman."

The professor shook his head and then called up the empty stairs, "Do you even know where we are headed?"

Marise Fermat's head popped back into view. She had some kind of smoky red lenses strapped across her eyes. "Of course!" She waved about aimlessly. "Strap yourselves in!"

The professor said, "But—"

"Best hurry."

There were little hinged panels all about the walls of the main room that folded down into stools, with leather belts hanging about each of them.

Cram's sat next to one of the windows. A moose and two mooselings stood out by the lake.

Marise said, "We have little time, Ham."

"Cram." He strapped himself in.

Marise Fermat turned to Henry. "Come with me. I want to show you something." The tall boy nodded, eyes wide, and followed her up a circular stairway and out of sight.

Her voice called down from atop the stairs, "Please do not touch this!"

With a *tink, tink, tink,* a ceramic flask dropped down the steps and broke on the floor. Something like red water flowed out of it, far more than could be in the little bottle. It *moved,* spreading itself over the floor and up the walls until it covered everything.

Cram turned to Athena. "Did she mean do not touch the vial, or do not touch the juice?"

"I don't know."

"What is happening, milady?"

Lady Athena shook her head, exasperated, and pulled her legs up onto the seat. Cram did the same.

The rumbling intensified, and then the room lurched. The red, covering the walls, floor, and ceiling, flashed gray and then disappeared. There was a mighty crack and then quiet. Cram felt seasick. The room was very slightly swaying. Outside the window the trees were sinking into the earth.

No, the house was rising!

Below, through the window, lay the meadow, growing smaller by the second. The moose and mooselings all looked up at Cram. One of the little ones was chewing on a mouthful of watercress. Cram waved. The moose didn't wave back.

The trees quickly turned from single trunks into a wide carpet of forest. The . . . house? laboratory? carriage? . . . slowed until it swayed just ever so slightly. Lady Athena unbuckled herself from the straps holding her in place. Cram assumed it was to head up the stairs and assess the situation, to talk strategy, to discuss their options. Leading them was her task and her duty, and nothing took precedence over that. Instead, she lay down on the cabbage rose rug and promptly fell asleep. What a mad idea. He perched his chin upon the rim of the porthole and took in the tapestry of treetops below.

Could she not see that they were flying?

CHAPTER 31

Liberty cannot be established without morality,
nor morality without Science.
—Elizabeth de Toqueville, *Travels in the Colonies*

Athena opened her eyes.

The sitting room was empty. She still lay curled on the rug, but someone had brought her a quilt with little sparrows on it. It was warm but hideous. The gloaming light of sunset crept through the window, and all was still. How long had she slept? She rubbed the sleep from her eyes and, after grabbing her blade, stumbled up the circular stairs. A maze of passages and pipes led to one spacious room cluttered with stools, a bank of levers, wheels, gauges, and a wide window. But no people.

She went back down the stairs and out the door. The cottage sat in a small clearing at the top of a bluff, a steep drop on all sides. They all were there, sprawled on blankets in the grass, huddled around a merry campfire as if they were on some sort of mad hunting trip. Cram waved at her and pointed to a bubbling stewpot, set up in the little clearing. She ambled over and sat down next to Henry. "A picnic? Should our progress be perhaps a bit more stealthy?" she asked no one in particular.

Marise Fermat looked up from a bowl of something steaming that smelled of armpit. "It's a lovely night, and speed is our aim now, not stealth. Besides"—she waved her hand about the bluff—"no one down there to see us but Algonkin, and they have no quarrel with me. They leave me alone, and I leave them alone. We'll start at first light, as soon as I can see to steer."

Cram quirked his head like a dog who had just heard a far-off thing. "But where?"

"I have a way to find my daughter."

"What is it?"

Instead of answering, Marise took a big spoonful of porridge and nodded to Cram. "Your servant prepared this for us. I have some corn in my stores. Take some. It's hot." She forced it down with a gulp, keeping her face remarkably still. "And . . . hot."

Athena took a bowl and found that indeed, she was hungry. "Thank you, Cram."

The servant boy nodded, eyeing her.

Athena looked over her shoulder at the cottage. Its structure was unchanged, save a blanket of patched-together canvas almost its size again. The blanket sprawled across the roof and the ground behind, connected by a neck of canvas down into the building. "That's not something you see every day. And thank you, Madam Fermat, for the transport. Even if we found you, I despaired of making it back across the wilderness."

The woman smoothed the panels of her dress and tapped her scuffed boots together. "No thanks are necessary. You came all that way for love of my daughter." She looked down at her food. "I daresay that makes you more family to her than I am."

The fire crackled.

Henry Collins waded into the silence. "Boyle, you should see the artifice when it is filled! It is an amazing feat of chemystral and natural engineering. The mechanisms alter the air to a lighter gas and then push it into the *vesica*, the cloth ball. The control room alone is—"

"So why did you leave?" It stuck in Athena's craw. This woman had abandoned Ruby in the cradle.

Marise Fermat gave her a tight grin. "You are not polite, sir."

"Not particularly."

Marise took a deep breath and met Athena's gaze with steel of her own, mixed with sorrow. "Something was more important."

"Than your child?"

"Do you think me one of your servants? To order about and question at your leisure?" The alchemyst's hand tapped her temple, dangerously close to the iron rod bound up in her hair. "You know not of what you speak, milord. Your role here is complete. You have fetched me, and you are unnecessary. Would you like to know what it is to hurtle through the air at high speeds? Or to have your body turn to liquid, to seep into the earth? Because if you persist in goading me, that is exactly what will happen."

Athena swallowed her words, but that just made her anger eat at her stomach. "As you say. My apologies if I offended."

Cram cut in. "Milord, more porridge? I found some crispy bits that had fell off the pot, and the crunch is brilliant—"

Athena stared into the fire.

"You know, Athen Boyle, the Grocers are a joke." Henry and Cram had gone to sleep in the house, and it was just Athena and Marise about the fire.

Athena adjusted a log, looking away. Ruby's mother had a way about her. She invited conflict. She reveled in it. It was at turns terrifying and refreshing, but that made Athena oddly shy. "I don't know anything of the kind."

Marise's teeth glittered in the firelight. The cold rage

from before had disappeared as if it had never existed. "Of course you do. You are a journeyman of the order, are you not?" Athena nodded. "Well then, you have seen your share of the program. Tell me of a Grocer plot that changed the world for the better, and I am happy to retract my assertion."

Athena's duty warred with her own reservations. "It is not so simple. Small actions can have large impacts, but only after a certain amount of time can one see—"

"Fine. What about Ruby then?"

It brought Athena up short. "What about her?"

"You were sent to secure Ruby and her secret by the Grocers, and you ended up where?"

"Well, currently in a little magic house perched on the side of a mountain in the middle of the wilderness."

She laughed, a musical sound. "Is that what Godfrey Boyle planned?"

Athena's head was spinning. "Well, no, but that is not his fault."

"Balance, twisting, pushing, pulling? Meddling with this queen to keep her armies at bay. Strong-arming this king for a few more crusts of bread for his nobles? And all for naught. Great powers and great people will not be managed, no matter how secret your society. The interference just makes things worse."

"So the answer is to run away? Across the mountains?"

Marise Fermat stared at her across the flames. "I left to keep it safe."

"What?"

"The secret." She tapped her forehead. "The one in here. The one that my daughter carries even now."

"But why did you leave it with her if you did not want it to be discovered?"

Fermat shrugged. "Because I wanted even more for it not to be lost."

CHAPTER 32

What makes a real trapper? Love. I loves them critters. But don't get me wrong. Love don't get in the way of killin'. This is a hard piece of thinking for some to untangle.
—Jimmy Two Hands, tracker

The next night they landed in a different, equally remote clearing. Ruby's mother disappeared down a long hallway behind a stout iron door. Much later, unable to sleep, Henry found himself knocking at the door. Marise Fermat eased it open, and heat billowed out, revealing a riot of pipes and instruments gathered around a small forge that looked as dense as the *Grail*. In a corner bubbled an angry yellow liquid trapped behind a sealed leaded glass vat. "Ah, the chemyst! You are up late, or is it early? We still have a few hours yet before dawn. Come in. Don't touch the container," she said over her shoulder to Henry. "Or the forge. Just . . . don't touch anything."

Henry clasped his hands behind his back just to make sure. They had a mind of their own when it came to chemystral artifacts, and the workshop beyond was packed with them. He eased inside. "Aqua regia?"

Marise straightened an alembic on the scarred stone worktable and flicked her finger on one of the heavy metal pipes that ran onto the table from the forge. The pipe rang, off-key. "We have a winner, ladies and gentlemen! Aqua regia it is! Aaaah-stonishing!"

Henry laughed. The captain had said she had left when Ruby was a baby. Across the years and the mountains, how was she so like her daughter? But not like as well. The mother was the same, but more . . . concentrated. Where Ruby was turbulent, Marise was volatile. If Ruby was vital, her mother was manic. Excitement fired Henry when Ruby was about, but the woman in this laboratory emitted effervescent danger. It was more than a little intoxicating.

The laboratory itself was a jewel box. The racks of instruments hung cleverly on screens, hinged like the pages of a book. The tables and stools moved on tracks laid into the floor. And the reagents! Oh, the reagents! The key to any Tinker's prowess was a ready supply of the chemystral components for her craft, and this little room had barrel after barrel and crystal after crystal of the rarest of rare ingredients. Blue vitriol. Mountain's Veil. Cuprite.

She was watching him.

"I'm sorry, I— It has been some time since I have been in a laboratory this well equipped."

"Not at all. I have been thirteen years without a trace of Science talk. I have missed it." She smiled. It was infectious, and he found himself smiling as well. "Who was your teacher before this?"

The old man had told Henry of Marise Fermat, that they had parted on bad terms and that she was interested only in her own self. This woman did match that description. Cautiously he offered, "Pierre de Fermat is my master."

She laughed. "Oho! Fermat, is it?" She leaned in across the worktable. "So we are like cousins, you and I! Apples from the same chemystral tree! How is he? You must tell me. I do miss the old man so."

"Well, I have heard from my companions that he may be in some danger—"

"I am certain he will come out of whatever it may be smelling sweet. Always has." She brushed the subject away. It was a little unsettling. She gave him a look full of mischief. "Would you like to see the compass? I suspect the others would not care for it, but you, as a fellow practitioner—"

"Of course!"

It hung on a fine steel chain she drew from within her smock. Her hand was as stained and scorched as his, and the artifice was dented and scratched with age. The size of her palm, the silvery white antimony disk carried no north or south but was most definitely a compass. An arrow wavered back and forth very slightly as Marise moved it widely from side to side. She looked at him, and there was something in the look. All at once he felt back in Fermat's study, the old man ogling him like an owl with a mouse. He realized he was to observe and inform. A test.

"The color identifies it as antimony."

"Melting point?"

"Incredibly high."

"You should see my forge. Observe further, please."

Henry turned about, then looked back down at the artifice. "It is not fixed on cardinal north."

"At least one of you knows his directions."

He cleared his throat. "By the amplitude of the swings and the fact that the arrow is not moving at all, whatever it *is* fixed on must still be very far from here."

She snapped her fingers shut over it. "Good. Do you know how it functions?"

"No."

"But?"

"But if I might guess—" She nodded permission. "I would wager it is attuned to the blood of your daughter."

Marise smiled. "Yes. Well done. Now. Why did you come knocking on my door in the wee hours of the morning?"

Henry chewed his lip. He had rehearsed the speech in his mind until he had gotten it just right, but all the words disappeared in a puff of smoke. "Your journal."

"Yes?"

"May I please continue to work on it?"

Marise cocked an eyebrow and pulled the journal out from a lower shelf, then laid it on the worktable. "This is cursed."

"Pardon me?"

"Cursed, I say, Henry." She tapped her fingers on it. "I made it as a way to guide my daughter to me when she was old enough and had enough skill or to unlock her own secrets if I was gone. Instead, the Bluestockings kept it for themselves and tried to kidnap my daughter. Now she's been taken by the Reeve. It sounds from your stories that once you acquired the journal you, too, have been pursued, by unknown agents and also apparently by two homicidal Catalan girls."

Henry swallowed.

"Nations may rise and fall for this information, Henry Collins. People will kill and people will die for it. You should be glad to be rid of it. Why on earth would you want to have anything to do with it?"

The aqua regia bubbled.

"Because I have to know," Henry said. His fingers tingled. "I understand all those things you just said, but the reason I could not sleep tonight is that I keep thinking about it. There is genius here, and I am on the very edge of comprehending it. I must know."

"I could tell you."

"Thank you, but I want to understand for myself."

She took a breath, and the mischief fell away for a moment, leaving deadly earnestness. "If you do manage to work it out, you will be just as hunted as Ruby. For what you know."

"I am already."

She laughed. "That is nothing. Why do you think I moved to the end of the world?"

There was only the thirst. "I want to know."

She slid the journal across the worktable, her eyes never leaving his. "Come find me when you finish."

Henry spent every available hour working at the problem of the journal. With Marise's aid his progress increased geometrically. She had also advised him he needed to make up his own traveling kit and had offered her stores freely for his use. He could barely contain himself. The breadth and depth of the reagents tucked into all the racks and drawers were difficult to comprehend. He had cut apart a stained and weathered leather apron to serve as a carrying pouch, and he was carefully arranging a series of small ceramic pots that he found particularly promising.

"Mademoiselle— er, Madam—"

"Master will be fine."

And there it was. Easy and free, an invitation to apprentice with her. "Thank you, but I have a master."

She laughed. The heartiness of it took him off guard. "But he was my master, was he not? You will not betray your lineage or your commitment if you serve under me as well."

He licked his lips. "Well—"

She rolled her eyes. "I am teaching you, am I not?

"Yes."

She looked askance at the journal. "I have provided you with a task, have I not?"

"Yes."

"And I will not be Madame'd or Mademoiselle'd, nor will I have you call me Marise."

It was all true, and she was brilliant. It simply fitted, didn't it? "Very well. Master."

She passed him a skin of rainwater, harvested from the catcher on the roof of the cottage. They shared a smile. Perhaps it was the fresh water on his lips, or perhaps it was his own new secret; but he felt strangely light. So he told her.

"Master."

"Yes, Henry?"

"Last night I solved the final equation. I know the secret."

She turned to him softly, almost scared. "Do you?"

"It is a schema, a method for the creation of a machine."

A few strands of hair flared white in the light of the moon through the window. "Tell me."

Where to begin? "Alchemysts all have Source. You have it. I have it. An internal reservoir of fuel that an alchemyst uses to break or unite the bonds of gas, liquids, solids, and catalyzers. If you pull too hard on it, or if you try to do too large a working, you can be seriously hurt or die."

"Yes, good. But this is common knowledge."

His mouth went dry. He could not say it all in one burst. "But what if everyone has that Source, that quintessence, they just cannot access it as chemysts can?" Tapping the Source was something that one in two hundred people could do.

She nodded, intent. "Indeed, and just imagine what great works some chemysts could do if they had access to all of that Source, to all that energy and power. Works the like of which the world has never seen." Then she asked him the question, even though she knew the answer. "So this machine. Is it a way to identify the Source?"

"Partly." He matched her smile and shook his head in wonder. "It is a way to harvest it."

CHAPTER 33

Betrayal is an Art of Life.
—Petra alla Ferra

It was a sharp they were running, Ruby was sure of it.

In the first place, they kept to the roads, in plain view of every Tom, Dick, and Winston. The path was filled with folk running from the troubles on the frontier in carts, or riding mules, or even on foot, weighed down with whatever they could carry, toting their lives back to the cities on the coast. At every opportunity Ismail crowed on about how hard it was back in Philadelphi and how glad they were to have gotten out of that "den of iniquity."

It was a classic old sharp, a play on the Sheepherder's Daughter, and Cole brought it off well, if a bit overdone. He wanted the refugees to think that they had come from Philadelphi and not the fort. Still, folk treated them with a great deal of suspicion. "Izzie the Weed Doctor" got never a whiff of custom for his herbal foot oil or palsy remedies, and travelers had only dark looks for his strange metal horse and his troupe of feral urchins.

They hucked on hard after lunch and made a camp just off the road, complete with a merry fire. Even though she had spent only a handful of nights with Gwath and the crew on island beaches, it didn't take long for Ruby to see that she was the one most used to bedding down under the open sky. Gideon Stump, in particular, jumped at every tiny crack or rustle out beyond the circle of the fire. For Ruby, the lack of walls and the bright stars twinkling above the canopy of leaves more than made up for any creepy-crawly intruders.

Avid Wake plunked down next to Ruby, close enough

that their knees touched. Ruby didn't move, and Avid stared a hole in her head. She bolted her hardtack and jerky, never looking away. When Wake wasn't chewing, she talked. "Stump is the strongest, the Curtsies are the meanest, and I'm, well, I'm me."

Ruby met her gaze. "The most puffed up? The smelliest?"

Wake chuckled, and she tapped Ruby on the knee rhythmically. "The one who can tap the Void."

It was true, and it galled Ruby that this jumped-up peacock had some deeper connection than she. Whether it was to change or do Works or just fly away, she didn't care. Cole lay on the other side of the fire, napping after dinner. "And?" Ruby said.

"Well, Sweetling, we are the best and brightest students at the fort. And I'm wondering, out of all this august company, what in the name of Providence you are doing here?"

"Leave off, Avid." Never Curtsie's lilt barely cleared the crackle of the fire. "She had as much choice as the rest of us."

"And she has to take your sass in the bargain." That was Levi Curtsie, his voice coming from . . . somewhere.

"Truth, Curtsies"—Avid hadn't stopped tapping Ruby's leg—"but we were chosen for our skills. What about you, Ruby? What do you have to offer?"

"It's simple, Avid. I'm surprised you haven't sussed out the thing you're all missing."

"Enlighten me."

"Brains, dear girl." Ruby tapped Avid's temple. "Brains."

Avid grabbed Ruby's wrist.

Ruby grabbed Avid's wrist.

"That's enough, children!" Ward Cole rolled up to sitting. "Stop your wailing, gather your bedrolls 'round the fire, and Doctor Izzie will tell you a story." His brown eyes gleamed in the firelight.

Ruby scrunched closer, eager to fight off the east wind and, truth be told, to put a bit of space between her and Avid.

In the shadows loomed the motionless Sleipnir, her breathing deep and even. She loomed over Cole like a vengeful spirit in the dark. Cole wore the most ridiculous outfit of them all, a riot of color and ribbons, half gentleman's suit and half mender's storeroom. Menders traveled the high roads and low, moving from settlement to settlement, fixing a bucket here, mending a sprained ankle there. Hooks hung from every possible seam on Cole's body, and a wild variety of flasks and utensils hung from the hooks. He clanked when he walked. He did well at disguise. If she had run into him in the street, would Ruby have known this man as the one who ran across the water so quickly and quietly?

His smile was as warm as Rool's was chilling. Ruby strained to hear his low voice over the crackle of the fire. "We have been asked to retrieve a set of documents," he said. "After a good long look our sisters and brothers have discovered the cowards who burned half of Boston this past winter. They are organized, and we fear they wish to do harm to the colonies and therefore the crown. Our job is to deal with that threat." The rest of the group leaned in, eager. This was what they had trained for.

Cole flipped a tin whistle around his fingers. "We've

traced a few of them to a salt metal mine near a village a few miles from here, and it's come to us that they have a list of schemers that goes much farther afield than that little hamlet, apparently as far north as New France and farther south than Georgia. If we can get that list and any other information they might have, we can be ahead of them. We can find them before they do more evil. There may be some danger involved, but if all goes well, the threat will be small."

Avid raised her hand. "Why us, Ward, er, Izzie?"

Cole nodded. "Because we have been tasked with it. That should be enough for you." But Ruby wondered. Rool had already said that he didn't trust all of the Reeve. Was he sending the cadets because they might not have been corrupted yet? Cole rubbed his hands together over the fire. "The list we must snake lies behind a back door to a mine outside Parkersburg. And that door . . ." He paused. Cole had a flair for the dramatic. "Our sources say that door is reached through the root cellar of the Parkersburg Home for Mislaid Children."

Never cocked her head. "An orphanage?"

"That's right," Cole said. "Which is the cause of the getups. If anyone asks, I'm taking you there to find you a place to make a life. Once we get into the cellar, they've dug tunnels that connect to the mine. Somewhere in those tunnels sits a chemystral safe with an alchemycal lock. That is where our friends keep their contact list, and where Robby Thatch here"—he nodded at Ruby—"will earn his keep. He's a wizard with locks." Cole smiled ruefully. "A fact that I know firsthand. Now, take care around the sodium metal from the mine. It is extremely volatile." He turned to Wake and held out the whistle. "Here. When we get to the cellar, blow it. The door to the root cellar—" A tree branch cracked loudly, and Stump jumped.

"It's not a ghost story, Stump," Ruby said.

But Cole didn't continue. The whistle fell from his fingers, and he looked down.

Red blood streamed down his buckskin shirt from the musketball wound in his chest.

Cole's mouth moved, as if he were trying to continue the story. There was a ruckus in the trees behind them, and the others leaped to their feet as shapes rushed at them out of the dark.

It was an ambuscade.

Never traded punches with a masked man twice her size. From the shadows, Levi started screaming. When she heard him, Never screamed as well: a terrifying banshee's wail.

Avid faced a big fellow with a cutlass in his hand. Ruby's father come to save her? But no, stupid girl, the blade was rusty, and this man was more muscle than fat. Piggy eyes shot out from over a greasy mask. He lashed out with the cutlass, and Avid dived under it and came up in a roll.

Out of the corner of her eye Ruby saw Stump take a wicked blow from a club and go down. Before she knew what she was doing, she had jumped up on a rock behind the woman with the club. She grabbed the neck of the woman's coat and held a spoon at the base of her neck. "Move and I'll cut ye!" Ruby whispered in her best Skillet voice. The woman—her mask was a red kerchief—raised her hands and dropped the club. Stump struggled on hands and knees, trying to get up.

It was getting ugly. The masked man had wrapped Never in a bear hug, her feet off the ground, and she wriggled like a fish, trying to bash him with the back of her head. Levi was still screaming from somewhere. The man with the cutlass had backed Avid up against a big shelf of rock, and she was bleeding from her arm.

Ruby risked a glance back at Cole. He didn't reach up and grab at his panniers for a weapon. He didn't yell orders for defensive tactics. He was still sitting in the same place. His brow furrowed, sweat all across it, and then the word came. He threw it over his shoulder at the motionless Sleipnir just before his eyes rolled up in their sockets.

"Aegis," he called.

With an iron roar, the gearhorse sprang over Cole and smashed chest first into Wake's opponent. There was a thump and then a groan, and the man did not move. Sleipnir's muzzle snaked forward, and her brass teeth crunched down on the shoulder of the man holding Never. He yelled and dropped her; then the horse, with a flick of her neck, threw him through the air into the trunk of an oak tree. He fell to the ground.

The woman whirled, wickedly quick, and her hand closed on Ruby's arm. "Clever, little reeve," rasped the woman, who had savvied the spoon. That voice. Did she know it? "But now you need to come with me." She had an iron grasp, and she spun Ruby, holding her to her chest as a shield. Sleipnir charged forward. "Stop!" the woman yelled. She drew a knife, and the blade pricked at Ruby's neck. The gearhorse skidded to a halt, just feet in front of them. Sleipnir's warm breath washed over her: the odor of sand on a sunny beach.

The clearing was still, save the woman's labored breathing.

"Very well," she said. It was a low voice, but it didn't stay regular. She was putting it on, pretending to be someone else. "Your pet there, she is a protector. Good. Step back, all of you, or I smash this one's head to jelly!" Avid and Never stepped back, hands in the air. Levi appeared from the brush, ear all bloody. A body and a musket lay on the ground behind him. Sleipnir did not move. "You, too, beast!" she yelled. "I know you don't want harm to come to your charges, so I'll just take my little shield here and bid you—"

Quick and dainty, Sleipnir lashed out a forehoof and clipped the woman square in the face. She collapsed without a word.

The mask slipped from her face. It was Ward Burk.

"Ward Cole!" Gideon cried. They all rushed over to their fallen teacher.

He was lying under the oak tree as if he were taking a nap, a contented smile across his face. But his eyes were open, and his chest did not move.

Ismail Cole was dead.

CHAPTER 34

Your brief, in short. Obtain tome and, upon your judgment, the holder, H.C. Transport to London with utmost urgency. With the coming troubles, nowhere in the Colonies is safe.
—Godfrey Boyle,
Worshipful Order of Grocers

They buried Ismail Cole under a willow.

They did it that very night, with the picks, spades, and shovels Cole had packed as part of their menders' disguise. After some discussion, they dug a trench for Ward Burk and the brigands as well. The soil was rocky and tight, and it took them until dawn to hack out the shallow resting places. The new-turned earth smelled fresh, but Ruby's mouth tasted of ash.

Levi Curtsie summed it up well. "What in the heavens is happening? This is absolute madness!"

"Levi—" Avid said.

The boy shook his head, a dog breaking a hare's back. "No, Avid! Don't you try to use sense here. Ward Burk just killed Ward Cole, and we are out in the middle of the wilderness, and"—he was kicking a tree and yelling—"we don't know who to trust!"

Avid grabbed him and shook him. "Stop it, Levi!"

He went for her ankle, a savvy move, trying to bring the bigger girl down. She pivoted with it and landed on him, knocking the breath from his body.

"Cadet"—she was nose to nose with him—"you're right. We are in the wild, and who knows who else is out there? Howl one more word, and I swear to you I will have Gideon sit on you until you until you are a little old man."

Never took a step forward grim faced. "Stop it."

Gideon said, "Avid—"

"Quiet!" Avid stood up. The leather tie on her hair came loose, and she bunched it back up, breathing heavy.

Nobody said anything. "We have a comrade to send to rest. Then we talk. Yes?"

They nodded.

The five of them stood by the grave as the rising sun crept through the tree trunks.

Gideon coughed. "There might should be words for Ward Cole."

Never had her hands in front of her, clasping her fingers together over and over. "And Ward Burk. And those men, whoever they were."

It was Levi who scrubbed his hands on his dirty breeches and said, "I don't know the Reeve words, but Pa taught us from the Gospel of St. Empirical. I could do that."

When no one piped up, Avid nodded. "It might not be what he wanted, but it's what we've got."

As if by some kind of hidden signal, they all bowed their heads. Ruby did the same. They had used the words of Empirical on the *Thrift* as well. It was fitting.

The improvised bandage made from Cole's shirt had crept up. Levi tugged it back into place over his bloody ear. He cleared his throat and scrunched up one eye, as if he could squint the words into being. Then he started singing. Sweet as a lark.

My days have been so wondrous free,

The little birds that fly

With careless ease from tree to tree

Were but as blessed as I,

Were but as blessed as I.

Ask the gliding waters,

If ever a tear of mine

Increased their stream betime,

And ask the breathing gales

If ever I lent a sigh,

If ever I lent a sigh.

His face had gone all peaceful while he sang, but it tensed right up as soon as he was done. He stared off into nowhere.

"That was real nice, Levi," Avid said. Ruby wiped some wet from her face. It must have been the morning dew. She didn't know what to feel. The Reeve had taken her from her family. She was as much a tool as Sleipnir, and the Swede was, well, harvesting her. And yet she didn't feel happy to see these people dead. She didn't feel victorious. Cole had been good to her. Burk had been good to her, but whatever else she was—secret assassin? A spy for the Grocers? An agent of whoever was starting this war?—she was dirt now. All Ruby was was hollow. And tired. And scared.

They all kicked and poked at the ground a bit, and then they came together around Sleipnir. After the last brigand had fallen, the gearhorse had gone still.

Levi looked at his sister, as if he didn't trust himself to speak.

"Who were they?" Never said. "And why kill Cole?"

Ruby knew what Athena might say. "He was the threat. A true reeve would have tipped the balance of that fight, especially with Sleipnir."

"But why were they here in the first place?" Never pressed on. "To stop our mission? To take Sleipnir?"

"Or for the Sweetling?" Avid said.

Was it for Ruby?

Avid clapped the dirt from her hands. "Well, none of

them can tell us. Do we stay the course or go back?"

Gideon broke in. "I think we should go back. The lord captain needs to know what happened. Something's wrong. This was a secret mission. How did they know where to look for us?" He straightened his ridiculous cook's hat. "If they found us, others might be looking, too."

Never Curtsie fiddled with Levi's bandage. "How's your ear?"

Levi shook his head and then growled in pain. "I'll be fine. We should finish this mission. It is what we are. Ward Corson says the task is what we are."

Avid slowly nodded. "I think Levi is right. We have a mission, and who knows how long we have to do it or whether this is the only opportunity?" She looked about. "We're baptized now. I say we keep on."

Never said, "I'm with you. What do you say, Teach?"

It surprised her that they even asked, but they all waited on her answer. Even Avid. The way ahead was filled with uncertainty. The way behind held only gray wood walls and more helpings of Swede. "Onward."

Ruby helped the Curtsies and Gideon break camp and repack Sleipnir's saddlebags. Avid, as the oldest, took on the part of the weed doctor. They had cleaned and salvaged Cole's clothes as best they could, and as Avid pulled them on, Ruby clearly saw her back for the first time. It was a map of raised skin. Burns, she realized. The others were busy with packing. The two of them were oddly alone.

"Avid," Ruby said.

The girl pulled down Cole's shirt and turned over her shoulder. "Teach?"

"What happened to you? To your back?"

Maybe it was the fight, maybe it was Levi's hymn, but Avid didn't sneer away Ruby's question. She looked at Ruby a moment. "Second mate and milliner, right? Your parents?"

"Yes."

"Not all of us had that."

Ruby caught the look on her face and took great care with her next question. "Is that why you're so good at Works? Whatever it is that happened?"

Avid pulled on the dead man's boots. "I don't know. I guess the Void comes easy when there's nothing you want to remember." She walked off to help the others. Ruby had hated her for so long. She was so smug, harsh, skilled . . . but Ruby was coming to realize that she was other things as well. Brave. Diligent. Tenacious. It was strange.

They set out.

Ruby welcomed the silence as they passed through the still-waking forest. It was a well-traveled road, and as the mist dispersed into the bright, warm morning, several travelers passed them, heading for the safety of the cities.

Parkersburg was a busy little village, full of bustle and grit, nestled up against a forested mountain. Their dirty faces fit right in in a town where mining was the only business. There was a pump and a long trough in the middle of the town square, and they all stopped for a drink. Levi filled a cup and held it out to Sleipnir, who actually sniffed it before moving her snout away. The gearhorse had begun to display more horsey qualities, but needing food and drink wasn't part of them. Evram had said her four sparkstones would last months. It was hard to think of her as an artifice. She looked, she *felt* so alive. After the ambuscade, had the gearhorse been walking closer to her? It was silly, maybe, but the thought that they might be becoming friends warmed Ruby all over. A big roan down at the other end of the trough wanted nothing to do with a metal cousin and snuffled and blew, giving Sleipnir a wild eye. Strangers in wartime, they all got more than their share of suspicious looks. Should they have come in at night?

Avid scanned the square. "Levi, find me that orphanage." The boy's eyes flicked to his sister, who gave the slightest of nods before he disappeared into the crowd. They all looked away studiously.

After a short time Levi appeared next to Ruby, drinking from the trough as if he'd been there since it was built. Barnacles, but he was good. As good as Ruby maybe. "Wake, I found the house." They gathered around as he took another drink. "Two wool merchants were going on about it."

"What did they say?" Avid and Ruby said at the same time.

"The wool merchants used to use the children to work on their finer garments, but they all packed up about a week ago. They said it's just louts and vagrants now. Follow me." And he headed back the way they had come.

Louts and vagrants? Was any of their information good? Were they walking into a trap? Was this all some intricate ruse by Wisdom Rool to rid himself of her for good? Ruby barely saw the gleaming green leaves of the forest as they wound their way through it, dappled with late-afternoon sunlight.

Gideon Stump said, "Ruby," and that pulled her back to the world.

A venerable wooden gate hung from one hinge of a split rail fence. A dilapidated sign announced cheerfully, RUPERT'S BAY COMPANY HOME FOR MISLAID YOUTH!, the letters barely legible from the menagerie of cute little animals that peered through *p*'s and perched atop the *o*'s.

"Charming," Ruby said.

A rough dirt track headed straight from the gate into a cluster of apple trees in the shoulder of the mountain.

"The ruts in the road are deep," Never said. "Heavier things than children in the wagons coming out of there."

Avid led them off the road and into the thick underbrush along the fence line.

Darkness fell, and they waited another hour or so. Avid turned to Levi. "Scout ahead for us, Curtsie? We'll wait here."

Levi nodded, twisting his waist this way and that. He disappeared into the orchard.

Hours crept by. The moon rose in a cloudless sky. Levi tapped Gideon on the shoulder.

"Gah!" Gideon spat. "Stop that, you demon! I nearly jumped out of my skin!"

Levi grinned. Filed teeth glinted in the moonlight. "I've found it. Follow me."

They wended their way through the white-blossomed trees until they stopped at the bottom of a high hill. Levi got down on his belly, and they all followed him up. On the other side of the hill sat a huge old house, backed right up against a high cliff. Parkersburg would be somewhere on the other side of the cliff, but from here the house was the only structure in sight. It was completely isolated.

Levi whispered, "Wait a moment. There." He pointed toward the wide front porch. A shadow rounded the corner and walked the length of the house, stopped for a moment and crouched, then disappeared at the back edge near the cliff. "The round takes about two hundred breaths. I watched three times." He pointed to where the shadow stopped. "Two double doors there, down to a root cellar."

Avid motioned them all back down the hill. "That guard's not just some lout. He looks like he knows his business. Mind your p's and q's, my friends. Whatever we are going into, it is not what was expected." She handed Ruby the tin whistle, the one Ward Cole had been holding. "Cole said to use this when we got to the root cellar."

Ruby looked the whistle over. "What's it for?"

Avid said, "You should ask Ward Cole. I'm sure he'll tell you."

Ruby gave her a look and pulled her picks out of nowhere with a flourish.

Avid blinked, and then she quirked a smile. "Cross me, Sweetling, and I'll come for you."

Ruby thought about holding her tongue for about two seconds.

"If I crossed you, you'd have a better chance finding a frog on a treetop." Was that how she wanted to leave it? No. She flexed her wrists. "I want this to work. You can trust me. We are in this together." As she said it, Ruby realized she meant it. She looked about at the other four: the Curtsies, primed to unleash their fury; stout Gideon, quietly poised; and Avid, the savvy leader. They were not the crew she wanted, but they were the crew she had. She needed them, and they needed her. And they were all of them headed full sail into unknown danger.

Avid set her jaw. "And we will watch your back, Ruby Teach, and protect you with everything we have."

Ruby checked her picks and got reacquainted with the night. "No use loafing," she said, and set off around the side of the hill.

CHAPTER 35

Providence is a comedian playing to
an audience too afraid to laugh.
—Voltaire

The sticks would have crunched under Ruby's feet, but she picked her way among them, a bird on a branch. The trees made excellent cover. She put her shoulders against the bole of the last one between her and the farmhouse. White apple blossoms hung fat from the branches, surrounding her in a cloud of green-tasting sweetness.

Ruby Maxim Eleven: "Be More Patient than the Guard."

After a few moments the patrol rounded the corner. He was a stout man, breathing heavily just from walking. But Ruby could see the handles of two pistols sticking up from his belt in the moonlight. She couldn't outrun a clocklock ball and didn't want to try, especially after what happened to Ismail Cole. The guard wheezed over to the root cellar and knelt, most likely checking the door. He levered himself up and moved on. When he rounded the back corner, Ruby counted to ten and then left the safety of the tree.

The doors were wide enough to fit a wagon and were set into the ground in an iron frame. However . . .

There was no padlock.

There was no keyhole.

The only things marking the perfectly crafted door were two pulls and a seam so clean a gnat couldn't wiggle through. Ruby couldn't even feel an edge when she ran her hand over it. Her thinnest pick wasn't thin enough.

A wheeze and crunching leaves announced the guard's return trip. She shimmied up a support onto the awning above the doors, she flattened herself to the roof, and then she blew the whistle.

Nothing happened. A bit of air came out of the little instrument, but no sound. Perfect.

She tried it again. Same result.

Ruby wanted to throw it into the night, but instead, she kept blowing, over and over. The guard rounded the corner. He worked his way down the windows, humming a jaunty tune.

Then, far off, the sound of hoofbeats. Gaining speed through the night. Coming right toward them.

Below, the guard stopped and took a breath, to yell or scream or chuckle, Ruby knew not what. She did not even realize what she was doing until she was in the air.

As she flew down from above, she glimpsed a big shape shooting across the open area between the trees and the house. Ruby slammed into the shoulders of the guard. She wheeled her arm around and stuck it, wool sleeve and all, into his mouth, only a jot before he began yelling for help.

He clapped his meaty hand across Ruby's wrist, but she could not let him not pull her away. She clamped her other hand down on her forearm and held on for dear life.

Sleipnir galloped up, skidded to a halt in the dirt, and bowed her head. Avid slid down her neck and launched herself into the guard with a knee to the stomach. He went down wheezing, fighting for air, and Ruby rolled off. Avid's fist slammed into his neck, and he stopped moving.

At the edge of the doors, the gallant gearhorse reared. It turned itself back the way it had come and cocked its head for a moment, as if it were listening. After a moment several somethings, each about the size of a harvest melon, dropped out of its backside. They landed on the doors with a series of clangs. *Cling. Clang Clingclingclang.*

It looked for all the world like a pile of metal horse manure. It began to hiss.

Sleipnir scraped her hooves back once, twice, and then galloped off.

"Help me," Avid said. She had half rolled the unconscious guard over the little garden wall but was struggling with his back end.

"Are you serious?" Ruby asked.

"Do it!" Avid whispered. "Hurry!"

The hissing from the metal dung intensified. Ruby put her shoulder into the prone guard. Together she and Avid flopped him over the wall.

"Come on!" Avid jumped over the wall and buried her face in the leaves. Ruby hurled herself over the wall and then down between Avid and the guard. He smelled like mutton.

Nothing happened. Ruby turned to Avid. "What—"

The night lit up.

A giant jumped on Ruby's head.

That's what it felt like.

When Ruby woke up, apple blossoms were dancing all around her in the air. The blast had thrown her across the yard, but Avid was still right next to the wall. She was standing, groggy in the firelight, with blood running out of her nose, trying to get her balance like a newborn colt.

The wall behind Avid leaned forward. Ruby yelled; but she could not hear herself, and neither did Avid. Ruby waved her hands furiously and ran for the other cadet. Avid blinked her eyes back into focus on Ruby, then turned. She threw herself to the side, just as the garden wall crashed down without a sound. Avid tried to get up but then fell back down on her bum, a drunk in a Charles Town alley. She would not stop looking at her hands.

The rest of the wall was burning, lighting up the scene like a gruesome fantasy. The root cellar doors had been ripped open, a raw hole punched through the metal down into the earth.

Still foggy, Ruby leapt through the ruined doors. Down the ramp a cloud of smoke roiled, masking the faint light of chem pots.

Shadows of men and women stumbled about in the smoke. One lay prone and broken; two more rushed past Ruby up the ramp, one leaning on the other's shoulder. Ruby tripped over another body, catching herself on something wet. No time for thinking or wondering. A darker spot in the smoke showed her the passage. The smoke thickened, so she dropped to the floor and crawled.

Around the next bend the passage opened up into a larger room. On hands and knees, she weaved her way between rickety chairs and rough table legs until her hand brushed up against what she was looking for. It was the stout door of a safe, the metal cool against her fingers, with a strange square-shaped keyhole.

This was the right place. A deadly chemystral lock, and Ruby defying all reason to pick it. Just like that day so long ago in Boston. The memory warmed her to the task, and she began.

Sweat stung her eyes. She closed them. It was not as though she needed them. The picks were in, and the only way to avoid a face dissolved by aqua fortis was to remain completely still. Any excess motion, and she'd end up a Ruby-size puddle. Where would they be then? Her crew was counting on her. Clear, calm purpose flowed through her. Was this the emptiness Corson kept going on about?

The first tumbler went down.

The second.

With her eyes closed, it felt quieter. More and more smoke crept into her chest. Her throat tickled. The tickle grew into a scratch. She couldn't give in to it. If she moved, she died. She desperately tried to control it, but the scratch blossomed into a demand. She couldn't stop it.

She coughed.

It was a hacking cough, a good gut-buster that went on for five heartbeats or so. It felt loud, though it still sounded as if it were behind a mile of alchemycal glass.

But there was no telltale stream of poison and no melting of hands or faces.

How had she survived? Mad, impossible luck? Maybe a fever dream?

The coughing subsided, Ruby said a thank-you to Providence and went to finish off the lock. That was when she knew. She could move her fingers, but her arms dangled from her shoulders as if their puppet strings had been cut. Changed. Some hidden urge had protected her, stopped the shaking of the cough from being transferred into the arms.

She finished the lock off with one hand propped in place and the alloyed glass pick in her teeth. The door eased open into darkness.

CHAPTER 36

Pigeon huntin,' By Jimmy. Writ down by Carl.
1. Head up that hill with a club.
2. Wait for a flock to come down on ye.
3. Close yer eyes.
4. Flail that club in the air.
5. You just hunted pigeons!
—Jimmy Two Hands, tracker

"Master, what do you make of those clouds? Should we set down before the storm reaches us?" The normally spectacular view through the back window was a wall of angry-looking clouds.

Something lit up Marise Fermat's face. Something Henry had never seen there before.

Fear.

Henry looked again, and the clouds had already

come closer. Much closer. The sky behind them was solid black, eating up the sunset sky. But the blackness pulsed and swirled, like smoke with an ax to grind.

"Henry, those aren't clouds."

"What then?"

"Pigeons."

Marise cursed and then hauled on the wheel that controlled their altitude, spinning it like a mad dervish. She looked over her shoulder and sucked the breath in through her perfect teeth. "Secure the storm shutters."

"Because a few birds might foul up the gear works?"

She kept looking behind her. "Henry, pigeon flocks out here run ten miles by ten miles. They tear down trees and flatten barns, and we are floating hundreds of feet in the air in a chemystrally lightened and therefore dramatically weakened container of wood. If that storm catches us, we'll be torn apart."

The flock grew as Henry watched. It was spellbinding.

"Secure the shutters now, boy!" Marise leaned down into the spiral staircase. "Cram! Athen! Strap yourselves down! Now!"

Henry hurried down the shutters that ran the length of the room, slamming and barring them. The wood felt light as air, literally.

"No, leave the rear shutter. I need to see the storm," she said. She slid a clever slat open in the one before her, allowing her to see just a little bit forward as well.

Calls, yells, bumps, and thumps came from below as the other two strapped in.

Marise looked back and forth between the rear window and the fore, muttering calculations under her breath.

"Henry, I need you to do something for me."

"What is it?" His pulse pounded in his ears.

"Take that." She nodded at a long spear, lying flat on the floor along the cabinet. The point was elaborate, bearing some kind of tapered alchemycal envelope in a reservoir behind the point.

He grabbed it.

"Good." The cottage yawed as she steered toward a hilltop, about a mile away. "Now I need you to take that through the trap in the roof and stab a hole in the vesicle."

She was mad. "I'm sorry?"

She did not look over her shoulder. "We need to drop more quickly, or the storm will catch us in the air. Oh, and be very careful with the tip of the spear. Don't let it strike anything else."

A thousand arguments for why he should not do it ran lightning speed through his skull, but he climbed up the little flimsy ladder and flipped the latch.

The door burst open, and a howling wind tore past. It was a storm in earnest. He inched his head up above the roofline, and the whirling air spun about him. Evenly spaced lanyards attached to the roof hung taut between the cottage and the gas-filled vesicle, floating a good twenty feet above. A shoulder-wide hole stared from the base of the vesicle, surrounded by a thin border of wood. From the border, flapping wildly in the whirling wind, hung a cloth rope ladder.

"Surely you jest," Henry breathed.

"Now, Henry Collins!" Marise's call filtered up from below.

Smothering a curse, he pulled himself up crablike up onto the roof, knuckles white about the spear and on the lip of the trap. He pulled his eyes away from the edge of the roof and the ground far, far below. The cloud was definitely closer now. Marise was right. It had to be ten miles wide if it was an inch.

The bottom of the rope ladder flailed about above him, out of reach. He pried his hand loose from the trap and pushed himself up onto his knees. The wind tore at his eyes so fiercely tears leaked from them.

He stood on the swaying roof in a windstorm half a mile above the forest.

The sky behind had gone completely black now, a pulsing, whirling curtain of beaks and claws. The wind howled even faster, whipping at his clothing. The ladder twisted about, as did the cottage below, ominous groans and cracks echoing up through the wailing wind.

He levered himself up one rung, then wrenched his elbow over the next. He pulled his knees up, muscles screaming, and then heaved his foot into the next rung. His bad foot. It twisted and then lost purchase, flying out into the air, with only his elbow between him and doom. He cried out, and a faint call echoed him. Marise Fermat was below, waving urgently.

He nodded as if he understood her and then found the strength to wrench his trembling limbs up two more rungs.

From below, fainter still, Marise yelled again. She pointed a vial upward, and a swirl of yellow gas tore up the ladder and wrapped itself about him.

Quiet. The wind was somehow gone. He could think. He was just under the vesicle. But if he stabbed its bottom, that would do nothing. Any gas above the level of the hole would still stay in the vesicle. So he gripped the spear by its haft, cocked his arm, and hurled it hard as he could up through the inside of the bag.

It flew straight and true in the silence.

It struck the top. A red cloud blossomed from the envelope. And then suddenly blue sky shone through the canvas, like a window back to another world. His stomach lurched. They were falling. He had done it.

He glanced over his shoulder. The storm of birds was upon them. Its curtain blocked out the sky, eclipsed the setting sun, a wall of wings rushing at him. He could see them now, individual shapes dancing inside the cloud. It was beautiful. It was pure math. It took him.

CHAPTER 37

The chemycal fires Blazed most Terribly, and Burnt all the town in the space of half an hour. The French brigands are everywhere. I implore you. Without soldiers from the Crown, we cannot count ourselves Safe.

—Letter from Esmerelda Williams to
Governor William Keith, April 1719

Inside the safe, among a jumble of artifices and lumps of metal, lay a rolled parchment secured by a wax seal. Ruby flopped her arm onto the shelf and grabbed it. She had to be certain. She popped the seal.

In the smoky flicker of chem pot light the title read:

"Use the Utmost Restraint and Care When Contacting."

A cramped list of names and scratched notations marched down the parchment.

Of the Reeve

Charlotte Dove—Reeve House, Boston

Kyra Burk—Fort Scoria

Of the Bluestockings, Philadelphi

Alice Dorn (Hearth)—Frayed Hem Roominghouse

Aquila Gaioso (Fish) —Chem ship *Deviltry*

Lazarus Cooper (Wagon)—Lazarus's Dry Goods

Name Unknown (Hammer)—Benzene Yards

Mary Nickerson (Badger)—Alembic Coffeehouse

Abel Ward (Long Gun)—Arden Farm smoke shack

Greta Van Huffridge (Scales)—Daughter of Lothor

Philadelphi

Elias Fell—Quaker Meeting House

Thandie Paine—Polus Library

London

Mary Tills—Invisible College

Godfrey Boyle —Clove and Camel

She knew those names. So many of them. The two reeves: had Burk engineered that ambush for the Grocers? The Bluestockings from Philadelphi, who had tried to keep her in their secret school. Godfrey Boyle, Athena's father. More names followed, many more, in Boston, in Charles Town, in Montreal. In Algiers, Lisbon, and Paris, by Providence.

They were the conspirators? The ones who set off bombs in Boston? The ones who were spurring the colonies, not to mention their parent countries, to war?

She flipped the parchment. On the cracked seal lay two symbols: a camel and a pepper mill. The symbols of the Worshipful Order of Grocers.

Another wave of coughs racked through Ruby, but she wrestled them to a stop. These names. People that she knew. Revealing them to the Reeve would be dooming them to unending pursuit and danger. For Ruby, it would mean success, a respite from the Swede, a chance for survival. If she did not bring back the list . . . the future tore at her.

Given the names on the list, might they not be trying to do something good?

But these people were starting a war. Burning cities. Destroying farms. How could she support that?

Yet, if she gave Godfrey Boyle's name to the Reeve,

could she ever look Athena in the face again? Or Henry? Or Cram?

No reeve could ever see these names.

She took the chem pot and lit the paper on fire.

She pull-crawled her way back down the smoky passageway, dark as a hold in a thunderstorm, her only company the unmoving shapes of the left-behind miners. She could barely haul her own weight on her jellied shoulders. Whether they were brigands and spies or fighters for freedom, they had to get out for themselves. She could not help them.

She scuttled up the ramp. In the center of the field, lit up by the burning house, the Reeve cadets crouched with Sleipnir, imps around a horse from hell. All Ruby could do was make certain that one foot landed somewhere near the other in the drifts of apple blossoms that had been blown to the ground in the explosion, their rustle a faint whisper in her head from miles away. A distant voice called out behind her, an ant yelling at her from a faraway mountain. A heavily muscled man emerged from the mine covered in soot, a huge mattock held easily in his hand. Ruby staggered backward, and he began running toward her.

She turned to run; but her leg caught on a root under the blossoms, and she fell to the ground.

The man with the pickax closed, veins bulging.

Shapes flitted past, one, two, three, four, and the cadets were on him, diving, rolling, punching, kicking. They were fighting *for* her. Avid had picked up a thick branch somewhere and came at him hard, overhand, but he easily sidestepped the blow, sending her reeling with the stock of the ax, full in her chest. She fell on her back like a stone. The Curtsie twins swooped in from both sides, bobbing and weaving, but Never went down with a gash in her forearm and Levi from a knee to his fruits. Gideon Stump caught the man a hard kick right in the chest, and the brute actually took a step back; but then the haft of the mattock came hurtling around from behind, clipping the big boy cleanly on the temple.

The man kept coming.

Ruby could barely get a full breath, let alone get to her feet. Red flashed in the sides of her eyes, and pain crept up from her arms as the shoulders ever so slowly began to harden. She vainly tried to hide in the blossoms behind her.

A shadow leaped over her from behind, topped by a cloud of red. Three strikes, one to the chest, one to the knee, one to the neck, and the man was down.

Edwina Corson turned to Ruby, concern plain on her face. *"Wooh hef de liss?"* she said.

Ruby shook her head. Pointed to her ear.

Corson repeated, louder and clearer, *"You have the list?"*

Ruby shook her head again. *"It wasn't there."*

Corson looked to the heavens, as if for guidance.

Satisfaction and guilt tore at Ruby in equal measure. Why did she feel guilty?

"Hold here and we'll go back in!"

The ward moved on to tend to the cadets, kneeling next to Avid. No one else's attention was on Ruby. She had some of her wind back, and with that wind came a desperate revelation. They would not find the list. Rool would cast her off. There would be no protection from the Swede. She eased herself to her feet, ever so slowly, then climbed on Sleipnir's back and whispered into her beautiful bronze ear, "Sea and Sky."

The horse's shuddering breath almost threw Ruby to the ground. Sleipnir craned her muzzle over her shoulder at Ruby, and her sapphire eyes shone warm with curiosity. She whickered.

Ruby wrapped her fingers in the braided brass mane. "Go, girl," she said, and they leapt together into the dark.

Sleipnir's eight galloping hooves rang out in the night. The gearhorse weaved in and out of the trees, veering past the trunks before Ruby could even see them. Ruby craned her head back to see if anyone was following, but there was nothing but shadow and moonlight. A branch stabbed at her shoulder, hard, and she twisted with its force, one leg flailing in the air. Still woozy from the smoke, she managed to wrench herself back up onto Sleipnir's back, but just then another shadow swooped down out of the night. Ruby ducked her head into the gearhorse's mane. The low-hanging tree limb cracked and smashed, and Sleipnir just kept going.

Ruby tried to get her thoughts straight, tried to get back on an even keel, but the images just kept plowing through her mind so fast it was hard to even see them. The explosion, the searing smoke in the mine, the list burning to ash, the cadets flying to her side. Corson.

Movement pulled her back to the present. Something was out there. A flicker in the dark, behind and to the left. Her imagination? No, there it was again. Something was pacing them, following.

"Faster, girl," Ruby whispered. And even through the whistling wind, Sleipnir heard. The gearhorse whuffed and craned out her neck, surging forward. Sleipnir cut left sharply, and it was all Ruby could do to hold on. If she fell, the horse could not protect her, though if she were paste smashed into the side of a tree, she would need very little protection. The wind bored into her ears, punctuated distantly by Sleipnir's hooves.

She let the wind in.

The whirling gusts were so loud they made a kind of quiet, and then something happened. It was almost as if her thighs had lengthened or widened about the metal flanks of her steed. She no longer had to struggle to stay on the horse. She gave up trying to guess which way Sleipnir would turn, and she realized she did not need to. She leaned further into her steed's back and plastered herself to it.

Ruby's senses fell into Sleipnir's.

The pistons pounded inside her chest, a gully came up out of nowhere, and the muscle in her back legs bunched up, then snapped open to launch her and the little thing on her back safely over. It felt good to run. There had been something holding her back, like a halter, hemming her in, but now she was free. A deep canyon appeared in front of her, so she turned back toward the eaves, racing along between the gorge and the edge of the forest.

An instinct, an inkling ripped Ruby out of her trance. The shape was back, in and out of the shadows, keeping pace with them through the trees. A person! It was impossible, but someone was running behind Sleipnir and gaining on them. It swerved around thorn brakes, disappeared into the gully they had just jumped, and then somehow ran out of the other side. The shape leaped up to vault over an outcropping, but it must have misjudged; its foot struck the top of the rock.

No. It *used* the top of the rock to plant its foot and then launched itself upward.

Flying through the air, hair wild and streaming, straight toward Ruby, the shape resolved itself out of the dark into Edwina Corson.

Ruby tried to duck, but strong hands wrapped around her torso and tore her from Sleipnir's back. Dark shapes of tree trunks flashed past, but somehow Ruby was deposited in a pile of leaves, Corson rolling to a stop a few paces away.

Her hair flamed like a halo above her blacks. She was breathing heavily. She put up her hand. "Ruby."

Ruby said, "Aegis."

A brass streak burned the air. Sleipnir came to a stop ten yards away and then cantered back to stand in between Ruby and Edwina. Ward Corson crouched on the ground. Just behind where she had been standing, a medium-size oak tree had been sheared off at waist height.

Corson held up her hands, and her words were slow. "Ruby. Tell me why."

"I didn't know." Rage and fear warred inside her.

"Didn't know what?"

That I would know these people. If I gave that list to you, you would hunt them. And then it would be my fault. She could not say that. "You need to let me go."

"I can't."

"Where did you come from? You weren't even supposed to be there."

"Burk disappeared, so I came after you. I found Ismail. And Burk. Give me the list."

"There is no list."

"Think of those who died in the bombs and fire. The men and women on that list are murderers, Ruby Teach. They were going to use that salt metal to create more chemystral incendiaries. Setting fire to barracks, to schools, to churches, killing innocents."

Was that who the Bluestockings were? Burk and Dove? Athen's father? Murderers? "But why?"

"Because they want to start a war."

"Why?"

"So there can be a new king in America."

"Well, I don't care about any of that," Ruby said.

In the dawn tree branches cast shadows across Corson's face. "If you wish to be a reeve, Ruby Teach, you must care about all of that. It is our Oath."

"I was never one of you."

"But you could be." Corson took a step forward. "I could teach you to protect those you love. A place in the Reeve means I can protect you from those who wish to harm you. It is a hard life, I agree, but you cannot stand alone."

"You all stand alone. Ward Burk killed Ward Cole! You saw it! I can't be empty like you."

Corson's eyes softened. "It's not the Void that powers me, Ruby. Or Cole. Or even Wisdom Rool. Cole had joy. Rool has duty. I have—" She grimaced. "You have to get empty only so you can know what to fill it with. I can teach you." She held out her hand.

"Stay back," Ruby said, and Sleipnir took a step forward.

"Aegis." It was Corson who said it this time. The gearhorse made no move. Corson's eyes widened in surprise. "You have made a friend, it seems."

Corson had attempted to take control over Sleipnir. Ruby thanked her stars for Evram Hale.

Instead of tensing, the ward relaxed even more. She was utterly still. "I do not wish to harm you, Ruby, or this mechanical."

Ruby stepped behind Sleipnir's flank. "That makes two of us. On your way then, Ward Corson. I hold you no ill will; you have been kind to me this last few months. But I must be going."

"I cannot let you do that."

"Watch me." Ruby reached for Sleipnir's mane, but it wasn't there. The gearhorse swung around, aiming a rear kick at Edwina Corson, who was sprinting at Ruby. Corson threw herself to her knees, flying forward, and arched her back. The rough metal hooves flashed through the air just inches above her nose. Her hand flashed toward Ruby's leg, but Sleipnir's body crashed down between them. Corson whirled and smashed her doubled fists into the gearhorse's face. It rang like a bell. A deep dent appeared in Sleipnir's cheek, but she just looked down at Edwina and let out a metallic snort. Corson shook her hands out and flexed them, bobbing back and forth. The gearhorse tore at the ward with her bronze teeth, and Corson cartwheeled away. Sleipnir charged right behind, all eight hooves tearing at the ground. The battle was joined, and Ruby's throat caught at the thought of either opponent losing.

For it was an even match. As hard as it was to believe, Edwina Corson held her own against the gearhorse. It was a dance of grace against fury. Sleipnir kept coming like a tidal wave, bucking and thrashing, hooves cutting through the air. But Corson was always a half step ahead, always a hand's width clear. A dozen times the mechanical had her cornered, and a dozen times she slipped out of reach.

Ruby's nails dug ever deeper into her palms. What could she do? She couldn't run. Corson would just keep coming.

Just then the inevitable happened. In a game of so

many narrow escapes, so many little things can go wrong. It just takes one to send you down to the bottom. The gearhorse had maneuvered Corson to the edge of the gorge, feinting and dodging, rearing up and slamming down over and over again. At last the ward seemed to be tiring. Her limbs were heavier, her twisting escapes ever more perilous. Sleipnir reared again, and Corson rolled back, just out of reach of the gearhorse's hooves.

But she was caught. It was an island of land that jutted out over the gorge, and she was boxed in by the gearhorse's big body. The mechanical reared once again, and Ruby could not tear her eyes away. Ruby was killing Edwina Corson, just as surely as the Reeve would kill all the people on that list. Was it just as she said? Kill or be killed?

So be it.

The hooves came down.

But just before they landed, Edwina Corson let out a cry that shook the leaves on the trees. The reeve's foot shot *down* into the ground, and a crack opened up. She leaped up and swung around the great gearhorse's neck to stand on its shoulders. All four of the front hooves came down with the full weight of woman and mechanical behind them. The crack in the ground opened, and the island slid forward. Corson *ran up* Sleipnir's spine as she was teetering, jumped into the air, and landed softly on the grass at the edge of the gorge. The great gearhorse scrabbled backward; but its momentum was too great, and Sleipnir tumbled out of sight with a confused whinny.

There was a terrible jangling crash.

Ruby could not see. Her eyes were clouded with tears. Edwina Corson approached her slowly, heaving and stumbling, barely able to keep her feet. Ruby did not run. A howling hole broke open in her chest. Sleipnir was gone, and by Ruby's hand, as surely as if she had ridden her over that cliff herself.

Corson put her hand on Ruby's shoulder. "I'm so sorry," she said. Then she did something with her hand, and Ruby's world went dark.

She didn't mind one bit.

CHAPTER 38

Your mind is a prison. I am here to break you free.
—Halvard de Anjou, *Bastionado*

Henry woke in a sea of white. He was alive. He rested snug in the fork of a tree, the ruins of the vesicle collapsed on branches all about him. The cushion of gas Marise Fermat had cast about him had been formidable indeed. He had fallen from the sky and had only a few bumps and bruises to show for it.

The white carpet lay across the trees and grass as far as the eye could see. But it stank. It wasn't snow. It was poo. Pigeon leavings. He flailed at the pigeony covering, flinging it down to the ground below.

Henry's heart caught in his throat. The cottage sat broken at the base of the tree, just feet from smashing into the wall of forest behind him. Marise had landed it somehow, but it would be a long time before it flew again. The roof was staved in, and the whole house listed to the side on broken beams like a drunken parson.

"Greetings, Henry Collins."

Henry looked down. He then wished himself anywhere but here.

At the base of the tree stood two people he had hoped to never see again: the girls from StiltTown. It was the tall one who had spoken, the one with black hair and buskins. She held an ax in one hand and a dagger in the other. "I did not have the opportunity to introduce myself when last we met. My name is Vera Medina, and my captain would like a word with you."

The serving girl from the King's Bum stood by her side, pistol leveled, wiping fresh pigeon stuff from her forehead with the other hand. She cocked her clocklock.

"Alaia Calderon. You pushed me into a swamp, and for that alone I would be happy to kill you. Please refuse to climb down."

Henry stared. "This is . . . well, it's not impossible, but it is highly improbable."

Alaia laughed. "Isn't it? You had given us the slip, dissolved into burning forest. We had abandoned all hope of finding you, but then something wonderful happened."

"What is that?"

"It was the strangest thing. A house flew across the sky, right in front of us."

They thrust him to the dirt floor. He twisted to land on his shoulder, protecting his bound hands. His captors had marched him down the hill to a no-longer-abandoned farmstead, a sturdy little house and barn out on the now guano-covered plains. Shapes moved about in the house. A hard-bitten man and woman guarded the barn, both clad in heavily used leathers and bristling with weapons. Shafts of light cut through gaps in the walls of the barn, and ancient hay lay strewn about, like the last hairs on a bald man's head.

"Well met, hero." The voice emerged from the shadows at the back of the barn.

Henry scrambled to sit up. "Captain Teach?"

Wayland Teach edged his drawn, weary face into a sunbeam. "Marise told us of your dashing maneuver. I never pegged you for a crow's nest man." The Blacks were there as well, Cubbins on the ground next to his mother.

"What happened?" Henry asked.

The captain gave a sad grin. "Suffice to say that while you are making a habit of saving folk, I am growing to be somewhat expert in being captured."

Cram, Athena, and Marise had been caught as well, escaping the crash with only scrapes and bruises. Except for Marise, the whole company had their bonds secured to hooks on the wall, hands above their heads. The alchemyst, however, wore something new upon her shoulders and head: a mask, or rather a helmet with two short chains attached to the chin. The chains ended in two manacles, pulling her wrists up to the bottom of her neck. The helmet had no eyeholes and only a small slit for food. A formidable lock secured the visor. It was a beautiful artifact, engraved with images of angels fighting flask-wielding demons, but designed to keep a Tinker pacified. For Henry the two girls had rigged up a halter around his neck, binding his hands at his chest in similar fashion. The cord was basalt, tight yet damnably slippery.

The blond girl, Alaia—no longer Jenny—smiled, a gap between her two middle teeth. "Count yourself lucky." She nodded over to the mask. "That was meant for you."

He counted himself very lucky. The conversation back in the laboratory haunted his thoughts. "Master, are you all right?"

Marise remained silent. The girls sauntered out, snickering to each other.

Captain Teach said, "Marise, they're gone. Are you all right?"

Her voice rang hollow from inside the mask. "Yes, dear Wayland. I'm dandy, in the way most chemysts are when they happen upon a friendly party of Tinker hunters. Your band of urchins lured me out of safety. Now what do you have in that legendary bag of tricks? What are you going to do to get me out of this?"

"Indeed. What are you going to do, Wayland?" The low voice crept in from outside, the other side of the barn wall. They all went silent. A shadow passed across the gaps in the boards. The speaker was coming around to the front door. "You all speak so freely of your lives, you know." The voice had a slight accent, Catalonian, like the girls'. "Your conversation was so intriguing that I could not help listening. Perhaps you should take greater care with your words." The shape, framed in the sunlight, opened the door. The two girls stood behind her, weapons drawn. The woman was neither short nor tall, in gray- and green-dyed buskins, shirt, breeches, and moccasins, her long black hair braided behind her in an intricately tied ponytail. A streak of silver shot through the black at one temple. She crouched down on the balls of her feet and looked Henry straight in the eye. She held the journal in her hand, loosely, as if it might bite her. "Is this yours?"

He swallowed. "Yes."

She nodded for a while. Then she smiled. "I admire your courage. The scarring on your hands certainly gives you away as a practitioner of chemystry, and so this journal could be yours, but you lie. I can smell it." She put her finger to her nose. Then she pointed it at Marise. "I think it is hers."

"Why?" he could not help asking.

"Because of the way your eyes darted over to her just now when I asked you and because of the other damned instruments my people found on her." She handed the journal to Alaia, with the pistol. She used a sweat-stained handkerchief to remove Marise Fermat's "hairpin" from her pocket. She spun the hand-size length of black metal around her fingers. "This is a chemyst's weapon. I have seen its like do terrible things to people I love. And it is powerful, too. Perhaps too powerful for you to wield."

"How do you know?"

She flipped it and held it out gingerly.

"Am I wrong? You might be able to use this innocent hairpin to even the odds, at the very least. Take down your captors, no?"

A twitch of her hand, and Marise had almost made the earth swallow them up with that thing. But she had never spoken of it or let him touch it.

He opened his hands in their bonds, and the woman put it in his palm. It called to him. It yearned for his Source. Then nausea hit him: brutal, overwhelming. He had to get it out of his hands. He dropped it. He retched.

The barn was quiet.

The woman's eyes were midnight. She reached out with her kerchief and gingerly maneuvered the wand back into her jacket. "Yes, it is a difficult thing to hold, is it not? The truly powerful chemyst must cultivate an iron will to master the forces inside such a tool. So, Vera, you were right in your choice to use the mask. The woman is the one we must fear. And now we know that she is called Marise. It is not an uncommon name. But I heard stories, years ago, of a powerful chemyst with that name. She disappeared, if I recall. I wonder if this could be her?" She turned back to Henry. "Forgive me. You are Henry Collins, are you not?

Henry saw no benefit in lying. He shrugged.

"My name is Petra alla Ferra. My people and I have been hired to bring you and this book to certain parties."

"What parties?" asked Wayland Teach.

She ignored his question. "You held this journal for a

while, but you were traveling to attempt to find its owner, were you not?"

"I don't—"

"Please do not dissemble. If you are Henry Collins, then this is Athen Boyle, this the serving boy Cram." If these people knew them, it was likely they had access to the Royal Navy or the Grocers. Either way, it was not a position in which he wanted to stay. Alla Ferra pointed at Winnifred Black and Cubbins. "These I do not know." She turned to Marise Fermat. "But for this one, I think, ladies . . . I think for her, our employers may give us a very large bonus." She stood.

Marise Fermat's voice rang hollow from inside the mask. "If you let me out of this thing, I would show you just who I am."

"Oh, I know!" Alla Ferra unsheathed from her belt the biggest hunting knife Henry had ever seen. She held it to Marise's neck. "You would pull the sky down upon our heads or burn us from the inside out. That is exactly why you will stay inside this." She tapped the mask. It rang like a bell. She turned to the rest of them. "Make yourselves ready. We will move with speed tomorrow, and I do not like waiting." She whirled to go, and Henry saw a green key hanging from a chain around her neck.

After alla Ferra had left with the two girls, the companions inched near each other as best they could and held a whispered council.

"I have heard of her," Marise said. "As a very young girl she helped lead a New Inquisition unit during the Tinker purges in Catalonia. They cut a bloody line from hidden workshop to hidden workshop up and down the coast."

"Who do they work for?" Cram asked.

"They are elite. Whoever hired them has a very large sum of money or very powerful friends."

"Purges?" Cram whispered.

Henry nodded, wide-eyed. "There was a fight, a bloody one, between the church and the chemysts in Catalonia."

"Who won?"

"Chemystry is no longer practiced there."

"Ah."

Vectors of possibility flashed through Henry's mind. Their future. These people were obviously after the plans embedded in the journal. Alla Ferra would question Marise. His previous master, Fermat, had told him of this "questioning." Either she would describe the machine after a great deal of pain, or she would refuse and die. Then they would question Henry. Or Athena, or Cram first, if they thought Henry himself was strong enough to resist. Or Cubbins. They would not stop until they knew the secret Marise had left in Ruby's blood or until they all were dead.

Henry called through the door, "Guard."

Athena whispered. "Henry, what—"

"Guard!" he called again.

The door opened, and a guard stood across the doorway, pistol leveled. "What is it?" she asked.

"Take me to alla Ferra. I have something she wants."

Captain Teach leaned forward. "Lad, what are you doing?"

"Saving us," Henry said.

The guard smiled, as if she were used to this kind of thing. "Come on then." She grabbed him under the arm and hustled him across the barnyard while Henry did his best to ignore the fierce, insistent whispers behind him.

CHAPTER 39

History is a pack of lies we play on the dead.
—Voltaire

Something poked Ruby. She woke.

She opened her eyes a slit, but there was nothing to see. Even with her eyes wide open, not a trace of light. She lay on a cool platform of some sort. She rolled over and reached out her hands. Her fingers brushed up against cold metal. Bars. She laughed. It was funny, she had to admit, that after so much—storming onto the *Grail*, sacrificing herself for her crew, training with the

Reeve, secret missions, midnight bombings, and, let us not forget, killing magnificent chemystral horses—she was back in a cage. But this was not Fermat's cage, with its bouncy floor and genial keeper. No, Ruby could guess who held the key to this lock, and he was another thing altogether.

"It is amusing, isn't it, Miss Teach?" Swedenborg's breath jangled through the fine silver mesh. He was close, just on the other side of the bars. Fabric shifted on metal. Ruby's memory flashed to a small chair that lurked in a corner of the laboratory, but the Swede almost never sat. Was there someone else in the room?

She had to play for time. "What's that? Forgive me, I am still groggy. What is amusing?"

Swedenborg's mesh echoed wetly when he chuckled. "Why, that you squandered your opportunity so spectacularly."

"I'm sorry, I don't—"

"The powers that be in our little fort gave you an opportunity to prove your loyalty. That loyalty might have kept you out of this cage. You carried out your task very well, by all reports. But then, and here is the part that just tickles me, after you had succeeded with your picking, even though there was no list—surely you could not be blamed for that—you still ran away and then, when caught, refused to return. Oh, yes. I know all the sordid little details, even the subversion of my poor Evram. Convincing him to give you the overcommand word was quite a feat."

Fear blossomed in her chest. "He did nothing intentional. I tricked him. You can't—"

Metal dinged, as if he had flicked one of the bars. "What I can and cannot do is none of your concern. The matter is between me and my apprentice."

It was no use fencing with this man. "Fine," Ruby said. "What are you going to do to me?"

"So fierce, Miss Teach. Beware your impulsiveness. It may be your undoing. Or, forgive me, it has already been your undoing." The metal scritch of fabric on the chair in the corner sounded again. There *was* someone else in the room with them. "Since you will no longer train with our fine cadets, we will accelerate our program of experimentation." Dread crept up Ruby's spine. "Our little laboratory here will be your home for the forseeable future. Do not worry, we will take excellent care of you. Your blood is, after all, of primary importance."

"No longer training?"

"Why, no. The Reeve have a very dim view of deserters. I feel fortunate that you were not executed upon your arrival. I suppose my intervention had something to do with it."

She searched for something to say. The silence dragged out.

"Two wards dead. A priceless artifice shattered. Do you have any regrets?"

She bared her teeth in a grin. "I regret nothing. Only that I don't have you in this cage with me."

The metal chair scraped back. Fabric brushed against fabric as someone stood up.

Swedenborg said, "Are you satisfied?"

Wisdom Rool said, "Yes. I've seen enough." Rool sighed. "Ruby Teach, it pains me that we should part. I had thought you would make a reeve, and a fine one at that. But alack alay, I must turn my eyes otherwhere. Your steel is too common for this work. We cannot have impurities cracking our tools at the improper time. Farewell."

His feet brushed against the stone floor, receding toward the door.

Something snapped.

Ruby yelled many things, until her throat was hoarse: pleas, promises, justifications, excuses. The lord captain of the Reeve did not respond or return. Eventually she found herself kneeling in the cage, fighting for air. Her breathing quieted until she was still again.

Clapping. Glove on glove. Swedenborg was applauding, quite enthusiastically. "Well done, Miss Teach! That was quite a performance! I do appreciate you driving the lord captain away. He remains so interested in you; I find it ever so inconvenient."

Swedenborg's voice crept closer. "We are alone together at last. Now, Miss Teach, put your arm through the bars again, please. I need a fresh sample. We are so close. The machine is almost complete. Please do not resist or attempt to do violence to me. I will simply be forced to secure you even more tightly. Do as you are told."

She put her arm through the bars. Swedenborg rolled her sleeve up quite gently, and the pinprick wasn't so bad.

So why did she feel as though she had lost something massive?

The door to the laboratory closed, and she went back to counting breaths, like the old days in Fermat's cage. The numbers eluded her, though, drowned out by reeves appearing through blossoms or horses falling into canyons. Gwath had always said that . . . but Gwath had never been imprisoned like this. Perhaps he would think fondly of her since she had just sent him a steed.

Corson had blinded her. She was blind. Ruby tried to lock that away in the strongbox in her belly, but it kept creeping out and clawing at her insides. She barely kept it at bay.

Keep busy. Ruby explored the cage. There was a pot for doing your business. It smelled of chem. Using her fingers, she found a keyhole in the door, but a careful inventory of her clothing revealed that in addition to her picks, anything hard or metallic, even the buttons, had been removed. She was barefoot. Ruby had grown strong in the past months, but not strong enough to bend bars. The simplest of latches was an unpassable barrier to a girl with no picks. Skillet had told stories of an infamous Sicilian thief who could open the most complex lock with just a thump of his fist. She tried it several times, but all she got for her trouble was a sore hand.

A creak announced the door's opening.

Ruby stayed silent. She wouldn't give the Swede the satisfaction.

"Ruby Teach?" It was a hesitant voice, quiet enough so that she had to strain to hear it.

Her stomach sank. "Evram?"

"I am here to feed you."

"Evram—" Ruby said.

"Please hold your face close to the bars near my voice. Doctor Swedenborg told me to remind you that you must be polite."

She did as she was told, pressing her face up to the bars. "Evram—"

"Please do not speak. It will interfere with the feeding."

She opened her lips. Warm porridge filled her mouth, and it was gooey heaven. The whole trip back to Scoria she had been unconscious; she had no idea when she had last eaten. "More, please."

"Open."

The second bite was more magical than the first, and there was something else. A hint of honey?

"Evram"—she pulled in a shuddering breath—"I am so sorry about Sleipnir."

His stifled sob filtered through the air and cut into her.

"I didn't know that Corson could stand up to Sleipnir. I panicked. She was so brave and strong. I thought she could protect me. If I had known that she would be in danger—" She stopped there. If she had to do it again, knowing what she knew now, would she have set the gearhorse against the reeve? A cold, practical voice down deep inside her said, "Perhaps."

Evram sniffed. "I know. You did not intend for Sleipnir to die."

His understanding made it worse. She reached her hand out of the bars, trying to find his. It was there, cold and a little bit limp. "No. Is that what happened?"

He pulled away. "Yes. The party came back with her body on a wagon late last night. Doctor Swedenborg is examining her. He says the overcommand word is a highly unusual innovation. I have been allowed to assist in the autopsy." Evram's voice filled with pride.

"Evram, are you in trouble?"

"I don't know. Should I be?"

The words tasted like lead in her mouth. "You gave me the word, and I ruined something magnificent that you had made. Sleipnir was also important for the Reeve. Won't Swedenborg be angry?"

His hand came back and held hers. "Do not worry for me. I crafted Sleipnir. They told me what happened. You used her words, and she befriended you. Why would the doctor be angry if she worked perfectly to design?" He squeezed her hand once, and then was gone.

Ruby lay back against the bars and stared into the distance. The black was endless, as if the blindness somehow extended her sight. Was it temporary? Forever? She had forgotten to ask. The quiet wound her in a cocoon, stifling all the rest of her senses.

A single spark of hope kept her warm. She still had one friend. For that, she thanked Providence and Science and all the saints whose names she had never learned. But what was to come?

CHAPTER 40

Negotiation is the marriage of a fierce purpose to a useful lever.
My favorite type of lever is a cannon.
 —Precious Nel, scourge of the Seven Seas

The inside of the abandoned house was cool. Henry poured sweat. They had tied him to a chair and then left him with alla Ferra and her two seconds. Weapons drawn, Vera Medina stood ramrod straight at the edge of a beat-up table, and Alaia Calderon lurked against the doorframe behind him.

Watching him as she ate, hunting knife laid across the top of a wooden plate, Petra alla Ferra gnawed fiercely and without apology on a haunch of venison. She cleaned it all—sinew, skin, cartilage—until the bone was pristine. She took out a handkerchief and cleaned her hands and face, never taking her eyes from his. She tucked the handkerchief away. "So. You have something I want."

"Yes. I can translate that journal." The journal lay on the table, lock opened, button key necklace lying next to it.

"Of course you can."

"But the more important question is will I?"

She leaned back in her chair. "Young sir, I have spent a very long time learning all manner of methods to persuade folk to speak, and speak truthfully. Some of them I am quite certain you will not enjoy. It might be difficult for you to resist our questioning."

He chewed his lip. Suddenly all this seemed like a very bad idea. He had thought to offer his services in exchange for the safety of his companions, much the way Ruby had on the *Grail*. But this woman was a predator. She fed on fear. If he showed weakness, she would pounce on it.

"I see that, and believe me when I say I do not relish

the thought. But what if I could resist you? Or what if the woman in the mask could? Or what if either of us lies? You have no way to tell if what I say is the truth or not." He took a chance. "Unless you have a chemyst with you?"

Alla Ferra still wore a smile, but it was a touch less catlike. "It has been long since I feared chemysts. When I was young, I thought they were godless demons."

"What changed?"

"I grew older. A chemyst is just a woman or a man. Your Science is no more or less a godless pursuit than the works of the church, or even my uncle Remei's goat farm. And that place stinks like Hades. I am simply the one paid to bring you in. My employer has tasked me with hauling you back and discovering what is in that journal." She bared her teeth and leaned forward to play with the hilt of the knife. "If I must, I shall cut that information out of you. If you do not wish for that to happen, convince me that there is another way."

Henry closed his eyes for a moment. The images he saw there did not help his composure. He opened them back up. "I wager you have heard of Fermat."

The fingers stopped on the hilt. "Who has not? The Breaker of France, the Terror of the Inquisition."

"He is my mentor."

Behind him, Alaia cursed. It gave him the strength to continue. "You wish to become an enemy of his?"

She shrugged. "If I must. We have had many enemies over the years. Tinkers, cardinals, princes of the fur trade, imams of Arabia. Coin is our friend, and our other friend is vigilance. They protect us from all manner of fairy stories."

"But must you make an enemy of him?" Henry asked.

"What is my other option, boy?"

Henry forced himself to smile, to try to do this as Ruby would, showing an ease that was not there. "What if we were partners?"

Alla Ferra frowned. "Well, what if?"

"You say coin is your friend."

"Indeed."

"What extra coin might you acquire if you could offer your employers access to not just the journal and me but a living version of the journal as well?"

"Living, you say?"

His pulse pounded in his ears. "My friends and I can take you to Ruby Teach."

"The famous girl?" Alla Ferra smiled. "Continue. I am listening."

Winnifred Black smelled.

She smelled of sweat, and earth, and trees. But Athena had come to realize, in the hours strung up in the barn next to her, it was not an unpleasant odor. It might have seemed that way at one time, compared with the roses, jasmine, and orange of the salons and gardens where Athena had chattered and dueled. But Winnifred Black did not smell of tameness. She smelled of rushing rivers and steep stone. She smelled wild.

And so, Athena realized, did Athena.

"Miss Black?"

"Call me Winnie, Athen. Prison is not a place for formality."

"Very well. Winnie." The others were listening, but Athena discovered she did not care. "Might I ask you a question?"

"Well, I do have many appointments and parties to get to, but since you insist . . ."

Athena chuckled to cover her unease. "Well, I have noticed that among these mercenaries men and women tend to share fighting responsibility and such. In fact, the three leaders of this military company are female. This kind of equality has not been my experience in the upper reaches of polite society."

The woodswoman grunted. "You are perceptive indeed, Athen."

"Thank you, but that is not my question."

"Ask it, then."

But how to? Just do, she supposed. "How do you, an accomplished woodswoman in a vocation dominated, I perceive, by men, carve out your own place in society?"

Winnifred Black chuckled. "I don't."

"I'm sorry?"

"I don't, lad. I discovered long ago that they don't want me, with my buskins and my knives and my baby, Cubbins, in their society. So I don't live in it. I live on the edges, in the woods and alleys, and in company that don't give a hoot for such truck. Much like I reckon these mercenary ladies do."

"Thank you, Winnie."

"You're welcome, Athen."

"Call me Athena, if you please."

Winnifred Pleasant Black looked her up and down for a moment. "Why tell me now?"

"Why not face my death with my true name?"

A trace of a smile appeared. "All right then. Athena."

Athena was the next to be chosen.

She had heard of the exploits of the sacred companies in the purges in Andalusia and Catalonia. Terrifying pictures haunted her mind as the guards hustled her across the waste-covered stretch between the barn and the little farmhouse. It had not been that long since they had taken Henry. Had he broken so soon? Or had his questioners slipped with their fierce instruments, ending the life of her friend once and for all? For he was her friend, no matter his own opinion on the matter. He was brave and intelligent, and she mourned his loss already.

As they approached the door, she steeled herself to

witness whatever gory remains of Henry their torturers might present her with.

The door opened.

She had not expected dessert.

A warm fire glowed in the fireplace, and the hunter, Petra alla Ferra, her two assistants, and Henry Collins all sat about a large pan of creamy golden custard, flecked with a beautiful brown crust.

The company leader pointed her heavy hunting knife at Athena. "Catalonian cream?" A chunk of sticky sweetness quivered on the flat of the blade. "It is Rafa's specialty." A brute of a man stood over a pot on the fire, brows knitted in fierce concentration over a tiny tasting spoon. "We eat to confirm our new friendship!" The woman and the girls had transformed completely. No longer grim, they were all smiles and cascading laughter. Athena had finally gone mad. It had only been a matter of time.

Henry Collins looked up at her. He had a streak of cream across his upper lip. He winked.

Petra alla Ferra pushed a dented inkpot and a feather pen across the table to Henry. "Just write the note and have your handsome witness sign it, and we are boon companions."

Henry picked up the feather pen and tapped it on his teeth for a moment. Then he wrote:

> Upon the rescue of one Aruba Teach, I, Henry Collins, commit myself and my companions—Athen Boyle, Cram Cramson, Wayland Teach, Winnifred Pleasant Black, her son, Cubbins, and the Woman in the Iron Mask—to the following: We will accompany Petra alla Ferra and her company to a location of her choosing, and we will deliver ourselves into the hands of her employer without resistance or complaint. Further, I will offer her any aid I can in the translation of one chemystral journal.
>
> By my hand and seal, this 7th day of May, 1719

Ruby! Henry had, *somehow*, convinced alla Ferra to help them. But this was not an honorable woman. She was a mercenary. "You are a hunter of chemysts," Athena said. "Known for it throughout the world. There is one in front of you, another in that barn back there. Do you expect us to believe that you will lay down your duty?"

The knife swished under Athena's nose and into the

creamy dessert. "I do," said Petra alla Ferra as she took another bite. "I do expect you to believe me."

"But why?"

"Because, young lord, 'duty' is just another word." She smiled. "My people and I are good at hunting chemysts. The best. We are also good at hunting murderers. We are good at hunting rebellious princes. Once we even hunted down a rogue actor. Now that was a challenge. We are skilled at this job, but if other opportunities arise . . ." She shrugged. "Besides, my task is the same. Bring the lot of you in. If this Ruby is as Henry says, then I will simply be doing a better job for my employer, and I stand in line for a nice, tasty bonus." She toasted Alaia with a bladeful of custard.

"How can we be certain of your intentions?" said Athena.

Alla Ferra smiled. "You can't. Nothing in this life is certain."

"Athen." Henry put his hand on hers. It was warm. "Trust me."

She looked about. The hunters were still smiling, but their hands hovered above their weapons. She was bound.

They had her sword. What use would it be to throw herself on them? And if Henry was indeed her friend, she had to trust him, no matter what lunacy he was up to. Besides, whether she and the others were officially captives or no, it seemed Henry had recruited a small army to aid them in getting Ruby back. It was a stroke of deft prowess.

She turned to Henry. "Brilliant. Tactical mastery. I bow to your genius." She cleared her throat and pointed at the letter. "Also, it is . . . Athena."

He raised his eyebrows. She nodded. He added an *a*.

He signed it.

Athena signed it.

The Catalonians cheered. Then there were embraces and kisses in the Continental fashion, and Athena felt embarrassed and strange but, also, just a little, hopeful. At one point, alla Ferra gave her a strange look while reading over Henry's letter; but it quickly passed, and Athena thought nothing more of it.

The pact was announced, and the camp transformed almost instantly into a festival of sorts. There were backslaps and toasts all around. Save for Marise Fermat.

Alla Ferra's one condition on their new mission was that the chemyst had to stay in the mask. Henry had reluctantly agreed.

Late that night, in the light of the dying coals, Petra alla Ferra found her.

She plopped down next to Athena in the grass. "Boyle is an interesting name."

"Is it? I have always found it rather common."

Alla Ferra sniffed. "But Athen Boyle is less common, would you agree?"

"I suppose."

"Athena, even less common." Athena did not answer. "Since I am now your comrade-in- arms, rather than your captor, I feel you should know something."

"And what is that?"

"Is your father's name Godfrey Boyle?"

"Yes, but what—"

"That is also the name of my employer." And with that, she rolled up to stand and walked into the house.

Athena stared into the coals for a long time.

CHAPTER 41

Everyone feels the evil, but no one has the courage
or energy to seek the cure.
—Elizabeth de Tocqueville, *Travels in the Colonies*

The days passed in a haze, or it would have been a haze
if she could have seen a single blasted thing. Ruby got
to know the inside of the cage very well, and the sounds
of the laboratory grew as familiar as the hidden reefs
off the coast of the colonies. Evram had a small hitch in
his step, and he never took any care to make his passage
quiet. Swedenborg came daily for blood samples and to
gloat. He also occasionally followed Evram on his visits,

lurking silently as he could near the doorway. He could not mask the jangle of his breathing. The Swede was watching her, and she took care to give him no cause for offense. She ate her porridge, did her stretches, and tried to be a model prisoner.

She had to stay hopeful. Her tools were gone: her picks, her status with Rool, her sight. Was it even possible to change some piece of this nightmare? She had to try. She held the pain close in her hands.

One time (she had no clue whether it was day or night) Evram came by himself. He fed her in silence; she put the low chamber pot through the slot near the floor, and he gave her a fresh one.

As he was going, she whispered, "Evram?"

"Yes, Ruby Teach?"

"Can you stay and talk for a moment?"

"Doctor Swedenborg was cross with me after we spoke on the first day."

"Just for a moment."

He paused in the dark. So. He still was not entirely committed to the Swede.

"How are you?"

Evram sighed. "I cannot work on reanimating Sleipnir. He says her independence made her fundamentally flawed. Besides, he has me working on the machine."

Ruby tried to sound casual. "How is it proceeding?"

"It is almost complete." Evram hesitated. "We will test it soon."

"Evram—"

"I must go, Ruby Teach."

"Just call me Ruby, Evram." She forced herself to smile.

"All right. Ruby. Good night."

Night. It was night. Evram's footsteps retreated, and she was alone with her thoughts. And the failing candle of her hope. She nursed it until it burned her fingers.

She slept.

After the next sleep the Swede came to see her. She rolled her fingers into a fist.

"Hello, Ruby Teach." He sounded absolutely jovial. She presented her left arm through the bars.

"Oh, no, thank you, Ruby." Swedenborg tittered. "I have no need of your blood anymore."

Ruby kept her face as flat as she could. "Why not?"

"It is exciting, is it not? My dear little repository of secrets, I finally have a secret to keep from you." His fingernails trailed across the metal bars and played a little piano on her forearm. She snatched it back. He laughed again. "Discovery is strong tonic to the system, Ruby. Perhaps you will have your own opportunity to experience discovery sometime soon." He walked away, whistling a jaunty tune.

The machine was finished. The Swede had come to her to gloat. Soon. He had said "soon." If he no longer needed her blood, then he no longer needed her alive.

She tried to count her breaths, but they came quickly and irregularly. She flexed her fingers and nurtured her hope, redoubling her focus. Would the Swede return to take her? Did she have any time left?

Later that day, Evram returned alone.

"Ready for my snack, O Keeper of Gruel," Ruby said, and forced a laugh.

The spoon scraped across the bowl. Ruby opened her mouth and ate the porridge. She swallowed. "Evram?"

His only response was the rasp of the next spoonful. She ate it.

"Evram?"

Nothing.

"Evram— If I have done something to make you angry, I am sorry. Have I done something wrong?" She racked her mind, going over everything she had said in the past days, even the way she had said it. There was nothing, no hint that he was angry or upset about any of it. Cold fear washed over her. "Are you all right, Evram? Has something happened?" After the next spoonful she grabbed his wrist with her left hand. "Evram, please. Talk to me. Say anything." He gently pulled his wrist away, and she let it go. "Well, I am sorry. For whatever I have done, Evram. I am truly sorry." His footsteps were slower than usual, but they walked away, just the same. The door opened and closed, and then the laboratory's quiet washed over her.

It was impossible to deny. She was now truly alone.

She let the emptiness take her.

The hours passed, and Evram returned to feed her, silent as the last time. He left, and the time, and the pain, stretched out until she found she was done with it.

She opened her hands and reached through the bars and found the keyhole. She found the keyhole with the thin, sharp brass picks she had grown out of her index fingers.

CHAPTER 42

Across the mountains they are neither beasts nor spirits. They are as we are. And so I fear them.

—Mother Green Foot,
Exodus Council, Keepers of the Western Door, 1702

In the days to come Athena discovered that she could smell worse. It might have been the constant running. Petra alla Ferra called her company Los Jabalís, the boars, and they certainly knew their way about a forest. They numbered somewhere between fifteen and twenty— Athena could never get a solid count—and at any time some of them were prowling about on the flanks and ahead, screening their passage through the forest. Los

Jabalís were hard and wild, and she counted her blessings that the company no longer held them prisoner.

To her surprise, Athena spent most of her time marching along next to Marise Fermat. Ruby's mother needed continual help navigating the treacherous roots and rocks. First it was Athena and Cram, but after a few hours Henry, the Blacks, and even Captain Teach himself took turns helping guide her through the forest. Such an odd group, and all united in the pursuit of this single girl. But what would happen if they ever found her? Henry had his allegiances. She had her own to the Worshipful Order, and what of her father, the mysterious employer alla Ferra had been going on about? Wayland Teach wanted nothing to do with any of them, and who knew what his wife wanted? And what of the Blacks? This forest, this land, was a place out of time; but she suspected that time had been passing in the rest of the world, and Athena feared its shape if they ever finally came back to it.

A few days later Athena was summoned to a point outside their most recent camp. The mercenaries had accepted her true gender without a moment's hesitation. Athena had told no one of their late-night chat, but she suspected that her status as the boss's daughter might have had something to do with her constant inclusion in alla Ferra's counsels. She found she did not mind. With the bonds off her wrists they could call her a duck, for all she cared.

"Girl."

The voice called from the cook's lean-to, pitched back in the woods. The shadows were deep in the trees, and the big cook, Rafa, loomed over a bubbling cauldron. The smell of garlic and spices drifted out into the leaves and set Athena's eyes to tearing. Los Jabalís loved their food murderously hot.

"Girl, come in here and help me for a moment, would you?"

Athena ducked under the lean-to and into the warm shelter. "What is it, Rafa?"

"Does this need salt?" he rumbled, and passed her a spoon.

She tasted it. It flowered and looped in her mouth, and then attacked her taste buds, in the most pleasant of attacking ways. "No," she gasped. "It needs nothing at all. Thank you."

"My pleasure," he said. "I just wanted you to have a hint of flavor, some reinforcements against the conditions. It looks like rain out there."

Why would she care about the rain? "Er, thank you."

He moved his head out of the shadows. It was not Rafa's face that hung there, but a smooth olive pate, with a stone earring in one ear. Ruby's teacher.

Gwath.

"Gw—"

He cut her off. "You have been summoned, have you not? You should get moving." The face moved back into the shadows. "I wanted you to know I am here if you need me. Be careful of boars. They are wildly unpredictable. You can't be too careful these days. Or patient."

"Yes. Thank you. I will."

Care and patience, he counseled. What in the name of Providence was happening? The last time she had been near that man, he had chucked Wisdom Rool over the side of a ship. Ruby had said he was dead, but he most obviously was not. She resolved to keep quiet, and she would indeed be careful of boars. She certainly could not tell Los Jabalís they had a spy in their midst, especially if it was a spy helping her.

A light rain did indeed begin to fall as she threaded her way, mind reeling, through the company to the base of a little hill. Vera and Alaia stood at the bottom. Vera tossed her black hair. "Up there."

Alla Ferra crouched in the underbrush with Wayland Teach and Henry Collins, and they passed Teach's chemystral monocle back and forth.

"Here," said Teach, and handed it to her as she knelt down beside them. "Up there, on the top of that bluff across the valley."

She fixed the monocle on the high bluff. It stood impressive and alone like a pillar in the river valley, and at the top, a fortress. A castle on a crag, just as sure as they had in the Scottish Highlands, and just as remote. "Stout walls, well patrolled, only one visible road up, exposed all the way to gunners or chemystry from above."

"And don't forget about the Reeve themselves," said Teach.

Athena lowered the monocle to look at the other

three. "We know she is in there?"

Henry nodded and showed her Marise's compass. It pointed straight at the bluff.

Athena ran several possible tactics through her head. She turned to alla Ferra. "If we try to take that place in a frontal assault, many of us, your people included, will not be coming back."

The hunter shifted on the balls of her feet. "I choose to not have my people die when it is unnecessary."

Henry frowned. "But our agreement—"

"Be easy, my friend. Los Jabalís are not abandoning you. We are committed with great passion to your cause, and besides, I need to keep all of you safe if I want my money. I agree with Lady Athena that a frontal assault will be a suicide."

Something dangerous flashed in Teach's face. "Make your meaning plain."

"I do not like plain meanings, sir. But I will force myself for your sake." She raised a finger. "What if we did not need to use the front door?"

CHAPTER 43

We are the stories we tell ourselves about ourselves.
—Wayland Teach

The hallway beyond the door lay quiet. Ruby wrapped it around her, a blanket of air, and trailed her fingers along the wall with the lightest of touches. Impossible to think of risk now or of foolhardiness. She had to trust that she had judged the time correctly and that it was deepest night. If a cadet passed by, barnacles, if Swedenborg had to use the loo, she was done and dusted. But she would not stay in that cage anymore. The Swede had made his intentions clear. Do what they might to her, she would not just sit and let it happen. If that meant flailing her way out of this madhouse blind, then so be it.

A new sound filled the hallway, from the left, past the first door. A ticking kind of hum. It actually pressed against her skin as it pulsed. It moved the air. It had to be the machine. Could she destroy it? Perhaps. If she could even see—ha—how it worked. Gum up the gears or knock it over, but then what? He builds another one, and Ruby is back in the cage.

Her fingers trailed over Evram's door, but there was no singing behind it. Steady breathing. That was all. She passed it by.

The door to the room with the desk opened easily to her finger picks. She navigated the trip wires, slipped the lock on the desk, and felt about carefully until her hands landed on the Swede's journal. Now that he had built what she carried, his notes might be less important to him, but they might be of great importance to his enemies. If he had any, Ruby would find them and help them in whatever way she could.

Back in the hall the thump of the machine was still there. Like a heart. She was inside a heart. But what beast was it powering? More important, how could she escape this beast of a place? Into the sand room and down the impossibly slick cliff face? Or slinking through the yard and out the main gate, under all their noses? A mad grin crept across her face. What else was there to do but move forward?

But there was something else she needed to do.

She made her way back to Evram's door. She had to say something. She could not just leave him.

A hand touched her shoulder.

Cold rain fell in a little waterfall out the front of Athena's tricorne. Alaia had taken them by cover of night out of the Jabalís camp through the forest, and now she called them to a halt at the foot of a very steep slope rising up into the night.

"That's too steep to climb"—Athena kept her voice low—"and too slippery in this weather." She cast a sidelong glance at Henry Collins. "I don't think we could get three feet up that."

With a bow and a flourish Alaia pulled aside a curtain of weeds and roots to reveal a narrow ramp curving upward.

Cram whistled. "How did you—"

"Miss Black is not the only one in the world gifted at tracking," Vera said over her shoulder as she started up the slope. "We've had our forward scouts all over this cliff as soon as we found it."

Cram muttered under his breath, "If Los Jabalís and the Reeve tangle, I want to be on an island far, far away."

"Agreed," said Wayland Teach.

Athena said a prayer to Providence that Henry's deal would hold up. Once this was all done, she just hoped the mercenaries would not sell them again to the highest bidder.

Ruby whipped around, but the hand that had grabbed her had done its work too quickly.

Light blinded her. She ground her eyes closed, bit her tongue to stop herself from yowling, and backed against the wall. She lashed out with her hand, and it hit a wrist.

A bone-hard hand clamped down on her own, and another shot over her mouth. She struggled but could not move. She opened her eyes a crack.

Wisdom Rool stared back at her. "Shhhhhh."

He was a spirit. A ghost. A demon. Whenever Ruby found hope, Rool appeared to dash it to pieces.

He had brought one of Swedenborg's lamps with him, and it lay on the floor. Dim white light filled the hallway. "You do not have much time," he whispered in her ear. "The good doctor could wake at any moment."

Wasn't he there to foil her? The scars on his hand chafed her shoulder. "How did you cure me?"

He wiggled his fingers. "Edwina performed a simple trick on you. Has to do with the fibers in your neck. You would have learned it in a year or two."

"How long have you been watching me?"

"Almost since I left you with the Swede." His eyes flicked to her brass fingertips. "Better than pumpkins, I suppose."

The ground was shifting under her feet, and she knew not where.

"Why did you let me get this far?" she said.

"I have a fondness for you Ruby. Also, you still owe me a task." Rool smiled down at Swedenborg's journal in her hand. "And look at you. You kept to your word. Open it, please."

Sweat trickled down her back. "But you said—the Swede—any moment—"

"Well, you had better get cracking." He plopped down on the floor in front of her.

And so Ruby Teach sat down in the belly of a Reeve fortress and picked a chemystral lock, while her greatest enemy looked on.

Was he her greatest enemy?

The lock was no match for the picks on her fingers. They were breathtakingly sensitive. The clasp popped open. Rool's paw swallowed the journal in one quick grab, and he stowed it away in his vest.

Ruby stared at him. "What now?" she whispered.

He frowned, puzzled. "Well, now you are free to go, Ruby Teach." He patted his vest. "You kept your side of the bargain, and as you know, I am a man of honor."

"But you said I could no longer be a reeve. You said you were done with me."

"And so I am. You would never make a reeve." He put a finger on his chest. "What I am is Duty to Country." He rested the finger on her shoulder. "Your loyalties lie elsewhere."

"Then why not just leave me to Swedenborg?"

"Do you think me a monster?"

"Well—"

"I can't have the good doctor ruining you. He would never have agreed to your release."

"You are lord captain."

"Even I must answer to higher powers. Besides, an open battle with our resident chemyst is one I am not certain I could win. Your escaping on his watch will cause him a great deal of trouble with our masters, as will the loss of his notes."

The ground was no longer shifting. It had dropped away entirely, and she was spinning through the air. But Ruby was no dummy. She knew an opportunity when it grabbed her by the throat. She nodded, and Rool released her.

It all had happened in near silence, the space just below whispers.

She went toward Evram's door.

"Not a good idea," Rool said.

"I have to say good-bye." He shrugged. What she did not say was that Evram was in danger, too. Perhaps Rool would let him escape as well. She eased the door open. The white light from Rool's lamp crept in with her. A shape sat upright in the chair, wreathed in shadow. It was breathing easily.

"Evram, I am so sorry. I know you hate me, but I think you should come with me. The Swede has it in for you, and I'm making a run for it. Will you come with me?"

Rool shifted behind her, and the light hit Evram.

Black veins crept up his neck from underneath his shirt and into his hair, cradling his ears. His eyes were bloodshot as well, except with tendrils of dark gray.

"Evram," she whispered.

He turned to her slowly, no expression on his face. His mouth opened, and a withered tongue lay there, like a spoiled carrot. The sound that came from his throat would haunt her dreams for a very long time. Before him, ignored on the worktable, lay an almost finished automaton. It was just a little longer than her forearm. Its shape was that of an otter, but its fur shone of brass. It had sapphire eyes. Next to it lay a slip of paper. A word was scrawled on it, as if by a child: *Ruby*. He must have been crafting it before *this* happened. She felt she might almost go blind again. His eyes followed her as she found a sack in the corner and laid the otter inside. She took it. Deep inside her something wailed.

Rool pulled her back into the hall and shut the door. "Told you it wasn't a good idea." He hurried her along the hall. "Doctor Swedenborg has added his own properties to your famous machine. It removes the will now as well."

The door at the top of the steps was firmly locked. The wood was gray and glistened. Cram got a picture in his head of a greasy, spoiled steak. His belly rumbled in hunger.

The professor looked back at them; Vera, Alaia, Lady Athena, the captain. Los Jabalís had insisted that the masked chemyst stay with them. Henry had the leftovers of Miss Marise's laboratory spread out on the stone in front of him, and he had an air about him. As if he were shoeing a mule from behind. "The lock and the door are chemystral make, and I have not seen either of their like before. Move back." They scarpered around the corners of the door, backs against the rock. Cram put his fingers in his ears.

Lady Athena looked at him. "What are you doing?"

He shrugged. "Seemed apropos."

His lady mouthed "apropos," but Cram didn't hear it because just then a loud pop rang out. The professor flew across the cavern and rolled to a stop.

He picked himself up, dusted himself off, and said, "That wasn't it," and hurried back to the completely undamaged door.

Lady Athena bared her sword. "Well, they know someone is knocking. I hope Los Jabalís are keeping them occupied on the walls."

From across the chamber, Alaia whispered hoarsely, "They'll be all worrying about the armed party down on the plain, never fear!"

Cram tried to keep it straight in his head. Strategery. The rest of Los Jabalís had circled the fort and were marching about with a big to-do, making like they had an interest in attacking. Alla Ferra had said something about a catapult, a flaming catapult. He shook his head. All a ruse, howeverward. The captain had called it a sharp. Draw their attention one place, while you dig into them in another.

The professor, muttering and cursing, finally applied two vials at once to the door, then flailed his hands over his head in protection. Cram closed his eyes. There was a fizzing and a smell of rutabaga. Cram opened his eyes. The door had a hole in it, the size of a mastiff. The professor's hair was smoking.

"Come on!" he whispered, hauling the Ferret compass out of his pack. "We're in!"

Rool hurried Ruby up into the sand room. A warm, wet wind whirled back and forth up from the river and down from the clouds. Rool pulled a coil of rope from his shoulder. "Your plan is still sound, and a legend will spread about your climbing down blind. Tie this off, will you?"

Ruby wanted to scream, but she couldn't. "I have to go back for him."

He looked up from the rope, a mad sail mender. "Do you not hear me? Evram Hale is gone, as surely as if you had thrown him from this ledge. You must accept this, Ruby Teach. Now. I am giving you a chance to live. You are a survivor. I saw you hesitate outside the workshop. You could have sacrificed yourself nobly, destroying the machine and damning yourself. I saw you pass Hale's door the first time, and you would have left him on his wee stool if I had not given you back your eyes. This is your chance to live. If you do not take it, I wager you will be sitting right next to your little inventor before the next day is out. Is that what you want?"

She shook her head. "But what if this is some trick?"

"Then you will slip it."

"I don't know what to do, where to go."

He chuckled and took her by the shoulders. "You are like me, my apprentice. You are a wild wind, a fire in the field. Destruction follows you wherever you go. That is your legacy. Hale is just another name to add to the list." He cocked his head. "Is it so hard to understand that I want you to live?" She had never seen him hesitate. "I have grown . . . fond of you, Ruby. And I wager your hatred for Swedenborg far outstrips your hate for me, and I cannot imagine that you will not do your utmost to stop him. Do you think he will be satisfied with young Evram? Give a man like that a sniff of power, and he will never stop searching for more."

"But how?"

"Follow your nose." His glance flicked down to the picks emerging from her fingers. "Besides, your solutions are becoming much more interesting than mine."

As he finished tying the rope, all she could do was look at him. He tested the knot and tossed it over the edge. It flopped down the rocks into the dark and mist below.

Rool cocked an ear. "You have guests coming. You may want to shimmy down that rope. Then again, you may not. The choice is yours. I will see you again, Ruby Teach." Then he sauntered around the corner to the changing room and was gone.

Whispers came down the hallway. She could not be discovered, not now, not so close to freedom. She threw all that had happened into the chasm before her and then lowered herself over the edge. One slip, one missed foothold, and she would be gone. The rocks cut slippery and sharp into her bare feet, but she made the best time she could. The wind whipped through her hair, and the rain was cool and clean. The task was pure. Climb down. If anyone died, it would be her. She was responsible for no one else.

The sound of hushed voices filtered over the edge. She went still. There was a tiny ledge, a shelf made by Providence in the side of the cliff, and she huddled in it, letting the rope twist freely. The wind and rain lashed hard enough that she might have been washed right off.

A head popped over the ledge, backlit, shadowed.

"Ruby?" Henry Collins called into the wind.

She did not move. She did not make a sound. Against all odds they had found her. But what was it they had finally found?

She called, "Here," and grabbed the rope, to start the slow climb back up.

≈ ≈ ≈

They all were there at the top: Cram, Athena, Henry, and her father. They stared at each other a moment, the fort shuddering the alarm. They had changed. Sun browned. Lean. Cram looked like a wolf, and Athena had a wild gleam in her eye. Henry was beaming, but there was something hard in his face. Her father, too. He looked almost shy. Two girls were with them, tough, with clocklocks and hand weapons. They all stared back at her. How had she changed? She hid her hands behind her back.

The happiness blooming inside her struggled to overcome a crippling wall of fear. Rool's words hung around her neck. *A wild wind, a fire in the field. Destruction follows you wherever you go.* Her words, though, tumbled out: "You shouldn't have come."

They were breathing heavily, just seconds ahead of the hunt. It was Athena who said, after checking over her shoulder, "What?"

"You shouldn't have come. You're all putting yourselves in deadly danger." She thumped her chest. "I'm a threat to you. You should just let me go." She stepped back toward the ledge.

They looked at her as if she had just grown an extra head.

It was Cram who broke the tense silence. He stepped forward and took her hand. "Ferret. We don't care about no threats, and we don't care about no danger. We're here for you, and if you climb back down that cliff, well, I guess we'll just have to follow you down it." He squeezed her hand. "We came for you."

That little squeeze, the looks on all their faces: they chased away the fear. At least for now. Corson's words came back to her. *You have to get empty only so you can know what to fill it with.* Emptiness—loneliness—was never where she would find her strength. *This* was her power. These people. This strange, courageous family. She wrapped herself in thoughts of them, and the picks molded back into her fingers as slick as summer sunshine.

"Well then, let's be about it. I'd prefer you didn't meet my recent acquaintances. At least one of them wants to turn this whole continent on its head."

Athena raised an eyebrow. "Well, we can't have that.

By the way, there's someone down below you should probably meet." She grinned. They all did.

Ruby could not help grinning back. Then they all were grinning at one another like fools at a fair.

Wayland Teach cast a look behind them. "About that meeting—" he said.

Ruby cut him off. "I'm sure they're lovely, whoever they are, but we really must be going, don't you think?"

Captain Teach took a breath and then nodded.

She threw herself into her father's arms just for a moment. "At last," he said, and then they tore down the gray wood hallways, toward escape, spiraling ever deeper away from the madness that lay behind.

≈ ≈ ≈

⟿ Acknowledgments ⟿

Recipe for a story:

Begin with a base of Anna and Bobo, the touchstones. Refer back to Dianne, a mother as ferocious as Marise, but who is always there. Tony, who taught me about stories. Julie, who taught me about people. Chris, who showed me that heroes are born in the forge of the wager.

Fold in The Gamers, who first witnessed Ruby's world: Crazystones, Aloysious Pleasant Black, Hieronymous Wodehouse, Violet McTavish, and Coldbrook McBiggerstaff. Add percolaters: Valerie Roche and Emmy Laybourne.

Catalyze with a brilliant agent, Susanna Einstein. Count yourself lucky. Refine and then explode and then refine and then explode and then weep and then do a jig with Editrix Adept Martha Mihalick. Count yourself thrice lucky. Further hone through the centrifuge of fantasticness known as Greenwillow Books: Sylvie Le Floc'h, Tim Smith, Katie Heit, Virginia Duncan, Gina Rizzo, Preeti Chhibber, and the rest of a small yet mighty army.

And then add people like you, who like stories like this. Drink the potion down.

Special thanks to those who helped me speculate about the fictional Algonkin: Joe Coulter, and the tome to which he referred me, *The Atlas of Great Lakes Indian History*, ed. Helen Hornbeck Tanner.

⤜

Read on for an excerpt from

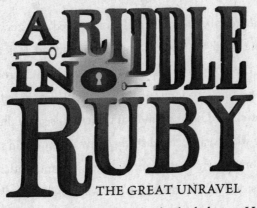

A RIDDLE IN RUBY

THE GREAT UNRAVEL

At the edge of the gorge she looked down. Her belly jumped up into her gullet. Far below, body breakingly, eye poppingly far below, lay a roiling river, the shores on both sides studded with rocks.

In front of Ruby, Cram edged forward, muttering under his breath, "There ain't no tonic like perilous danger. There ain't no tonic like perilous danger . . ."

Alaia brought up the rear.

Cram shuffled forward quickly, but not quickly enough, alternating death grips along the guide ropes. The "walls" of the bridge were nothing but a cat's cradle of frayed cord holding up a floor of two thick parallel cables, each about as wide as Ruby's waist. The very long, very scary structure bowed across the river like an upside-down rainbow to the far side of the gorge. The white water rushed hungrily below, daring her to fall. Behind her Alaia muttered, "Faster, faster," like some kind of prayer. And Cram did go faster. They were at the bottom of the curve now, halfway across. The company came into focus as they scrambled closer: a cluster of hunters, hard, lean women and men poised on the rocks, bristling with weapons and steely of eye. Ruby could see their faces more clearly now, a mix of tension and anticipation. Athena stood among them, but she was pointing back across the gorge, behind them. Ruby risked a look back, and her blood went cold.

One of the fastest reeves, a lanky girl in gray with curly brown hair, had made it to the bridge and was running toward them at an impossible speed, her hands not even holding on to the guide ropes. Ruby's pulse skipped a beat. Avid Wake.

Alaia's blowpipe hissed again, but whether it was too far or Avid was just more prepared for it, the reeve cadet threw herself to the side, and the dart sailed past. The bridge wobbled back and forth now, but the girl righted herself and kept coming. "Run, run!" Alaia waved them forward. "If she gets to us, we are lost!"

A clunk echoed out across the bridge, followed by several more.

Axes flashing, four burly hunters were chopping at the ropes.

Cram ran, a shuffling, jerking, wobbling run, holding

on to the guide ropes as much as he dared, but he ran. Ruby scrambled after him, and she forced her eyes forward. No use watching Avid gain on them. The bridge shuddered with every axe blow, and the wobbling got worse and worse. Would they cut it with the three of them still on the bridge, even Alaia, who was one of their own? Cram's breath was reduced to a tortured whistle; but he kept scuttling, and the back of Ruby's neck tingled with expectation. It might have been half a minute, but it felt like the longest moment of her life.

When they clambered onto stone on the other side, Ruby had never been so happy to bang her shins on a rock. The three of them threw themselves down in relief onto the solid ground.

"Now, now!" someone yelled. The axes doubled in speed, raining down upon the ropes. And then all at once, with a *pock pock pock pock* like distant gunfire, they broke.

The bridge lurched and snapped like a flinching snake, cords trailing into the mist like spiderwebs. Avid was halfway across.

She fell.

Ruby's heart leapt into her mouth.

Then, somehow, Avid did something with her feet in midair and, by Providence, caught herself up in the ropes. She hung, bum over head, as the bridge tumbled away into the gorge. No one spoke.

Across the gorge the full weight of the bridge hit the remaining supports, and they groaned in protest. Somehow, Avid twisted her body *just so* to get the mass of cables between her and the rock face before the bridge slammed into it. She hung there, stunned, but still moving.

Against her will, in spite of the pain and desperation of the past months, Ruby's heart swelled with pride. Her rival was a truly gifted reeve.

A crossbowman took aim at Avid, but Ruby lunged, quick as lightning, jostling the man's elbow into the stock. The bolt sailed to the right, skittering off the rocks. The man turned to her, enraged. "Stupid girl! If one of them gets to us, just one, who knows what evil might come to pass?"

"*I* know what evil might come to pass. Believe me." Ruby rode the sudden wave of her own anger to move nose to nose with him. "And that reeve, hanging by her ankles on the other side of a by-Science *canyon*, is no immediate threat to you."

"Listen to the girl, Nic." A wolf of a woman flowed up, the silver streak in her hair matted with wet and mud. "We are clear. No need to poke the jaguar any further."

The hunter blew out a long breath and then lowered the weapon. "Yes, Captain."

The woman inclined her head to Ruby. "I am Petra alla

Ferra. These"—her wave took in the pack of hunters—"are my people, Los Jabalís. You have us to thank for your rescue. I hope you will not interfere any further with their attempts to keep you safe." Her stare nailed Ruby to the rock underneath her.

Before Ruby could respond, Petra alla Ferra turned away. She ran her eyes over her company, and a tense silence fell on the lip of the gorge.

Then, with a huge grin, she thrust her hands in the air.

The hunters exploded with hoots and hollers into what Ruby could only describe as a carnival, with the Jabalís swapping jokes and pounding one another on the back. From somewhere instruments were produced, and an impromptu jug band sprang up.

She looked about in disbelief. "Cram, what is happening?"

Head cocked like a puzzled terrier, he watched the cold killers kicking up their heels in a jig for a moment. "The Jabalís are, well—hmm. You see—"

Petra alla Ferra appeared behind him. "We are triumphant, young Sam."

"Cram."

"Yes. We are triumphant, and we celebrate our victories. This is a victory, yes?" She ruffed his hair.

"But we need to go," Ruby said. "We need to keep

running. If they catch us, we all will die."

The woman lifted an eyebrow. "All the more reason to celebrate now, is it not? Even if only for a few moments." She chuckled. "As you so eloquently pointed out, the reeves are on the other side of a canyon so wide not even their finest could leap across. It will take them days to find another way around. By then we will be gone. So now? We celebrate. We have a reputation to uphold. The world needs to *know* what hearty band of mercenaries came right into the den of the reeves and tweaked their noses. And they need to know that in the face of fear, when others cower, we laugh." The smile disappeared. "Have no fear, Ruby Teach. I will protect you and yours. After all, you are very, very valuable to me." She snagged a wineskin from a passing hunter and was gone.

Ruby looked at Cram.

He shrugged.

The spectacle of the moment was Avid, and wagers began flying fast and furious over whether she would get back to the top of the bridge. The growing crowd of reeves on the other edge began to organize to get down to her, but in the end she did not really need the help. Hanging ipsy-dipsy, she swung herself back and forth with her arms in ever-wider swings. Then, at the top of a swing—and Ruby had to give her credit—the girl hinged at her belly and then grabbed on with her hands above her feet. The mercenaries cheered good-naturedly. Cram whistled low.

Ruby and Cram crouched in the rain on a rock like two grasshoppers, and Captain Teach, Athena, and Henry drifted over until they all were watching the show. Seeing Avid—her bully, her rival, her companion, on the brink of attacking them, then in grave danger, and then escaping in such brilliant style . . . it stretched Ruby's insides. She didn't know whether she was sad, or glad, or just plain addled. "I know that girl."

Cram looked at her for a bit, perplexed. "She your friend?"

"My friend?" Ruby sighed out a long sigh. "Honestly, Cram? I have no idea."

He cracked a grin. "Well, at least you got us to protect you."

She wiped the rain from her eyes, and she took in her rescuers for a moment. "But who's going to protect *you*?"

Avid had finally reached the top guide rope, and she pulled herself hand over hand back to the crowd of waiting reeves. The press parted in a wave for Wisdom Rool. The reeve lord captain hauled Avid up to the lip of the canyon. The mercenaries gave a rousing cheer, and Avid curtsied in response. She was tall, but the lord captain of the king's Reeve topped her by more than a head, and he seemed twice as wide. Rool clapped Avid on the shoulder with encouragement, and they had a word, after which she nodded. She turned back and gazed across the gorge. Her eyes met Ruby's, and for a breathtaking moment Ruby thought the girl might try a Work to jump across. It was too far. A hundred yards, at least. Even Wisdom Rool couldn't make a jump like that. Could he?

Still, excitement fluttered in Ruby's chest. When the young reeve cadet turned about and made her way back into the crowd, Ruby couldn't help feeling just a bit disappointed. A pang of . . . was it loneliness?—struck her. The Jabalís clustered about them, faintly ridiculous in their strange carnival, and none of them knew what Ruby had gone through in the past year. Nor did her friends. One of the only ones who truly might understand had just disappeared into the press of reeves standing united behind their leader.

The rain hammered down on Wisdom Rool. It was too far across to see the ropy scars that twisted all around his body, but they burned in Ruby's mind's eye as the man lifted his hand to his mouth. "Ahoy, the gorge!" His voice rang out raspy clear over the wind and rushing water.

Petra alla Ferra stepped forward, leaning forward carelessly over the edge, one hand grasping a stump of guide rope. "Ahoy, the Reeve!" she called. Los Jabalís snickered among themselves. Like the crew of the *Thrift* loved Ruby's father, they loved this woman, this woman who had led a band of unruly outlaws against the Reeve and *won*.

"I am Wisdom Rool, lord captain of the king's Reeve! To whom do I have the pleasure of speaking?"

Alla Ferra tucked a stripe of silver hair back behind her ear and hesitated. Ruby sympathized. The smart move here would be to make up a name, a false identity to throw the Reeve off the scent. Buy some time.

"Captain Petra alla Ferra at your service! My stouthearted companions here are Los Jabalís!" Another murmur rose up around Ruby: one part fear but two parts approval. Ruby ground her teeth. Didn't they know they were giving away their advantage? Heedless. Careless.

"A brave company indeed to steal from the house of His Majesty, especially in times like these!" Rool called.

"Tell your friends! We are always looking for work!" Los Jabalís laughed in appreciation. "Besides, this massive gorge between us bolsters my bravery! And I am not certain I understand. What is it we have stolen from you? A bangle? A set of solemn churchman's garb?"

Rool smoothed down his reeve blacks theatrically in response and then pointed at Ruby, sitting exposed on her rock perch. "That girl. She is a prisoner of England, and we would have her back!"

Ruby's head spun like a top. He was putting on a sharp, a show for the other reeves. He didn't want her back. In fact, Wisdom Rool was the one who had let her go. He had given her a rope to climb down the cliff, for Providence's sake. The lord captain and Ruby had made a deal to steal the notes of the tinker they called the Swede. Ruby had lived up to her part, and Rool had helped her escape to her friends. The rest of the Reeve didn't know that, though. The crowd of black and gray teachers and students loomed behind Rool: a storm waiting to be unleashed.

Petra alla Ferra swung her head about to peer exaggeratedly at Ruby, as if she were some strange bird. She projected relaxation, amusement even. She pointed at Ruby. "This girl, eh?" She held up her hands in an elegant shrug. "Alas, sir. This is not English soil. The bears and wolves are constables here, and it is their law we obey. Besides, even if this"—she tapped her foot on the rock—"were your land, it is currently on the other side of a canyon from you!" At this, Los Jabalís erupted in cheering and jeers. A few of them had gathered some flowers and began tossing them into the gorge like pining lovers. Ruby shook her head. These people were mad. The Reeve would pursue them to the ends of the earth. Ward Corson and Avid were already leading a detachment scaling down the remains of the bridge. Ruby guessed they could cross the river and get up the sheer face of the canyon before nightfall.

Wisdom Rool stood motionless on the other side. He waited until the cheering subsided.

"Very well then! Please remember that I did ask nicely! When next we meet, perhaps it will be within arm's reach!"

Petra alla Ferra laughed. "Come if you will, Sir Wisdom! If you catch me, I will give you a kiss!" She blew him one then and stepped back onto the firm ground, igniting a new round of cheers from the Jabalís.

Wayland Teach was waiting for her. The moment of sun was gone, and the rain had taken up again in earnest. Distant thunder rumbled in the distance. He leaned in and muttered something in the huntress's ear. Alla Ferra's gaze flitted over to Ruby and then back to her father. She nodded once.

Teach walked over to Ruby and said simply, "Come with me."

What was he about? As the hunters burst into action, finally making ready for their escape, her father led her farther into the little clearing on the other side of the bridge. A small woman stood motionless amid the jumble, her features completely hidden in a metal mask. Ruby's friends had followed behind, all their mirth suddenly gone. As one they looked to Ruby's father.

He stared at Ruby, beard dripping in the rain, mouth open as if he were trying to catch the words of a once-remembered song. A kind of fear took her. Her pulse thundered in her ears. Teach offered Ruby his hand, and she took it. He walked her down into the clearing until she stood opposite the woman in the mask.

"Ruby—" said the captain.

She looked up at him, but he said no more.

Petra alla Ferra had followed them. "Only for a moment," she said to Teach, "and then we must be on our way."

He looked at Ruby, then nodded.

Alla Ferra cast her eyes about the clearing at her people. Her voice cut through the downpour. "Ready your weapons!"

Muskets, axes, bows, and swords flew into hands. Three hunters took positions just behind the woman in the mask, weapons ready. The one in the middle was a huge brute, and the edge of a wicked carving knife lay between the masked woman's shoulder blades.

Ruby scanned the faces of her father and her companions for some hint of information. "What is this?"

No one answered.

What was this grand opera about? Who was this masked woman who struck fear into a company of hardened hunters? Why, in the name of Science, stop their flight from the full might of the Reeve for some sort of overblown mummer's show? Petra alla Ferra drew a chain from around her neck. At the end of the chain was a green metal key. She held it out to Ruby.

"I don't understand," said Ruby. A creeping dread scrabbled up her spine. "I say again, 'What is this?' "

The masked woman had not moved this whole while, hands clasped up under her chin, as if in prayer. Short chains ran down from just below the engraved ears, binding both her wrists in place. The mask itself encased the woman's entire head. Its weight rested on two broad shoulder supports. The face was that of an Athenian statue, classic and grave. The eyes were plugged, and a tiny hole opened at the mouth. Twisting across the features, engraved chemystral demons warred with scaled and winged angels.

The rain pounded down. It coursed around the iron eyebrows, rushing across the sculpted, empty eyes and down the cheeks, spattering on the rocks at the woman's feet.

The wearer of the mask waited, the wrist manacles carved with equations that skittered from the eye. Ruby looked about at the circle of staring faces, witnesses half lit in the rain-swept morning.

The huntress handed her the key. "This is for you to do."

Ruby almost dropped it, slick in the downpour, but

caught herself and willed her hand to stop shaking. It wouldn't. Using both hands, Ruby managed to get the key into the keyhole, just below the right ear of the mask.

She turned it.

Click.

A small handle popped out of the mask at the right temple, and Ruby pulled it across, the metal face opening like a door on hidden hinges. Time slowed as the pieces of the puzzle fell into place. A woman who could terrify an entire clearing of hard cases. The deep concern for Ruby writ large on everyone's faces. The way the woman stood, like a mirror to Ruby's own body. It could be only one person. Ruby put her hands down at her sides, clenched tight, and willed herself to look.

Inside the mask, shadowed but dry, lay a face that almost matched Ruby's, tangled hair yellow instead of black, tiny bird's tracks at the eyes where Ruby's were smooth.

"Hello, Ruby," said her mother.

Ruby Teach quieted her shaking hand, and then she punched her mother square in the face.